BLOOD BRAIN BARRIER

To ALVIN,
   In GRATITUDE,
HOPE YOU RNJOY!
GRRAT MRRTING
YOU.

           Pete

BLOOD BRAIN BARRIER

BY

PETER ACKER

Karjeda Publishing
Goldens Bridge, New York

BLOOD BRAIN BARRIER
© 2014 by Peter Acker

First printing 2014
Printed in the United States of America

ISBN 978-0-9851144-2-8

This book is dedicated to Gila, Karen, Jessica and Daniella.

In memory of Bill Herman

Acknowledgments

I owe gratitude to many people. First, to all my teachers at Manhattanville College: Joanna Herman, my first writing teacher; her husband, Bill Herman, who read and helped edit several versions, John Herman, who taught me so much about the novel; Jeff Bens who helped with an earlier version; Brian Morton, who led a one-week workshop (as part of the Manhattanville Writer's Week) in which an early version was discussed; Jim Weilkart and the gang (Jon Groszjc, Barbara Nachman, and Marian Michelotti), who workshopped a later version and have provided ongoing encouragement; my sister, Caroline Acker, who gave a much needed critical read of the book; Jennifer Leahy, who edited an earlier version; Catherine Curnin, Judith Dupre, Jan Shallman, and Doug Puder, a fellow pediatrician, who read earlier versions and gave me extensive feedback; to all the people of SEAK who sponsored a weekend medical thriller course led by Michael Palmer and Tess Gerritsen, and finally, to my wonderful family.

Chapter One
August 20, 2008 1:30 AM

Eric Egan, MD, stifled a yawn as he put the last stitch in the forehead of a squirming two-year-old girl. He stepped back, inspected his handiwork, and with a satisfied grunt, snapped off his latex gloves. He placed a small bandage over the repaired laceration.

"Okay, kiddo, your boo-boo is all fixed." He undid the Velcro straps of the restraining papoose board, lifted her up, and handed her over to her mother. When the woman had come in with her daughter, he had barely glanced at her. Now, he tried not to stare as he noticed her long blonde hair and toned body.

He had been heading toward his on-call room in the back of the pediatric ER, ready to collapse onto his cot, when he had heard the girl's crying, signaling that he was not done for the night. He had turned back irritably and strode into the treatment room, where Tina, the night nurse, a rotund Jamaican of indeterminate age, had already expertly placed the girl onto a restraining board.

As he had worked with tight-lipped focus, wearing magnifying goggles and with a bright light shining on the laceration, he had become increasingly aware of her: a haze of blond on the far periphery of his vision, a glimpse of a sinewy forearm. He had picked up a whiff of perfume that seemed to accent rather than cover up a faint odor of her sweat. It came at him in different proportions as she shifted her position and he felt at times her breath on the back of his neck as she spoke softly to her daughter.

Now, as he looked at her, he felt embarrassed and averted his gaze.

"You do such nice work, doctor."

He nodded while scratching a spot under his beard that always seemed to bedevil him whenever he did a procedure wearing sterile gloves.

"I'm Chelsea Brookfield, by the way" she continued. "Thank you for this." She extended her hand and Egan lowered his hand from his face to take it.

"You're quite welcome. Just keep the area dry for the next few days, and change the bandage once a day. A dab of bacitracin is not a bad idea to prevent infection. In five days come to the follow up clinic to have the stitches taken out."

"Will you be the one in the clinic to take them out?"

"Not necessarily—depends on the schedule, but I tell you, anyone can take them out."

"I'd like you to take them out." She looked at him coyly until he looked away.

"Well, we'll see what we can do."

She reached into her purse and pulled out a card and handed it to him. "I'm in real estate. Here's my card." He took it reluctantly. "If you're ever in the market," she said, "give me a call."

He watched her walk out, holding her daughter's hand until she turned her head giving him a smile.

"Nice body, huh?" Tina said. "And boy, she really had the hots for you."

Egan felt his face become even warmer. "I have no idea what you're talking about."

"Yeah, right. 'Oh, doctor, I'm a single mother. Oh, do you work out? It's obvious you do. Can you personally take the stitches out?'" Tina chortled as she imitated the mother's flirtatious manner.

"Tina, can you control your imagination—delightful as it is— long enough to let me know if this is it for the night? The only thing on my mind is sleep, sweet sleep."

"I don't know about that. She's going to slip and slide all over your mind, honey."

"Tina! A simple question: Am I done for the night?"

"Yes, sir boss, the waiting room is empty so you are free, free at last. Thank God almighty you're free at last." Tina gave him a little shove and he shambled down the corridor to the ER on call room.

He slumped onto the narrow on-call room cot. His feet ached. So many patients, just relentless, one after another. He felt his heart pounding against his chest and pulsating in his ears. He thought of the blonde woman and sighed. Glancing down at her card, still in his hands, he imagined being out of the hospital, in a fancy midtown restaurant, sipping wine with her. He tried to enjoy the fantasy, but patient after patient intruded, marching through his head: the new onset diabetic, the Tylenol overdose, a whole family with lice, innumerable coughers, and vomiters. His last thought before falling asleep was of a job he had on a farm one summer picking strawberries and at night when he closed his eyes, all he would see was red.

* * *

"A four-week-old baby just came in." Egan opened his eyes open to see Tina staring down at him. He closed them again.

"Come on, Eric. I need you to take a look at this baby." He opened his eyes again and blinked a couple of times, confused. *What's Tina doing in my apartment?* He looked around him. "I'm in the hospital."

"Well, you're certainly not in Kansas."

"I wish I were, even with all the tornadoes."

"I'm sorry, Eric. You look so damn tired. I really wanted to let you sleep a bit longer, but I don't know. It may be nothing, but I just have a bad feeling about this baby."

He wanted to scream, but got to his feet, dragged himself over to the sink and splashed cold water onto his face. He stood leaning with both arms on the sink and stared into the mirror. A red-eyed stranger, with a tempestuous sea of unruly brown cowlicks covering his head stared back at him. He made a desultory attempt to neaten his appearance before shuffling down the corridor to one of the examining rooms.

"Good morning, I'm Dr. Egan. What's going on with your baby?" He glanced down at the chart and noted the chief complaint: "won't stop crying," and then looked at the baby, sleeping peacefully in his mother's arms. *Good God, I got woken for this?*

"Thank you, doctor. I'm Suzy Gold; this is my husband Ralph." She paused, regarding Egan. "I'm sorry. It looks like we woke you up."

The baby stirred, and she looked back at her baby and began to sway back and forth. Egan looked at the two of them. Suzy Gold was a lean thirty-something brunette, who appeared to have taken the time to apply makeup with some care before venturing out with her sick baby. Ralph looked at least fifteen years older and had the weary expression of a husband waiting for his wife to pick out a dress at Bloomingdale's.

"Goes with the territory," he said kindly. "Tell me what's happening."

The baby let out a small sigh and a hint of rooting reflex began to appear. The mother took a pacifier and placed it into the baby's mouth and looked at Egan.

"I'm not really sure. Sometime yesterday afternoon, Robbie seemed a bit off, sort of cranky, but I didn't make too much of it. I began to worry because it seemed like I couldn't quite settle him down."

Egan nodded. "What about his feeding? Did that seem to be affected?"

"I'm nursing and it was going quite well, but last night he wouldn't get comfortable at the breast."

"Don't forget," her husband added, "that he vomited twice."

"Right, and then he looked sort of pale and for the last two hours, he's been crying, though of course he seems fine now that we're here."

"Yeah, know what you mean. It's like taking your car to the mechanic and the engine sounds just fine once you get there. Is this your first baby?"

"Why, yes," answered Mr. Gold with a slight laugh, "is it that obvious? Maybe we're overreacting. Maybe it was that curried chicken you had yesterday." He took his wife's hand.

She pulled her hand away. "I may be a first-time mom, but I just have a feeling something's wrong."

"But, honey, remember how much you worried during your pregnancy? And how during the delivery, you were gloom and doom the whole time until a healthy baby popped out?"

"Ralph, you never think anything is wrong."

"Excuse me," interrupted Egan, "I just have a few more questions."

"Oh, sorry," she apologized, offering by way of explanation, "we haven't slept much."

"I know the feeling. Where was your baby born?"

"He was born right here," answered Mr. Gold. "Dr. George delivered him."

"Any problems with your pregnancy?" asked Egan looking at Mrs. Gold.

"It was perfect, Suzy's worrying notwithstanding," laughed Mr. Gold again.

"Easy for you to say," she rejoined giving her husband a glance. "Actually the pregnancy was a long time coming—years of trying, various diets, tests, hormone therapies. Ralph even gave up smoking. Finally we resorted to in vitro, but Ralph's right, except for some mid-trimester spotting and one bout of premature labor, there were no major problems."

"You see, doc, we've been through a lot with this, so it's natural that Suzy would worry."

"Ralph, will you stop and let the doctor come to his own conclusions?"

Egan suppressed a sigh. "How about the delivery?"

"No problems really; it was long, somewhat, but the baby came out looking like a rose." She added triumphantly, "Mr. Bigshot here fainted when my water broke."

"I got a little woozy from standing up too quickly, that's all."

"Was there any fever?" asked Egan, trying to hide his impatience but anxious to finish the history taking.

"No."

"What do you mean 'no'? I call 100.5 a fever. Am I right?" Mrs. Gold looked over to Egan for confirmation.

"Well, I'd characterize it as borderline. So in a sense, you're both right."

He took his stethoscope from around his neck, placed the ear pieces, and leaned forward to place the diaphragm on the baby's chest. He felt relieved to be listening to the regular rhythm of beating heart and breathing lung rather than to the discordant voices of the couple. It had always reminded him of scuba diving, quiet except for the muted sounds of the deep, a whole new world. He listened for a long time, moving the diaphragm around the chest, first concentrating on the lungs and then the heart.

The regular rhythms of the heart sounded like oars cutting into water. He had been out on the river sculling the weekend before, his oars taking deep bites of choppy East River water. The sun had been just visible above the Brooklyn skyline as he stroked upstream against the tide. He had grunted with each stroke, taking him incrementally away from the hospital, his legs and arms working with coordinated bursts. His world reduced to include only his scull, the water around him, his breathing, the pounding of his heart, the contractions of his muscles, and his sweat.

He took the stethoscope from his ears. Both parents were staring at him.

"Is everything okay, doctor?" asked Mr. Gold. "That was quite a long listen you took."

"Yes, I'm sorry. I usually take my time. He sounds fine."

He continued to examine the baby, feeling the belly, moving the extremities, looked carefully at the fingers and toes. He finished his exam by looking at the ears with his otoscope. There was nothing obviously wrong with the baby, yet an uneasy feeling kept him from clearing the kid for discharge. He looked at the parents who were staring at him expectantly.

"The baby looks quite well. It could be something as simple as gas. But I do want to get a better look at his ears, and he's got some ear wax blocking my view. Give me a minute, I have to get a small curette to clean the wax out. I want to make sure he doesn't have an ear infection."

He left the room. In truth, his view of the baby's eardrums had been unimpeded. The ear drums were pristine, shining like the inside of an oyster shell. An actual ear infection would have made his decision easier. Antibiotics and a la casa! He needed time to think.

He entered the resident's lounge, a small room in back of the nurse's station. He became aware of a distant siren, coming closer. *Shit, I hope that's something for the adult side.* He poured himself a cup of coffee, sat down, leaned back, and tried to think while struggling to ignore the increasing intensity of the siren. He began to run the possibilities through his mind.

He had always liked the challenge of pediatrics, having to diagnose patients who often couldn't talk. "Veterinary medicine" one of his medical school classmates had snorted on match day, the day when all fourth-year medical students find out what residency they had "matched with." His friend had matched at the medical center in dermatology, and he could almost picture him in a bow tie driving his Mazda Miata to his beach house. When Egan was questioned about his choice, he often joked, "I was told that pediatrics was where the big money is. I was simply misinformed."

He looked at his watch, stood up, swaying slightly, and put his hand on the adjacent wall to steady himself. For an instant, he thought he might faint. He felt a familiar sense of panic that had been plaguing him intermittently since the beginning of medical school. He shook his head and the dizzy feeling was replaced by a roar in his head and he felt the pulsation in his ears again. He reached into his lab coat pocket, felt the vial of pills he always had with him but rarely actually used. Just knowing they were there, calmed him.

The siren suddenly stopped, and he tensed as he listened to the doors of the ambulance port open. *Please go to the adult side.* He remembered a night when one of his fellow interns had simply encountered one too many calls and had gone into his on call room and refused to respond to his beeper. Egan had been called in from home to complete his beleaguered colleague's call. The memory made him want to crawl into his own on call room. Then he heard an overhead page: "Trauma surgeon to Adult ER, stat." *Thank God, it's not mine,* he thought with a relieved sigh.

"So, what do you think?" Tina had entered to the room silently and her voice interrupted his reverie.

Egan turned to her with a wan smile. "Actually I was feeling downright sorry for myself, and was thinking about how tired I am and how good it would feel to lie down right now. What do you think?"

"I don't know. I just have a funny feeling about that baby."

"Tina, I did a full exam, and I can't find a thing wrong. Tell you what; I'll refer them to morning follow-up clinic and I'll instruct the parents to come back if anything changes."

"Okay; you're the doc." Tina shrugged.

Egan sat down at the nurse's station and began to fill in the ER sheet. He had gotten to the discharge instructions when he put down the pen abruptly and stared at the wall. He couldn't get that mother's face out of his mind. That vision was replaced by the grizzled face of one of the older docs intoning that a mother's facial expression is like a barometer picking up all the nuances of a baby's condition. A mom is observing over a 24-hour-period while we get to observe for five minutes. Of course, parents worry, but there are gradations and variations of worry and just like an Eskimo's familiarity with types of snow, a pediatrician can similarly extract reams of information from a mother's furrowed brow. He rubbed his eyes and turned his eyes back to the wall, staring silently for another 30 seconds, thinking again of his on-call bed.

"Oh, hell," he muttered to himself. "I'm going to work this baby up." He stood up heavily. "Tina, get the spinal tray out."

"Dr. Egan, it's all set up and waiting for you in the treatment room."

Egan gave her a hard look while Tina gave a familiar shrug with a slight smile before heading back to the exam room.

Chapter Two
August 20, 2008 2:35 AM

"A spinal tap? Why do we need that?" asked Mr. Gold, his voice raised and somewhat panicked, as his wife broke into tears, clutching her baby tightly. The baby let out a shriek. "You doctors are so aggressive. How safe is it anyway? I hear that it can cause paralysis."

Egan looked first at him and then at her. His face tightened. "Okay, okay, let me explain. The early signs of bacterial infection can be very subtle, especially in young babies. There's a very good chance that nothing is seriously wrong with your baby. But, it is possible that something more serious could be brewing and if we catch it early we can treat it very effectively."

Egan paused, looking directly at Mr. Gold and then continued. "As far as the safety goes, you should know that spinal taps do not cause paralysis. The principle risks are introduction of infection, but that is extraordinarily rare because we do it under strict antiseptic conditions. Bleeding can occur but that is usually minor. Bottom line: The risks of not doing the tap and risking missing meningitis are far greater than that of the spinal tap itself."

Ralph Gold glanced at his still crying wife and looked back at Egan. "Look, doctor, I mean no disrespect, but you seem young. I mean are you even fully certified yet?"

"Well, I'm not board certified in pediatrics yet, but I am a medical doctor."

"Wouldn't it be a good idea to call in somebody more senior, maybe get another opinion?"

Egan colored slightly. He steeled himself and took a breath, discarding the first ill-considered words that had leapt into his brain before answering.

"Mr. Gold, you're right, I'm young, but I'm not totally wet behind the ears. I'm well trained. I'm more than happy to call a more senior person, but you should understand, it's almost 3 AM. Most grey eminences are at home fast asleep. To get a physician in from home will take time. In my judgment, the time to act is now."

Gold and Egan held each other's gaze. Mrs. Gold had stopped sobbing and was also looking at Egan.

"Ralph, let him do it."

He stared an instant longer at Egan and slowly nodded his head.

The couple left the room, and Tina began to set up for the spinal tap. Without another word, Egan, who had been scrubbing while Tina set up, reached over to the tray and picked up gloves and put them on, careful to avoid touching the outer surface.

Tina placed the baby in a "folded position" with the lower part of the baby's back bent and protruding through sterile drapes. He swabbed the lower portion of the back with a Betadine swab. He palpated the baby's spine, feeling for a small vertebral interspace. He located it, and kept his finger there.

He took the spinal needle with his other hand and inserted it through the skin right next to his finger pressed against the baby's back. The baby cried and wiggled, but Tina expertly tightened her hold as Egan slowly advanced the needle, angling it upward slightly until he felt a faint pop that told him he had entered the spinal canal. He stopped pushing and carefully removed the stylet from the needle and was gratified to see drops of clear fluid drip out. After collecting small amounts of fluid into each of the five plastic tubes, he replaced the stylet, removed the needle and applied pressure for several minutes to allow the puncture wound to seal. He held one of the tubes to the light. He looked more closely at the tube and sniffed the top. He detected a faint odor. *That's not normal!*

He hurried to the small lab in the back of the ER, and with his hands shaking, he prepared a slide. He placed it on the slide holder of the microscope and brought it into focus. A sea of white blood cells and blue stained microbes filled his visual field.

Egan leapt to his feet and rushed down the hall.

"Tina, this baby has meningitis. Call the ICU and page the chief resident, and while you're at it, the infectious disease fellow. I'll be right in to start an IV after I talk to the parents."

The blue cocci, dancing in his mind's eye, energized him. His fatigue had left him and a purposeful and commanding manner supplanted the sleepy lethargy that had characterized him just 15 minutes before. Mr. Gold, his arm around his sobbing wife, looked at Egan.

"It's not good, is it?"

Egan willed himself to talk in soft measured tones, though he was anxious to start the treatment as soon as possible."

"No, I'm afraid not. Your baby has meningitis. But you should know that we're catching it early. I am going to start an IV and give the first dose of antibiotics."

Egan reached out and placed his hand on the father's shoulder. "Are you going to be okay?"

Gold pulled his sobbing wife closer to his chest. "Doc, don't worry about anything else; just do what you have to do." He left the parents and hurried into the treatment room, where Tina with quick, sure movements was assembling IV equipment. He put his finger on one of the baby's arms and gently palpated searching for a vein. He did the same thing on the other arm and then the legs. *Damn, not a thing.* He looked at the neck and wondered if he should try a blind stick for a jugular vein. He took a small IV catheter that consisted of a plastic tube over a hollow needle and felt the skin once again to see if he could palpate that slight spongy feeling that can signify a vein. He felt nothing. He picked a spot in the forearm where he knew a vein should be and penetrated the skin with the needle. Slowly he advanced it, watching carefully for any signs of blood in the hub of the needle which would indicate that the needle tip had found a vein. He had no success the first try and tried several more times. The baby, who initially cried vigorously, began to respond less to each needle stick.

Egan looked up at Tina. "Having no luck with this IV." He looked back at the baby. "Tina, let's get another set of vitals. I don't like the way he's looking."

Egan continued to try to get an IV started while Tina took the vital signs.

"Heart rate is 210, temperature 102.3, blood pressure 60/30."

"Christ, Tina, I need access and I need it now! Where the hell is the chief resident? He should have been here by now!" He paused for a moment and then softly, "Tina, get an intraosseous needle!"

She handed it to him hesitantly. "Don't you want to get parental consent?"

"No time; we'll get it after the fact. This baby is going into septic shock."

He began to scrub an area just below the knee.

"Dr. Egan, have you done this procedure before?"

"No."

She watched him with pursed lips while he felt a flat area just below the knee on the inner aspect of the tibia and firmly pushed the needle until he felt a sudden give and a crunch indicating that the needle had penetrated into the bone marrow. He connected the hub to IV tubing.

"Excellent, doctor; it's flowing beautifully."

"Okay, Tina, we're even. Let's give him 250 milligrams of ampicillin stat followed by 300 milligrams of Cefotaxime, followed by 250 cc's of normal saline."

The antibiotics were given and Tina was starting to give the saline when the ICU team arrived, including Chief Resident Dr. Doug Barrett

"Okay," Dr. Barrett said, "I'll take over."

Dr. Egan reluctantly ceded leadership to his senior.

Egan and Barrett had known each other for years since their freshman year of medical school and had never liked each other. Egan had finished first in his class to the surprise of many, including Barrett, who finished second. Egan's at times sleepy manner bordering on affectation disguised a sharp competitive intellect. Egan, who was in a MD/PhD program, took the two years after medical school to get his dissertation research underway and hence began residency two years after Barrett. It continued to rankle him to find himself under Barrett's supervision.

"Intraosseous needle! Being a bit aggressive there, aren't we, old boy? You never could resist trying a new procedure."

"Hell, Doug, this baby is in septic shock! I wasn't about to let his brain continue to fry from poor blood flow and bacterial toxins."

"Okay, okay," rejoined Barrett as he peered at the fluid and antibiotic bags hanging above. "Wait a minute. Isn't this baby only four weeks old?"

"Yeah, Doug, so what?"

"How come you've hung cefo instead of genta? That's not the protocol for a baby this age."

"Doug, this baby has pneumococcal meningitis."

"Pneumococcal at four weeks? Are you sure? That is pretty uncommon at this age."

"Take a look for yourself," Barrett demurred, reluctantly realizing that Egan with his extensive lab experience knew his way around a microscope slide.

"Boys, boys," Tina broke in. "What do you say about tending to this baby and you two can square off later at the gym?"

Both chagrined, they turned their full attention to their sick charge, communicating in short staccato bursts as they struggled to treat the baby who was looking sicker by the minute.

"Dopamine drip, 2 micrograms per kilo per minute."

"Okay, Eric. Tina, intubation tray. Get respiratory therapy to set up the vent."

"Blood pressure down to 50 over 25."

"Okay, up the dopamine to 3."

"Heart rate dropping to 65."

"Cardiac compressions, start bagging the baby, .5 milligrams of atropine."

Gradually, the pediatric team began to turn the tide against the microbe induced shock and stabilized the baby enough for transport to the ICU, the gurney surrounded by residents, IV poles, monitors and nurses as it made its unwieldy way to the elevator. Trailing behind, the parents followed with anguished disbelieving expressions.

Egan and Tina, grim-faced, watched them leave the ER. Egan turned to Tina. "Do me a favor; if in the future I hesitate even for a millisecond to follow your instincts, will you promise to give me a hard kick in the ass?"

Tina laughed. "Why, Dr. Egan, it would be my pleasure to do so. Kicking ass is something I'm particularly good at."

"Pneumococcus...who would have thought? How the hell did a four-week-old get pneumococcal meningitis?"

"I don't know. But it's not the first one I've seen. We had another one about six months ago. A bit older though; that baby was six weeks old as I recall.

Egan looked at her, his eyebrows arched up in surprise. "Really? That's strange. Are you sure the other was pneumococcus?"

Tina gave him a stern look, her arms akimbo. "Sure, I'm sure. Are you already looking for a swift kick?"

"Sorry, sorry. I promise never again. Do you remember the name by any chance?"

"No, but I can check the ER log." She walked to the front of the ER and opened a large notebook and turned back several dozen pages. "There it is." She pointed to an entry. "Jamie Reed, six weeks old, diagnosis: meningitis, presumed pneumococcus."

Chapter Three
August 20, 2008 3:15 AM

Egan strolled back to his on call room. He sat on the edge of the cot and took a moment to exult. *I made the diagnosis!* He went over the sequence of events minute by minute. He lay back, keeping his eyes open, a smile on his face, suddenly in no hurry to sleep. He thought of his mother and felt sad that she was not around to share this. When his mother died while he was in high school, his family had fallen apart. He pictured her excited, smiling face that had greeted him whenever he told her of an accomplishment. "Eric, my little Einstein, you have done it again!"

Shortly after his mother's death, his dad had come to watch the state high school sculls championship, something he had never found time to do before. He had seemed astonished at his son's victory. A year or so after his wife's death, he had left his high-level executive position and now spent a good deal of his time at a country cottage alone on the porch.

Egan's younger brother was battling a drug habit and was in and out of rehab. Egan had thrown himself into his studies and it seemed to him that he only heard from his family when he was needed to deal with some crisis or another. He forced these thoughts from his head and began to think about the blonde mother he had seen several hours before, and thought to himself, *it's been too long,* as he finally drifted off.

"Dr. Egan, Dr. Egan." It was Tina and her voice had a sense of urgency that began to penetrate to the deep recesses of his brain and stirred him to consciousness. He glanced briefly at his watch and winced in disbelief as he saw 4:30.

"Shit, Tina, not again."

"Don't you 'shit' me. All hell is breaking loose. One of the OB attendings just rushed in with his two-year-old son. The kid is comatose."

Egan sat up abruptly and fought a wave of dizziness as he tried get his rattled brain to think. Coma! "Come on, Eric; the doc in there is having a shit fit. Newhouse is on his way in, plus the neurology attending."

Without another word Egan raced down the hall to the treatment room he had left just a little more than an hour ago. On the gurney was a young child in a diaper and tee shirt, seemingly asleep. Hovering over him, Egan recognized Dr. John Oden, one of the recent additions to the obstetrical staff. Next to him was a blond woman in her late twenties sobbing loudly.

Dr. Oden, a large man in his early thirties, prematurely bald with a large compensatory mustache and known for his cool efficiency and confidence in the OR, was in a state of extreme agitation, sputtering as he spoke. "We found him like this on the bathroom floor, not 20 minutes ago. My God, what on earth can be wrong with him? He's never been sick a day in his life." His eyes flitted back and forth as he spoke.

Egan, stunned by the scene before him, felt a wave of vertigo and panic. He gripped the edge of the gurney and stared at the toddler. Coma, causes, differential diagnosis, think, think, but first evaluate, ABCs, right, airway, breathing, circulation—a cascade of disjointed thoughts tumbled through his mind.

"Doctor, do something. I can't lose another child." Her sobbing words intruded upon his internal mental cacophony.

A glance at both parents and his training asserted itself. He took two steps to the head of the bed and observed the child's breathing. Okay, airway patent. He listened to the chest. Good breath sounds. Color, a tad blue at the fingertips.

"Tina, oxygen by mask, put on a pulse monitor. Get a bag of normal saline ready. Let's get a cervical collar around his neck."

He examined the child's head looking for signs of trauma, but found none. Tina moved her ample girth in quick efficient movements, starting the oxygen, placing the monitor and readying the IV solution.

He had just placed an IV in the child's arm, when Egan heard the familiar stentorian voice of Dr. Jack Newhouse, director of the Pediatric Intensive Care Unit, emanate from the corridor.

"Where is he?" And then rapid footsteps and he was in the room. *Thank God,* thought Egan.

Newhouse gave Oden a quick squeeze on his shoulder and turned to Egan.

"Okay, buddy, what do we have here?" His voice was calm and almost conversational and Egan could feel the tension drain from his shoulders.

"Two-and-one-half-year-old, previously in good health, found by Dr. Oden and his wife lying on the bathroom floor, unarousable. On arrival here, I assessed him at Glasgow coma scale 10, vital signs stable and no outward signs of trauma. I've sent a complete blood count, chem profile, and tox screen, and alerted radiology to fire up the scanner."

"Good job, buddy. Any history of trauma the last few days?"

"Apparently not."

"Wait a minute," broke in Dr. Oden. "He was at the park yesterday with his nanny. Honey, didn't she say something about a fall off the swing?"

"Yeah, but he seemed fine afterwards. Do think something happened from the fall?" Oden's wife voice rose with panic.

"Have to consider it. Epidural or subdural hematoma could give a delayed onset coma. Better alert neurosurgery." Newhouse leaned forward and began a meticulous head to toe examination of the child. "What did you say his Glasgow coma scale was when you did it?"

"Ten."

"Not good. I get him at 8 now. I bet he has a subdural. We'd better intubate. This kid could stop breathing at any time."

Egan nodded his assent.

"Eric, would you like to do the honors?"

Egan flushed with pleasure. Despite the gravity of the situation, Newhouse trusted him to make the first attempt at the intubation.

"Okay, buddy, got all your equipment? Laryngoscope, suction catheter, better get three different sizes of tubes ready."

Egan sat at the head of the gurney, took a deep breath and leaned over the child's mouth and placed the laryngoscope blade at the tip of the tongue and began to slowly insert it. As the blade pushed the tongue to one side, first the pharynx, and then the larynx came into view. He lifted the blade to get a better view of the vocal cords which marked the entrance to the trachea and peered into the oral cavity, his face almost touching the child's mouth as he strained to see.

He became aware of an odor. He took a sniff. He had not noticed it when he first examined the child. What was that odor? It lapped tantalizingly at the edge of his brain and suddenly a chain of associations fell into place.

"Eric, what's the matter? Are you having trouble visualizing the landmarks?" Newhouse asked in an urgent whisper.

Egan withdrew the laryngoscope with one swift motion and looked up at Newhouse.

"I've got an idea. Tina, get me an amp of a 25 percent glucose solution."

"Eric, what the hell are you doing?"

But Egan already had his hands around a 50 cc syringe and before Newhouse could utter another word, had found the rubber IV port and pushed in the glucose solution. Almost instantaneously, the child had bolted up from the bed screaming for his mother.

Chapter Four

Egan and Newhouse stepped into the corridor leaving Dr. Oden and his wife crying and laughing as their now fully awake son squirmed within their tight embrace.

Newhouse paused and stared at Egan. "Eric, how the hell did you know that the boy was in a hypoglycemic coma?"

Egan was tempted to say, "Elementary, my dear Watson." His chances of having another situation where he could give this answer before the brilliant but baffled Dr. Newhouse were slim to none, but he decided to suppress it. God knows, flip answers had never been career boosters in his experience.

"I guess I was a bit lucky," he said modestly. "As I was bending over ready to intubate, I became aware of an odor that at first I didn't recognize. Suddenly I realized it was mouthwash, the minty fresh scent of Scope, to be exact. In that instant, I remembered an article I read in *Contemporary Pediatrics* several months ago. Toddlers are attracted to the brightly colored bottles and might drink enough to develop alcohol-induced hypoglycemia. That they found him in the bathroom made it seem even more likely to me."

Newhouse stared at him open-mouthed, "Wow, excellent. Excellent observation, excellent knowledge base, excellent deduction and decisive action. Most second-year residents wouldn't know that toddlers react to even small amounts of ethanol with a dramatic lowering of their blood sugar, let alone be aware of the mouthwash connection. Excellent, excellent. As for myself, I'm mentally chastising myself for leaping to the wrong conclusion. I was so sure we were dealing with a subdural."

"Dr. Newhouse, that was a perfectly reasonable conclusion."

Newhouse let a loud guffaw. "What's wrong with this picture, a second-year resident comforting the experienced attending? Anyway, let this be a lesson for both of us; medicine can be humbling no matter what your position."

Newhouse continued to gaze at Egan. "I must say, I have always been aware of your cognitive abilities, but frankly your olfactory capabilities were totally unknown to me. You've got quite a schnoz."

"Well, yeah. I never thought to put that down on my residency application. It's a bit of a curse, actually. I'm often aware of and bothered by odors that no one else seems to even notice."

"I suppose so, but it sure stood you in good stead today. By the way, I was going to call you today anyway. Do you have a moment to talk?"

Egan took one quick longing glance at his on-call room down the corridor before answering brightly, "Sure."

They stepped into a nearby lounge that was deserted at that early hour and settled into chairs.

"I think you'll be happy with what I have to tell you. It concerns the perinatal immunology fellowship."

Egan's ears perked up. The O'Neil perinatal fellowship was a much coveted and prestigious post-residency position that most of the residents gunned for whether or not they admitted it. Unlike most fellowships that simply asked for applications, this one solicited none but merely tapped the person the institutional powers felt was the most qualified among the residents. In the ten years of its existence, not a single designee had ever turned down the offer.

Newhouse regarded Egan with what appeared to be a faint smile of knowing amusement as if he could follow Egan's rapid thought processes that were precipitated by the mention of the O'Neil.

"I won't keep you in suspense any longer, Eric. The selection committee has authorized me to inform you that you are one of four finalists for the O'Neil. And believe me, your performance this morning will do nothing to hurt your chances."

Egan felt a rush of euphoria and could not contain the broad smile that enveloped his face.

"Wow, I don't know what to say."

"How about a simple: Dr. Newhouse, thank you, I'm honored."

Egan smiled and repeated. "Thank you, I'm honored."

"Remember what I have tried to tell you in the past—learn to be diplomatic. It won't kill you to learn to be a bit political."

"I'll do my best. Do you really think I have a chance?"

"Of course. You definitely have the smarts plus the research experience. The key obstacle will be your rather obstreperous tendencies. Now, you may or may not know that it is our tradition to invite the four finalists to my house in the country for a weekend. We have scheduled it for Labor Day weekend."

Egan frowned. "I think I'm on call that weekend."

"Don't worry; I already checked. You're on that Monday. You can come up on Saturday morning, and you can come back with the rest of us after dinner on Sunday. It's only two hours away."

"That's great. Who else will be there?"

"Besides the two of us, Blake George, of course, the three other finalists, and Michael Meiselman since he'll be starting the fellowship next year, Dr. Johnson and the pediatric department chair. And, of course, John Oden, who you just met. One other thing, you're welcome to bring your significant other if you have one.

"Significant other? Are you kidding me? The work you attendings saddle us with leaves us very little time for romancing."

Newhouse laughed. "Back in my day, we were even more overworked and still found the time!"

"Yeah, yeah, I know and you probably had to walk fifteen miles to the hospital in blizzards," he laughed, glancing at his watch. "Oh, look at the time. I've got to get to rounds."

"Okay, buddy, I won't hold you up."

They shook hands, and Egan left the ER and rushed down the hallway and past the elevator banks and sprinted up four flights of stairs. He stopped at the top to catch his breath still with the same smile that he had when he left the ER. "Significant other," he muttered to himself, and his smile faded a bit. What are the chances, he wondered, that I'll have one by Labor Day? He looked at his watch again and picked up the pace even more. Shit, old Johnson will be furious. A fastidious man, Dr. Herbert Johnson was obsessively punctual and accepted no excuses for being late for rounds. Once, Egan remembered, he had been fast asleep in the on-call room and was woken by the chart rack crashing into his bed. He had opened his eyes to find the whole ward team assembled at his bedside with Dr. Johnson at the head of the group. "If Dr. Egan will not condescend to come to rounds, then the mountain will move to Mohamed. Present your first case."

He left the staircase and took rapid steps toward the pediatric ward.

"Hey, where's the fire?"

Egan recognized the voice of Michael Meiselman. He slowed to allow Michael to catch up with him and then resumed his previous pace. Michael, a thin, almost cadaverous young man with a wide teasing grin, slung a friendly arm over his shoulders.

"Michael, can't linger, I'm late for rounds, yet again. Johnson's probably having a shit fit as we speak."

"Don't worry about it. What's one more tardiness on your record? Probably Johnson would faint with shock if you were actually ever present when rounds start, so slow down."

"Michael, I'm serious, I've got to go." Egan attempted to wriggle out of Michael's tightening grip.

"Just hold up for a minute, will you?" Michael pulled him to a stop as a cowboy would a runaway horse. "There, big fellow. You got to learn not to be so uptight about everything. I have to check that you're presentable for rounds." Michael turned Egan so they were facing each other.

"Yes, yes," Michael continued. "Not too bad. Those scrubs look like they've been around the block a few times, but a few blood stains are de rigueur for a busy resident like you. Lab coat stylish at mid-thigh length, pockets packed with your Harriet Lane handbook, pen light, and pens. Stethoscope casually draped around your neck. Yes, very nice."

"Jesus Christ, Michael, will you let me go? I'm in no mood for this."

"Patience, my friend." Michael again tightened his grip on Egan who continued to struggle. "One more thing I have to check." He leaned forward and for one moment an astonished Egan thought Michael was going to kiss him. "Open your mouth." He commanded which Egan did without thinking.

"Excellent," said Michael after sniffing. "Your breath is suitable for rounds. I detect the minty freshness of Scope. It's not every resident who takes the time." Michael was barely able to finish his sentence before he emitted a loud chortle.

Egan looked at him with astonishment, but was unable to contain a broadening grin.

"Jesus, you heard about that already?"

"Yessiree. Your latest exploit is being disseminated far and wide by Tina. I spotted her in the coffee shop not ten minutes ago loudly extolling your diagnostic virtues to a growing group of nurses and residents."

"Well, what can I say? Talk about luck!"

"Please, your modesty is most unbecoming. What most impresses me is that you managed to pull off this coup right under, dare I say it, the nose of the top attending in the whole place. You, my good Dr. Egan, are the man. You are deserving of a new moniker. Henceforth you shall be known as Dr. Mouthwash."

Michael paused for a moment, lips pursed. "No, no I got a better one, Dr. Schnoz."

"Okay, I can see that your creative juices are flowing, but I've got to get to rounds." Egan spun around before Michael could grab him and made his escape.

"How about Dr. Snout?" Michael called after Egan who was already 10 yards down the corridor, the sides of his lab coat flapping as he hurried down the corridor.

Chapter Five
August 20, 2008 7:09 AM

As Egan had feared, rounds were already well in progress when he arrived. In addition to the attending, Dr. Johnson, the group consisted of the third-year resident in charge of the ward, two second-year residents, three interns, and five medical students. It's easy to determine who is who, thought Egan idly. The one with old sneakers and jeans was the third-year resident, and as you went down in seniority, the dress steadily improved until you got to the medical students with shoes shined and ties knotted tightly at the top, and eager puppy dog expressions on their faces.

Egan tried to slip unobtrusively into the group, straining to keep his breathing slow and silent, but Dr. Johnson, despite having his head deep in a chart, sensed his presence.

"Ah, Mohammed, you have decided to honor us with your presence!"

Egan had learned from past experience to allow this to roll over him, and simply nodded in greeting and tried to clear his brain in order to concentrate. One of the medical students was presenting a case and Egan, who usually listened with half an ear, knowing that medical students tended to mention every detail no matter how obscure in order not to leave anything out, now turned to listen because a new patient was being presented.

"Can you briefly summarize for Dr Egan?" intoned Dr. Johnson while giving Egan a stern look.

"Certainly. This six-year-old white male was transferred from a local community hospital with a chief complaint of chronic diarrhea. He was completely well until approximately one month ago when he began to have five to six very loose bowel movements, sometimes with blood. This was accompanied by intermittent vomiting.

"After a week of this he was admitted to the community hospital in a state of extreme dehydration. He was successfully rehydrated with IV therapy and discharged after four days but presented again three days later, again severely dehydrated. He has remained in the hospital since then with waxing and waning diarrhea requiring IV therapy at times. His workup has consisted of stool cultures, negative for salmonella, shigella, campylobacter, yersinia, clostridia and E. coli, stool for ova and parasites, upper and lower GI series. Colonoscopy was also performed and was completely normal. He was transferred here last night under the care of Dr. Jack Pierro."

"What about his labs?"

"Everything normal. He is not anemic, his white blood cell count is normal, and his eosinophil count was okay."

This student is pretty good, thought Egan, as she continued to speak. She mentioned just the relevant labs and didn't list every damn sodium level the patient had as some students would. He leaned over slightly, trying not to be too obvious and read her name tag: Gail Roscoe. She had a slight accent that was hard to place—somewhere southern, Virginia maybe—and her words poured out in neat paragraphs. She had a way of shaking her head slightly to move back a recalcitrant lock of straight light brown hair that encroached upon the left side of her face. Each time she did so, deep blue eyes were revealed.

Egan tried to maneuver himself a bit closer, vowing to follow this woman around until the end of his days, or least until the end of rounds, whichever came first.

The group now crowded into the patient's room where the boy laid on the bed playing intently with his iPhone. A well-groomed woman was seated next to him on the bed. She immediately sprang to her feet and held out her hand to Dr. Johnson. Her smile was broad and seemed a bit incongruous with that of a mother hovering over a sick bed. After introducing herself, she immediately launched into a long rather garrulous account of her son's illness, which ended with her presenting Dr. Johnson with a bucket containing her son's latest bowel movements as if she was handing over a particularly rare species of orchid. Dr. Johnson peered into the container and noted an impressively large volume of watery stool. The medical students jostled each other to get a better look.

"Now, students," began Dr. Johnson, "this is an excellent chance to review fluid balance. Let's look at the intake and output sheet."

Egan yawned and thought, *Oh no, not fluid balance.* He knew this was a particular interest of Dr. Johnson's. He also knew he couldn't stand to hear it one more time. His mind drifted off and he edged out of the room. He was surprised to find the medical student, Gail Roscoe, in the hallway, her head deep into a book. "You're not listening to the lecture?" He gestured toward the patient's room.

"Oops, you caught me," she said sheepishly. "I just thought I'd learn more by looking at this. I've heard Dr. Johnson on fluid balance three times already."

No ass-kisser, this one, Egan thought approvingly.

"Don't worry, I won't tell!" He grinned at her. "I'm Eric Egan, by the way."

"Yes, I know; I've heard all about you."

"Really? I had no idea I was well known among the med students."

"Actually, it was just this morning, at the beginning of rounds, from Dr. Johnson. Apparently when he is not discussing fluid balance, he likes to talk about the chronic tardiness of one Dr. Eric Egan." Gail looked directly at Egan, her blue eyes shining and a faint smile playing on her lips. Egan held her gaze, noticing concentric circles of varying shades of turquoise, beryline, and aquamarine.

He smiled back. "Oh, yeah? What did he say?"

"I think he began with 'where the hell is Dr. Egan?' threw in a few comments about how in his day, it would never be tolerated, how insulting it was, etcetera, etcetera, and ended with a little rant about the consequences of an incomplete education. I was beginning to think when you showed up it would be on a motorcycle with a 'rebel without a cause' tattoo on your arm. I must say you look rather like a typical resident to me."

Egan laughed. "Hell, if I had a motorcycle, I probably wouldn't be late. By the way, you said that you'd heard Johnson on fluid balance three times before. Isn't this your first day on this floor? I'm sure I would have remembered you if you had been here before."

"You're right. It is my first day on this rotation. But Johnson is famous for rounding up groups of medical students for impromptu lectures. The guy is a total teaching nerd."

"Miss Roscoe."

Egan and Gail in their tête-a- tête had failed to notice that the group had emerged from the patient's room and both started. "You're right. I am, as you say it, a teaching nerd. Now if you don't mind I'd like to hear from you how to calculate the sodium requirements for a 10-kilo baby who is 7 percent dehydrated. And as for you, Dr. Egan, I would think that having arrived late for rounds, your attention would be that much more focused. God forbid you may need some of the information that is typically imparted in early rounds to treat a patient." He paused briefly. "Miss Roscoe, if you please."

Egan, a bit red-faced, listened to Gail explain the steps of the calculation with economy of language and exactitude. Egan was impressed, and he could tell that Johnson was too, though for the uninitiated it was not too obvious in his guttural harrumph before continuing to the next patient.

Dr. Johnson mercifully became cognizant of the time and rounds continued apace. In rapid sequence, the group visited a three-year-old boy with an infection around his eye, four kids with asthma, and three more kids with diarrhea and dehydration. Finally, rounds were over and Johnson strode off.

Egan watched him go and smiled, shaking his head slightly. He turned to Gail. "Look at old Johnson, looking smug and satisfied. He had everyone squirming and almost brought one of the interns to tears with his questioning. He has once again exposed the incredible and shocking ignorance and unpreparedness of the heralded house staff of this august institution and he is, of course, pleased, and now is disappearing to wherever attendings go for the twenty-three hours a day that they are not torturing people on rounds. Of course, he made numerous suggestions most of which create tons of the most odious forms of ward chores. You, by the way, were the exception. You really exhibited grace under pressure in answering that sodium question."

"Well, thank you," answered Gail with a smile and opened her mouth to say more.

"Hold that thought, Gail."

"Okay. Folks, let's gather around." It was Dr. Joan Richter with her loud, and to Egan, grating voice.

"Uh-oh, here we go," whispered Egan to Gail.

Joan Richter was the third-year resident who was in charge of the ward this month. She was staring at her clipboard where she had dutifully noted each and every one of Johnson's suggestions as the group gathered around her.

"Okay," began Joan still staring hard at her clipboard, "people, let's get organized here, lots to do, lots to do. Interns, let's make sure you know what bloods to draw on your patients."

Egan began to edge his way out of the group.

"Eric, not so fast. The interns are going to need some help, so I'd like you to stick around. The diabetic in three needs a post prandial glucose, the seizure in five needs a therapeutic phenobarb level, and the heart in seven needs a pre op clearance. Eric, are you writing this down?"

"I'm making mental notes."

"Do me a favor; write it down."

"Yes sir, boss, but wait, didn't we just get a phenobarb level yesterday?"

"Please, Eric, not an argument each time; just do it." And back and forth they bickered. It's not that Egan was against work, as he told Gail later that day, "but the unnecessary work generated by one of the most anal-retentive people I have ever met, and that's saying a lot here in this institution where compulsives are bred like lab rats."

All dispersed. Egan managed to collar Gail to help him out.

"Okay, Gail, you are in for a rare treat. You get to watch an experienced resident organize a massive assault on a scut list."

"This is very exciting," she answered with a little shake of her head and amused smile.

"First, we divide it up into categories. Let's start with bloods. I like to note which tube I need for each one. Here, for example, the diabetic in room three needs a spun crit, a complete blood count, lytes, and a glucose so we will need a capillary tube, purple top, a grey top, a speckled top, and a red top."

"A red top? What's that for? By my count we have four tests and five tubes."

"I'll explain. Here's where the savvy resident factor comes in. It's a didya tube. Inevitably when we send a blood test, some genius who out ranks us shows up to ask, "didya" send a porcelain level or some other equally obscure test. So we'll be ready with our extra tube to send off."

"I see. My goodness, you are brilliant," Gail said with a smirk.

"You've seen nothing yet. Let's go."

They set off with a myriad of tubes jangling in their lab coat pockets and methodically went down the list. Finally they ended up in the small ward lab, loaded down with blood.

"Okay, Gail, all these with their lab slips go into the pneumatic tube over there, and all we have left to do is to spin these capillary tubes."

Gail took each capillary tube and placed it carefully into a small desktop centrifuge and closed the top.

"Ready to roll," she said as she reached to turn on the centrifuge.

"Wait," said Egan as he put a restraining hand on her forearm. "Remember, the devil is in the details. Aren't you forgetting something?"

"Oh, shit, the restraining cover." She reached over for the flat medal plate and screwed it into place over the capillary tubes, closed the cover, and turned on the centrifuge.

"I could have let you have experience as your teacher, but I didn't have the heart. Last year I forgot once to put the restraining cover on and I had, jeez, maybe twenty tubes in there. I tell you, the sound of twenty capillary tubes going crunch in the early morning is a mighty dispiriting sound when attending rounds are only ten minutes away."

"Well, I feel most honored to learn at the feet of a master."

"Hey, watch the sarcasm—I just may let you blunder next time." Egan said with a smile, his gaze fixed on the slightly crooked smirk playing on her lips.

The centrifuge spun while they talked and enjoyed the closed off intimacy of the small room they were in. He was half falling in love for the second time in 24 hours. It happens quickly around here, he thought. Not much time, so most of us fall in and out of love several times a day. We're sort of like mayflies, trying quickly to mate before our cells go off.

Chapter Six
August 20, 2008 12:45 PM

Later that morning, fatigue hit Egan like a freight train as he struggled to find a vein that had not been traumatized by previous intern attempts. Finally, he found a miniature blue line on the patient's inner wrist. He carefully inserted a 24-gauge needle and inched it forward until a small drop of blood emerged from the hub. He held the needle as still as possible, though he could not control a slight involuntary tremor, and with his thumb, pushed a small plastic nub connected to a catheter that encased the needle. He felt a slight resistance and knew that the catheter tip was on the verge of the hole in the vein created by the needle. A bit more pressure, a slight give, and he snaked the catheter home into the vein.

"Thank, God," he muttered to himself, a line of beaded sweat collecting across his forehead.

The rest of Egan's day seemed to stretch interminably ahead of him. He could think only of the subway ride at the end of which he would find his bed. There seemed to be endless tasks that he needed to complete before finishing the day. Then it hit him: It was Wednesday, his clinic day! This meant he could sign out his ward responsibilities to the other second-year resident and go down to the outpatient clinic where he would see his roster of patients and with any luck be out by three.

After a quick lunch, he arrived at the clinic to find that he was double-booked. "What's going on?" he demanded. "How can I see all these patients?"

The clerk, used to this sort of outburst, was unperturbed and calmly replied, "Come over here and take a look at this list."

He obeyed and peered at the list, still in irritable disbelief.

"See those little marks next to the names of the extra patients?"

He grunted yes. The little marks indicated that the doctor had previously approved the additions. As often happened to him, during the week various patients would call and each would have a particular compelling reason that he or she had to be added. Just as a user of a credit card is often shocked by the number of things bought the previous month, Egan was perpetually surprised at the number of approvals he had issued the week before. His fluent knowledge of Spanish put him in big demand among the largely Hispanic clinic population.

"Okay, send the first one in."

"*El es tan flaco! El no quire comer nada,*" said his third patient's mother, a diminutive Dominican talking about her nine-month-old baby, who was one of the largest infants he had ever seen. He patiently showed via weight and calorie charts just how well nourished this child was.

"*Mira, señora, el esta 95 percent por su pesa. Es muy bien.*" She looked at the point on the graph with some suspicion. She seemed unconvinced and merely repeated her lament. Egan smiled to himself, knowing that the maternal instinct to feed is deeply entrenched and is not so easily dislodged by graphs and a second-year resident. Yet most mothers liked his earnest manner and the sincere attention he gave their complaints. It was a ritual that seemed to meet the needs of both doctor and patient.

Finally his clinic was over. He glanced at his watch as he walked out of the hospital. "Three-thirty, not bad at all." The subway was crowded, but he managed to squeeze into a seat. The car didn't move as passengers flung themselves at the closing doors, pushing their way in. Finally, on the fourth attempt, the doors closed with a slam. Egan felt a brief wave of claustrophobia, hemmed on either side and with standing passengers hanging over him.

His bottle of pills was wedged deep down in the bottom of his pants pocket. He thought to reach for them, but realized his leg was tight against the leg of an enormously muscled man with large tattoos on both biceps and a seemingly indelible frown on his face. The car began to move, slowly at first and then with greater momentum, and the car began to sway slightly back and forth.

He closed his eyes and practiced some breathing exercises he had learned and was able to calm himself. He thought of all that had happened during his shift and various disjointed images flashed through his brain; Tina's muted "I told you so" expression, Dr. Oden's son coming to life like Lazarus before his eyes, stained cocci looking like a huge field of blueberries. This last image lingered in his mind: pneumococcus in a four-week old. The second one in six months. *What was the name again? Jamie Reed!* Right before he dozed off, he made a mental note to go to medical records the next day.

He awoke with a start and saw a commotion in front of him. An obese middle-aged man in jacket and tie lay collapsed on the subway floor. "What's happening?" Egan asked a woman next to him. "He just keeled over about ten seconds ago. He was clutching his chest." *Heart attack,* thought Egan, and instinctively leaped to his feet. The Hell's Angels man was already kneeling next to the man feeling in the neck for a pulse.

"I'm a doctor," Egan announced more loudly than he intended.

The tattooed man looked at him. "I'm an EMT. Let's get to work. I can't feel a pulse."

Egan reached his hand forward to the man's neck. "I can't feel one either. He's probably in full arrest."

Egan briefly tried to rouse the man and attempted once again to feel for a carotid pulse in the neck. He could feel none and whether this was because of a fat neck or because the man was in full cardiac arrest, he could not tell.

"We better start CPR. This man has heart attack written all over him."

"You're right," answered Egan and leaned forward with his two hands together ready to start chest compressions.

"Wait," said the Hell's Angel. "We need better exposure." He quickly loosened the man's tie and then opened his button down shirt with one swift motion causing loose buttons to fly all over the floor. Egan leaned over again, scanning the now bare chest to correctly position his hands for cardiac compressions. It was at this precise moment, with the sound of the buttons rattling along the subway floor still ringing in his ears that the man's eyes fluttered open. There was an awkward pause as both men eyed each other.

"Let me help you up, sir," stammered Egan as he attempted to close the shirt.

Egan glanced over at the EMT, who had magically disappeared and was back in his seat.

The man looked down at his exposed chest and open buttonless shirt and back at Egan two to three times, looking nonplussed.

"I guess I must have fainted. These subway cars are hot." Egan helped him to his feet and sat him in his space on the bench. The next stop was Egan's and he stepped onto the platform with alacrity. One last backward glance revealed the man still looking with a puzzled expression at his open shirt and the tattooed man next to him with his expression just as implacable as before, but now with a hint of amusement at the corners of his mouth. He gave Egan a wink of the eye before the doors slammed shut once again.

From the subway stop, it was a five-block walk to his apartment, and he trudged wearily toward it. The door to his building was ajar. He sighed. Better call the super once again about fixing the lock. He started up the stairs slowly, pausing briefly at each landing. On the fifth floor, he leaned against the door of his studio apartment while he searched for his keys.

He pushed the door open and surveyed the room he hadn't seen in thirty-six hours. Dishes were piled in the sink, the floor was dirty, and various articles of clothes were strewn in a line leading from the door to his bed. He sighed again. He stripped off his shirt as he made his way to the bed and added it to the collection on the floor. He sat on the bed, exhausted but eerily awake. He lay back and stared at the ceiling, a crisscross pattern of cracks and peeling paint. Like a boy staring at the sky and seeing faces and figures in the clouds, he began to make out a craggy old man looking down at him with a frown. "Oh, shit," muttered Egan. "I got to get out of here."

Ten minutes later, he was outside in shorts and a tee shirt jogging up 75th street toward Central Park. After one lap around the reservoir, he slowed to a walk and entered a large meadow. He stopped to watch the activities of various people there. A number of young women were stretched out on towels, enjoying the late afternoon sun. A group of young kids were engaged in a spirited game of tag, while their nannies stood by.

He spotted a gray sixty something man walking a large black lab. The dog periodically stopped and put his nose to the ground and sniffed deeply. His owner matched the pace of the dog and allowed all the time needed for these intense olfactory investigations.

Egan watched, impressed. So different from the more typical dog walkers that insist on a more jaunty uninterrupted gait. Smell must be like vision is for humans. That dog must know every animal that passed by here during the last 24 hours. *It's a whole world I know nothing about. Must be damned interesting, such intense sniffing and scurrying.* Hospital corridors have a special smell, courtesy of those armies of men who engage in the Sisyphean chore of keeping the floors clean. Sometimes we smell a diagnosis. He smiled as he recalled the toddler who drank mouthwash then frowned as he recalled the odor of the baby's spinal fluid. A chill went down his back. *Good God, I almost sent that baby home.*

He trudged slowly back to his apartment, now ready for sleep.

Chapter Seven
Spring 1999

John Maynard Maitland III dove into the pool and glided several feet underwater before slowly emerging, the water dripping off his smooth features and close cropped black hair. He slowly breast-stroked his way to the shallow end, climbed out of the pool, and with a satisfied grunt settled into an adjoining Jacuzzi. He could feel the tension drain out of his aching muscles, which that day—the first day of his Cancun vacation—had been devoted to frenetic physical activity. Deep sea fishing, scuba diving, singles tennis for two hours with the resort pro, and then forty-five minutes of weight lifting all done with the intensity and skill which had propelled his meteoric rise to be one of Goldman Sachs top energy analysts at the tender age of twenty-eight. He stared up at the deep blue sky beyond the waving palm trees.

After twenty minutes of pleasant contemplation of his day, he pulled himself out of the Jacuzzi. A nearby pool attendant was there with a towel and he dried himself, slowly, methodically, almost loving-ly as the towel glided over well-developed pecs, abs, and quads. At the far end of the pool, he noticed a young woman staring at him over the top of her book and he paused in his bodily ministrations to look back at her and smiled, revealing straight white teeth. She held his gaze for a moment, before returning to her book. He resumed his toweling and began to whistle softly. Yes, this vacation was looking very promising.

Later that evening, he stepped into the bar, scanned the room and spotted the woman from the pool, in one corner, alone except for her book. He strode over to her table, noting her long straight raven black hair, olive skin, and lithe body. If she noticed his approach, she gave no sign of it and remained deeply engrossed in her book.

"So is Dorothea still married to that jerk Casabon?"

She peered at him over the top of her book, a slight smile playing across her angular face. "So a man of literature, hardly what I expected to encounter in a bar in Cancun," she answered while putting down her copy of George Elliot's *Middlemarch*.

"Hey, I had to read the whole damn thing for a lit class at Brown. You're the literate one, reading it while on vacation. May I join you?"

"Sure, as long as you don't tell me how it ends."

"Don't worry, do you think I remember?"

She laughed. "Oh, I bet you remember, and I would venture that you actually enjoyed every bit of it."

"Okay, okay, I admit, it wasn't the worst novel I've ever read. Can I buy you a drink?"

"Sure, a beer would hit the spot."

He waved over a waiter. "*Por favor, un dos eques para la senorita y para mi, un vaso de tequila, con un poquito de juego de naranja y limon.*"

"Wow, and fluent in Spanish. I'm impressed."

"Don't be, I was forced to—language requirement, you know. Now enough about me. What do you do?"

"Not too interesting. I'm a second-year associate with Cravath, doing grunt work for the partners, sixteen hour days, the whole bit. This is my first vacation in a year. And it's been great."

"Past tense?"

"Yeah. Unfortunately, this is my last night here."

"And have you been alone all this time?"

"Not that it's any of your business, but yeah. You're the first one to pass the literacy test."

"Well, then we don't have much time. What's your name, by the way?"

"I'm Joyce. You're awfully sure of yourself, aren't you?"

"Pleased to meet you, Joyce. I'm John. I suppose I am. I just know what I like and where I want to go. No reason to dillydally. You are obviously no slouch—an associate at a premier New York law firm and clever enough to use a novel as man bait."

"Man bait? Why you ...." She began and then broke into a laugh. "Okay, what do you like and where do you want to go?"

"You and dancing," he said leaning toward her staring intently into her hazel brown eyes.

The next few hours were taken up with dancing to a five-piece Mambo band, a long walk on the beach, and a late night drink in John's three-room luxury suite. He walked her back to her room. They stood looking at each other for a long minute.

"I want to see you again."

She smiled and gave him a light kiss on the lips. "Shouldn't be a problem since we both live in New York." She went into her room. He walked out into the night air with a big smile on his face and turned back toward the beach to walk, too excited to sleep.

* * *

Early the next morning, Joyce's New York bound jet accelerated down the runway. Joyce stared out the window as the jet lifted off and down at the beach where she had walked with John just a few hours before. It faded from sight and with a sigh she took out her novel and tried to read. She finally gave up putting the book down with another sigh. *Is he the one? God knows I like him. Okay, he is a tad arrogant, but that's just a front I think. He was so sweet and soft when we walked on the beach. And not trying to sleep with me the first night. I've been lucky all my life, getting my first choice of schools, jobs, great parents, great friends, but never a man I could really go for, who can match me and not be intimidated. I'm not getting any younger and I want to have kids. Whoa, girl, you're getting way ahead of yourself. You just met him. Plus look at the problems. He's not only not Jewish, but he might as well have "WASP" tattooed on his forehead.* Joyce's head fell back and she slept until the abrupt sound of the jet wheels deploying during descent startled her awake.

Two nights later, she was at her desk working late on a brief when her phone rang.

"Shit," she muttered and picked up the phone. "Yes?"

"Counselor," boomed the low baritone voice on the other end, "I am in deep trouble. I need a really good lawyer."

"What? Sir, I'm not a criminal lawyer. How did you get this number?"

"Doesn't matter. Word on the street is that you are the very best."

"What are you talking about, I'm a second-year associate doing corporate law. Let me transfer you." Joyce grabbed a directory and started fumbling through to find the number of the criminal division. Then she heard loud familiar laughter at the other end of the line. "John, is that you?" The laughter only grew in intensity. "Okay, John, you've had your fun. Where are you anyway? Are you calling from Cancun?"

John finally was able to stop laughing. "Hi, Joyce. No, I left Cancun this morning. I am as a matter of fact in a bar a block from your building and hoping you can join me for a drink."

"Why did you cut your vacation short?"

"The best part of Cancun left two days ago."

"So you expect me to drop everything and run down and have a drink? My senior partner will be pissed if I don't get this brief tonight."

"No worries. I'll just wait. Remember, I'm still on vacation. I got nothing else to do."

Joyce looked at her watch. " Okay, give me an hour."

Joyce put the phone down and smiled. *He is the one!* She turned back to the screen and began to type furiously.

* * *

Summer 2000

They honeymooned at the Golden Oaks, a small exclusive country resort in a small town nestled in the Blue Ridge Mountains of North Carolina called Blowing Rock. On the second day, they had finally ventured out of their luxurious suite equipped with every amenity including a hydro thermo massage spa and were on horse-back heading up the Blue Ridge trail with prospects of an enchanting view of the whole valley.

"John, slow down."

John, who was some 50 yards ahead on the trail, pulled on the reins to stop his mount and turned his head to look back at his bride with a smile.

"Can't keep up, huh? You presented yourself as an experienced rider. Any other misrepresentations, counselor?"

Joyce urged her horse from a stately walk, to a slow trot to catch up with him.

"Do you realize how sore I am? I can barely sit on this saddle. And it's your fault, lover boy." She leaned toward him and they kissed.

Soon they reached the top of the trail and spent some minutes silently, almost reverently, contemplating the valley below, the morning sun burning off the dew and fog covering the verdure of thick forest punctuated by large swaths of bluegrass pastures.

John finally broke the silence. "Joyce, I feel bad about my dad."

"What do you mean?"

"Dad at the wedding. He wasn't exactly warm and fuzzy."

"Don't worry about it. I'm sure the whole Jewish wedding thing was a bit overwhelming for him."

"You can say that again. He is real old school wasp."

"Well, I married the third, not the second," said Joyce while leaning over from her horse to give John another kiss. "And anyway, once we have kids, I'll bet you he'll soften."

"Oh, yeah, as long as it's a boy named John Maitland the IV."

"That's a nice Jewish name," said Joyce with a laugh.

* * *

Later that day, they hiked on foot up a trail to the famous Blowing Rock. It commanded a magnificent view of the valley below. A faint mist hung over the forest below and the sunlight reflecting off that and the trees cast a distinct bluish hue.

"So now I see why they call these the Blue Ridge mountains. What a sight."

"It's beautiful." She said, taking John's hand. "Take a look at this." She pointed to a large bronze placard entitled "The Legend of Blowing Rock."

"Legend has it that a Chickasaw chieftan brought his lovely daughter, to the Blowing Rock to protect her from marrying outside of her tribe. One day the maiden, while idling on a large boulder, spotted a Cherokee brave in the woods below. They met and he courted her with songs from his tribe and they became lovers. One day the chieftain discovered them and ordered the young brave to leave forever. He could not stand to live without her and decided to fling himself off the large boulder into the valley below, despite the maiden's entreaties that he not do so. He leaped into the void, but a gust of wind blew her lover back onto The Rock and into her arms. Her father witnessing this miracle relented, and they were married with great pomp and ceremony. Ever since that day a perpetual wind has blown up onto The Rock from the valley below."

"Wow!" said John. "Quite a story. It could be about us, lovers from different tribes getting married. I would just add one thing to the legend."

"What's that?"

"That they had many children."

Joyce stepped toward him and they embraced and kissed on top of Blowing Rock while a brisk wind blew against them.

Chapter Eight
August 21, 2008 7:00 AM

Egan trudged into the medical center. Despite a full night's sleep, he still couldn't shake the fatigue that had stalked him throughout his residency. He took a long swig, emptying a triple espresso as he made his way down the wide main corridor.

"Hey, Dr. Egan, wait up."

He stopped and turned his head to see Dr. John Oden hurrying to catch up.

"Eric, great to run into you. I was planning to track you down today. Man, that was a fine piece of work. My wife and I will be eternally grateful."

"We all get lucky sometimes. How's your son doing?"

"That wasn't luck. You are a superb diag-nostician—and only a second-year resident. Just incredible."

"Please, stop, you're making me blush," answered Egan, though his broad, pleased smile belied his words.

"And my son—he's back to his old mischievous self, though as you can imagine he has not been out of our sight. And I went over the apartment with a fine-tooth comb checking for anything with the remotest possibility of risk. But mouthwash; who would have thought?" Oden put a hand on Egan's shoulder. "Do you have time for coffee?"

"I'm always up for coffee—wait, I better not," he said, glancing at his watch. "I'll be late for rounds and I'm already on the top of Dr. Johnson's shit list."

"If you are already at the top, it can't get any worse. Anyway I'll have a chat with that old fart. Christ, I remember him from med school. We used to call him the grill meister. Guess he hasn't changed, huh?"

"No, he hasn't. So you went to med school here? Did you do residency here also?"

"No, I was in Boston for that. Did a fellowship there also."

Egan allowed himself to be led into the coffee shop.

"So, Eric, what are your plans for the future? If you plan to open a practice around here, I'll sign my kids up for your care in a heartbeat. Plus, I will recommend you to all my patients that have kids."

"Geez, thanks, but I'm not sure I plan to go into general practice, though maybe I'll specialize in all disorders related to mouthwash. Actually, I just found out I'm a finalist for the O'Neil Fellowship."

"That's great. Maybe I can help you. Who are the attendings on the selection committee?"

"Well, let's see. Dr. Newhouse, Dr. Ken Roy, and, who else?" Egan put his fingertips together and looked up at the ceiling. "Trying to remember, a couple of others—Blake George." He lowered his head eying Oden with a grin. "Perhaps you can help me with him since you're in his department and all.

Oden's eyebrows shot up. "I'd love to help you, but Blake is pretty independent. I'll do my best though."

"What's he like?"

"Blake George is world famous, obstetrician to the stars, and of course, the in vitro maven. No question he's smart, though he probably takes on too much. It's very unusual for an in-vitro person to also do deliveries, but he does it. No question he's got a mega ego. And Christ, the fees he charges! You'd almost have to be a Saudi prince to afford him. By the way, I imagine my son's case is probably the most interesting thing you seen in a while. I mean, peds, it's an awful lot of runny noses and worried mothers. Means you really have to stay on your toes for those rare cases."

Egan laughed. "It's not quite as boring as you make it sound. In fact, there was something really interesting not too long before you came in."

"I'm all ears and ready to stand corrected."

"A four-week-old came in looking well, but with borderline low grade fever. Christ, the baby looked like a rose," he said, referring to an expression used by doctors about patients that looked really well. "But something kept nagging at me. So I did a spinal tap. The kid had meningitis, and not just any meningitis; the bug was pneumococcus."

Oden looked at him, his eyebrows slightly raised. "Pardon my ignorance, but isn't pneumo a fairly common peds pathogen?"

"Yes, but not in babies under two months of age. And to top it off, there apparently was another case a few months ago, though slightly older, six weeks or so. Once I get a little free time, I'm going to look into it."

They sat quietly for a few minutes. As Egan stirred his coffee, he was thinking of the baby with meningitis and he could still picture the mother's facial expression and a second mother's face appeared in his mind's eye. He lifted his head from the swirling coffee he had been staring at, looking at Oden, who had a half smile on his face as he watched Egan.

"Dr. Oden," he began.

"Please, call me John."

"Okay, John, I just remembered something that your wife said in the ER." Egan paused for a moment. "Did you have a previous child?"

Oden's smile faded and he looked away.

"I'm sorry, I shouldn't have asked."

Oden looked back at Egan. "No, that's okay. We did lose a child, which made our ER experience that much tougher, especially for my wife and why our gratitude to you knows no bounds."

"What happened?"

"Not something I really want to get into." He answered with a catch to his voice. "Some other time."

"Once again, I'm so sorry to intrude."

"Eric, don't worry about it. In the meantime, don't you have rounds?"

"Oh, damn, I just remembered who the fourth guy on the committee is: Herb Johnson—and I'm late for rounds. Where's the check?"

"Eric, you go, I'll take care of it. And remember anything I can do for you, let me know. Stay in touch."

Eric nodded appreciatively before heading out at a full sprint.

Chapter Nine
Saudi Arabia, Spring 1992

Prince Fasi Abdul-Khalid bin Saud, fifteenth son of his father and thirty-sixth in line for the throne now occupied by King Abdullah, his uncle, urged his horse, with a swat of his riding crop, to go faster. Some twenty yards ahead was another rider on a black stallion whose features were obscured by a loose full body robe and hood. He could feel the roar of the wind and the stinging from particles of sand kicked up by the rider ahead of him and smiled as he drew inexorably closer.

"Slow down, slow down!" he shouted with a laugh. Suddenly, with a skillful jerk of the reins, the leading stallion was brought to an almost complete stop and the prince behind who had just yet again urged his steed to greater speed, dashed by. By the time he had slowed his horse and come around, the other rider had leapt from the mount and was running toward a nearby grove of date palms.

With a shout Fasi bounded off his horse and chased on foot. Just as the hooded figure reached the grove, he caught up, grabbed the top of the hood and pulled it down, releasing a full mane of hair. "I got you!" She turned and they embraced. He pulled her closer and could feel the rapid beating of her heart. They continued into the grove to a secluded area that had a large Persian carpet and they sank down upon it. Their embraces and kisses became more urgent and frantic until finally she pulled away.

"Fasi, that's enough. There will be plenty of time for that after we get married."

"Oh, Farah, you know I love you." He reached for her again, but with a smile she intercepted his hand. He smiled back at her and dropped his hand resignedly and looked out over the desert.

"Oh well, one more week. I suppose one more week won't kill me, but then again," he said looking back at her with a wicked smile, "why take the chance?" He playfully wrestled with her and finally settled down with his head in her lap.

They had stumbled upon this small oasis early in their courtship and had gradually outfitted it with rugs, pillows and a silk sunshade. Forced by Saudi convention to be covered up and demure, Farah had shocked Fasi with her bold desire, though still holding on to the ultimate prize. Whenever they could manage to shake off various brothers and other protectors of Farah, they would sneak out here.

"Fasi, how many children do you want?"

He smiled up at her. In truth, he had given the matter very little thought. But as he looked at her, the curves of her body faintly visible under the folds of her robe, he thought, Yes, it is my duty as a Muslim and a man to have babies.

He sat up and looked at her. "Farah, I want many." He paused for a moment. "Especially sons." The idea took hold and for the first time since arriving at the oasis his mind drifted from the lascivious fantasy of his future bride's naked flesh to thoughts of holding his son, walking proudly with his son, teaching him his place in the sun of the Arabian peninsula, the way of the Saudis and their horse loving Bedouin ancestors. "Yes, sons," he murmured as he allowed his head to drift back into her lap.

Chapter Ten
August 21, 2008 11:30 AM

Rounds, which had seemed more interminable than usual, were finally finished. Egan checked with his interns to make sure that there were no problems. Quiet reigned and Richter was deeply immersed in chart review. The moment was opportune.

He made his way down to the first floor of the hospital where the coffee shop was situated. He walked in and saw that Gail was sitting by herself reading. He approached her booth.

"Hi. Do you mind if I join you?"

Her eyes drifted up from the page and met his. "Oh, hi, sure."

He slid into the seat across from her. "Did you order yet?"

"No, I just got here."

Egan waved for the waitress and within minutes he was sipping from a large mug of black coffee, while Gail had her lips locked on a grande cappuccino.

"Ah, that hits the spot," said Egan putting his cup down. "So, Gail, tell me, what's a nice girl like you doing in a place like this?"

Gail put her cup down and wiped off most of the foam from her mouth with the back of her hand and then ran her tongue along the sides of her lips to get the rest. Egan barely suppressed an audible gulp.

"Well, I'm sure it's a familiar story. I discovered at some point in middle school that I was good in science and math. Being somewhat socially inept at that point, I began to revel in all the positive feedback I got, so I kept working hard, winning science fairs. Before I knew it I was in college and it just seemed the path of least resistance to go premed and here I am."

"Path of least resistance, huh? First time I've heard organic chemistry and the like described that way."

"Well, you know what I mean; it just puts off having to make a decision of what to do for the rest of your life. Being a student is not so bad. How about you?"

"I got into it from the pure science angle. Originally thought in terms of getting a PhD and doing research, but I figured I might have an easier time getting grants if I had an MD / PhD. So I'm in the combined program. In the meantime I've gotten pretty interested in clinical work and patient contact, so I'm a bit torn at the moment."

"Yeah, I know what you mean. Even though going into medicine was not some well thought out plan, I'm just amazed at the number of things you can go into. I got a bit turned on by emergency room medicine where I rotated last month. I liked the action, the quick decision making. I think peds should be cool also."

Egan yawned, yet again. "You're right about action. The ER kept me hopping the night before last."

"Anything interesting?"

"Well, yeah. It was probably the most interesting and eventful night of my residency so far." He told her about the young baby with meningitis.

"What is puzzling is that this baby was so young. Usually the main players at that age are E. coli, group B strep, or listeria. Tina, the night nurse, told me that there was another case of a baby a bit older but still under eight weeks with pneumococcus. I'm going to check that baby's records and look for other cases."

"Wow," exclaimed Gail, leaning forward with a smile, "that is amazing. Say, do you mind if I help you with this? I've been looking for a project to satisfy the senior research requirement."

"I'd be delighted," Egan smiled back while leaning forward. *Ah, he thought, seduction, residency style.*

"I've got some free time. I'll review the literature and then dig around for other cases. Doesn't the hospital have a database that you could search for cases of meningitis over the last two years?"

"Yeah, but it is restricted. However, I have a pass code since I'm working on my PhD dissertation. Tell you what. I'll give you my password and see what you can dig up and then we'll meet to try and organize the data. If we get a paper out of it, you'll be first author."

"First author? Sounds great. In that case, let's not waste any time. I can get started right away."

Egan smiled at her eagerness and leaned forward to suggest they meet later to discuss it further, when he noticed her eyes flitting up and a radiant smile suffusing her lips. She lifted her hand and gave a little wave. "Michael, over here."

Egan turned his head to see Michael, walking quickly over to them, smiling broadly.

"Hey, do you two know each other?" Asked Egan.

"Yeah, I was doing a two-week rotation on the toxicology service and he was the resident. Smart guy."

Michael slid into the booth giving Gail a kiss on the cheek.

"Well, well, Eric, how did you escape the floor? Richter's not keeping you busy enough?"

"Oh God, I couldn't stand it one more minute. I had to escape even if only for half an hour."

"And I see you dragged Gail with you. Is this the right example to set for a young impressionable and if I may so, gorgeous, medical student?" Michael let out a loud laugh and Gail joined in. Egan's laughter was more muted as he looked at the two of them.

They continued to chat and laugh until with a groan Michael glanced at his vibrating cell. "Oh, criminy; they need me in intensive care. Eric, you going to the resident's dinner tonight?"

"Free food? Are you kidding me, I wouldn't miss that for the world."

"Great, let's go over together. Gail, see you soon."

Egan watched Michael stride off and turned back to Gail. She was watching Michael as well.

"You two seem to know each other pretty well."

"Oh, yeah, he's quite the charmer and smart too."

Egan was quiet staring down at his coffee. Finally, he looked up. "Are you two…?"

"Dating? No," she said with a laugh. "Like, I said, he's a charmer and fun, but not really my type. Why do you want to know?"

Egan blushed slightly. "No reason, just curious. Anyway, let's talk about our research project."

Chapter Eleven
August 21, 2008 7:05 PM

Egan and Michael arrived at the Upper East Side address out of uniform, their sweaty scrubs piled up somewhere in the cavernous basement of the medical center. Their showers had eliminated most of the last vestiges of the stench of patient care. Egan with some difficulty had been able to locate a blue suit that had not seen the light of day for a year or two. Michael, more sartorial, was resplendent in a navy blue Brooks Brothers suit, its lines reflecting the latest in men's fashion.

The doorman looked up and said, "For Dr. Newhouse, I presume?" The two young men nodded and entered the building. On the elevator ride up, Michael grinned at Egan.

"Nice to be out of the funhouse. What do you say to cutting out just after dessert? There are a couple of nice bars I know in this neighborhood."

"Sounds great, but Christ, Michael, it will be a miracle if I stay awake until dessert. I'm still trying to catch up on my sleep from my call the night before last."

"So you're going to wimp out on me. Oh well, one of these days."

"Sorry, Michael."

Michael merely laughed as the elevator stopped at their floor. A few moments later they were being ushered into a spectacularly large penthouse apartment by a uniformed butler.

Michael whistled softly. "So this is how the other half lives."

Egan did not answer, looking around in awe at the luxurious furnishings.

"Let me take your coats, gentleman. Hors d'oeuvres are being served on the terrace," said a tall erect man dressed in traditional English butler tails.

They made their way to the terrace which was lighted with small oriental lamps and offered a view of Central Park. Newhouse, a drink in hand, had his back to them and was gazing at the view. He heard them coming and turned to greet them.

"Ah, good, the first arrivals. Welcome, welcome. How nice to see my two top residents."

"Thanks, Dr. Newhouse," said Egan. "I'll bet you say that to all of us."

"Yeah, flattery goes a long way toward keeping us in line," added Michael with a laugh.

"Well, it has certainly worked so far. Since you are first let me take the opportunity to show you around, grab a drink and follow me."

They went into an improbably large living room, the far wall dominated by a large painting by David Hockney. The motif of the room was decidedly modern in its furniture and fixtures, but had an eclectic array of objects on every available surface. Egan recognized artifacts from at least a dozen different cultures such as African, Chinese, and even Eskimo, which bespoke of the fact that Newhouse had traveled widely and collected avidly.

They proceeded into a book-lined room, comfortable and less pretentious, obviously Newhouse's study. Egan noticed a number of first editions and wondered to himself how a busy academic like Newhouse could have the time or money to collect so much.

Newhouse was pulling a book from the shelf, when Egan asked, "Dr. Newhouse, how is the Gold baby?"

Newhouse turned around, holding the book he had just pulled.

"Holding his own. You had quite the night. Early diagnosis in meningitis is key, but despite that, the Gold baby's prognosis is guarded."

"I was puzzled by the fact that the bug was pneumococcus."

"Oh?" asked Newhouse lifting his eyebrows. "I didn't realize the culture had come back yet."

"Well, presumptive pneumococcus—it surely looked like pneumo under the scope. I'm planning to dig a bit and see if there are some other cases. Tina, the night nurse, seemed to think there had been a pneumococcal case in a six week-old a while ago."

"Well, my dear Dr. Egan, I commend you on your enthusiasm, but remember, rare doesn't mean never. And anyway, I'd wait for lab confirmation before wasting too much time pursuing it." With that, Newhouse, put the book down on the desk and led them into the dining room.

One entire wall was a fish tank filled with tropical fish. Egan wanted to stop and linger, but sensed Newhouse's desire to show them the whole apartment before the other guests arrived.

"If you like fish, let me show you something else." They followed Newhouse into a smaller room that had a long narrow pool, of the type that allows a person to do stationary swimming. Egan noticed that the water was flowing rather briskly and was surprised to find that a number of fish were positioned facing up current.

"Wow," exclaimed Michael, "are those trout?"

"Yes, indeed they are. Took a while for me to get conditions just right. They like cold clean water, flowing at about five miles an hour. I feed them worms from the vegetable garden on the terrace, which in turn feed upon rotting leaves that I gather in the park. Rather a nice ecosystem, don't you think? And of course I am in the enviable position of being at the top of this particular food chain. I do love pan-fried trout."

The uniformed man who had opened the door for them entered. "Sir, some of the other guests have arrived."

"Oh, good. Boys, we will continue this discussion later. Shall we return to the terrace? The hors d'oeuvres are probably out. Oh, and Michael, I haven't forgotten your peanut allergy—it is totally nut free. "

Newhouse walked out ahead of them. Egan remained for a moment staring at the fish.

"Come on, Eric," said Michael, putting a hand on his shoulder. "What are you staring at anyway?"

"Oh, nothing really, just watching those fish pointing up current and swimming just to stay in one place. Reminds me a bit of a day on the floor—the more work you do, the more there is to do. I often feel like those trout."

"I agree it is an outstanding metaphor for our predicament, one of your best efforts. But tonight we are not in the hospital and it's a short distance, downstream I would add, to some outstanding food and drink. So come on."

Egan looked up from the fish and smiled and together they walked toward the terrace.

Michael spotted a tray with caviar carried by a young attractive female caterer. "I'm going to start right here."

Egan left his friend feasting and flirting and moved onto the terrace where a considerable crowd had gathered. He joined a group of his fellow residents who were attacking a sumptuous array of delectables. They were a giddy group, delighted to be out of the hospital and soon Egan was stuffing his face, and drinking and laughing with them. By the time dinner was announced, he felt already slightly full and a bit tipsy.

Chapter Twelve
August 21, 2008 8:15 PM

Egan found his place card and sat down. He was momentarily startled to see that he was next to Dr. Johnson. Johnson smiled at him.

"Dr. Egan, I see that when it comes to dinner, you know how to arrive on time."

"Okay, I guess I had that coming," he answered with a laugh, thinking that old Johnson was much easier to take with a couple of glasses of wine.

Across from Egan was Michael ensconced between Joan Richter and Betty Freidman, an infectious disease fellow. As usual, Egan noted, Michael was carrying on, laughing, and skillfully dividing his attentions equally between the two women. Egan looked down at the other end of the table where the chairman of the pediatrics department sat, with an amused expression as he surveyed the rather raucous scene of residents laughing, engaging in rapid fire repartee and teasing. It was as if all the tension built up over months of hard, mind numbing, stress-filled work was spilling out.

Next to the chairman was chief resident Doug Barrett, who seemed to be trying to engage in a more serious discussion, but the chairman's eyes continued to turn away from Barrett, distracted by the entertaining scene of residents capering before him.

Egan spent a moment gazing at the table décor. A Tuscan theme had been chosen and each plate featured a different Italian painter. Each fork knife and spoon had an ornate handle patterned after a Michelangelo sculpture. Egan recognized a Botticelli painting on his plate. The tablecloth was finely spun cloth with a pattern that Egan could imagine fitting quite nicely on a tapestry hanging in a Tuscan church.

A clinking of glass caused Egan to look up from his examination of the table fixtures. Newhouse, at the other end of the long table, opposite the chairman, was on his feet, wineglass in hand.

"I would like to start things off with a toast. We have been very fortunate to have at the medical center a dynamic, hardworking group of residents. We, as an institution, are incredibly lucky to have you; a cadre of talented, energetic young people who quite literally are the heart and soul of the medical center. You are, quite honestly, the cream of the crop. I know because I personally reviewed all your applications. We were lucky in that we got virtually everyone we wanted out of an extraordinary group of applicants.

"I'm sure each of you has a couple of friends, not as bright, who are already moving up the ranks of business, banks, and law firms, earning outsized salaries. You instead have chosen a nobler path of deferred gratification, and you should be proud of yourselves. But if your experience is anything like mine was, there is plenty of immediate gratification—having a six-year-old wake up after life-saving surgery, and seeing the joyful smiles of his parents, of picking up an unusual diagnosis and making a real difference in the ultimate outcome.

"Dr. Egan, for example, just the night before last, acting on an instinct that usually doesn't kick in until after years of experience, made an early diagnosis of meningitis and instituted a gutsy, aggressive treatment plan."

Egan reddened a bit at hearing this unexpected praise. Across the table, John Oden caught his eye and lifted his wine glass.

Newhouse continued. "Our institution has become a world renowned center for pediatric transplants and while there have been some techniques and even some basic immunologic science pioneered right here at the medical center, a large part of our success has been the skill and willingness of our residents to take meticulous, detailed care of our post-op transplant patients. The devil is in the details, folks. There is no substitute for minute-to-minute observation of vital signs, electrolytes, and all the parameters that can signal the alert resident of an imminent rejection crisis. I know the surgeons get the glory, but you guys in my mind are the unsung heroes and to all of you I lift my glass." Wine glasses were lifted in unison and for a moment all was silent as they took in these words of praise so artfully delivered.

Egan began his salad, but then stopped and stared at the salad with the fascination of the slightly drunk and noted with interest a wide variety of greens and vegetables, some of which he could not identify. He was peering at something impaled at the end of his fork when from his left he heard for the first time since the meal started, Dr. Johnson.

"That, my young man, is arugula."

"Is it really? And I thought that I had just discovered a heretofore undescribed species and was ready to make my own personal contribution to the botanical lexicon. Whatever its name, it actually tastes quite good."

Johnson smiled at this reply. "That's what's wrong with America's youth—they can't identify vegetables. I was in the market the other day. I had a long wait at a checkout line because the cashier didn't know what a rutabaga was. I told her what it was and she went off looking for a manager to ask the price, but had to come back twice to ask—'What do you call that again?'"

This poor guy, thought Egan. *Can't even go to the supermarket without being bothered by the appalling ignorance of the populace.*

The next course was now being brought in: lightly grilled oysters on the half shell.

"Ah," exclaimed Johnson with evident satisfaction, "oysters, my favorite."

"Me too," answered Egan. "Can you pass the catsup?"

Johnson looked briefly stunned, but saw Egan's slightly mocking smile. He smiled back and said, "The irreverence of youth. Seriously, I should take you and some of your colleagues out for some real food. There is a French restaurant not too far from here with escargot—snails—to die for."

"I'd be game, though I must admit I prefer to eat members of the animal kingdom with a backbone. These oysters, however, are delicious."

"Eric, I understand you are an MD/PhD. What area is your research in?"

"You're right about the MD part—the PhD is not quite finished. I have probably a year to go on what has proved to be a recalcitrant project. I try to sneak over to the lab from time to time, but between my ward duties and trying to learn the names of all the vegetables of the world, I've had very little time. I may have to defer it until after residency."

He paused to finish chewing.

"But to answer your question, my research is in transplant immunology. Some years ago, I was thinking about the fact that the immune system early in its formation has to learn to distinguish the tissues of the organism that spawned it from foreign tissues. At some point in fetal development, the immune system takes a hard look at all the proteins of the body—if you permit me to be a bit anthropomorphic—and in essence learns to accept them as self. There is, as you know, a developmental window in which the immune system, normally such an aggressive attacker, learns to accept whatever he is been exposed to during that crucial period of time. Sort of like a gang of boys in elementary school—they bond, but once in middle school they attack any new boys while remaining loyal to their original gang. It's well known, of course, that if you introduce a foreign protein at that critical time, the immune system will learn to accept it for evermore."

Egan leaned forward, his face shining with enthusiasm. "My idea was this—to prepare a mixture of foreign proteins of another species say a pig and to inject it into a fetus during that critical time. The immune system would accept those proteins as native. The pig, of course, would be part of a huge herd of clones with identical DNA.

The fetus is born and say years later needs a kidney transplant. A pig kidney is harvested and theoretically at least would not be rejected. It really is like an immunization in reverse designed to circumvent the rejection process."

"Bravo," said Johnson, clapping his hands, caught up in Egan's spirited delivery. "A grand visionary idea—but I can imagine technical problems abound."

Egan's smile faded. "You can say that again. Rounding up pregnant women for my experiments has been an absolute nightmare— just kidding. I have been using rats as the recipients and guinea pigs as the donors. Just developing the techniques for introducing material into the rat fetuses has consumed months, and creating 'essence of guinea pig' for introduction has been unexpectedly difficult. I naively had visions of tossing a guinea pig into a blender and taking some of the mixture and injecting it into the fetus. In addition, because of a funding problem, I have had to master for myself the microsurgical technique of transplanting a guinea pig kidney into a rat myself rather than hiring a surgical tech."

"Wow, that's impressive. Can you do that transplant now?"

"Recently, my technique had improved. I'm hoping to refine it next month when I have my research month."

"Well, my young Dr. Egan, I am starting to understand why you look so sleepy on rounds. Very impressive."

The waiters were now bringing in the main course, a choice of either quail cooked in Madera with leeks, venison in a red wine sauce with wild mushrooms, or fresh pan-fried trout. Egan chose the trout. His survey of vegetables of the world continued as he eyed the specimens garnishing the trout.

"That's endive, quite good," whispered Dr. Johnson.

Once again a glass could be heard clinking, this time from the other end of the table. The chairman of pediatrics had stood. "I would like to offer a toast. My appreciation of our residents knows no bounds, but I don't think I can match Dr. Newhouse's eloquence.

All I can say is that I echo his words and emotions. A word of appreciation for Dr. Newhouse: Our institution has been extraordinarily fortunate to have Dr. Newhouse for six years now. You all may know him as the attending who is constantly available to teach, who is able to inspire incredible efforts out of those below him through sheer dint of his energy and enthusiasm rather than through authoritarian intimidation. It is no surprise that he is voted by the residents as their favorite attending year after year.

"I, of course, am privy to other sides of him. He has had a galvanizing effect on this institution—the pediatric ICU has been built into a preeminent facility attracting patients from all over the Northeast. Our pediatric transplant program has been a marquee act of the medical center—truly a high wire performance, the crown jewel of our department. Our results over the last five years have been unparalleled and patients travel to us from all over the world for their transplants. This happy situation has largely been due to the efforts of one man—Dr. Jack Newhouse."

All raised their glasses and Newhouse took it all in, his facial expression a precise balance of confidence and humility. Egan gazed at him once again and marveled at his preternatural grace in this situation. To Egan, his face almost seemed to reverberate between the two, like one of those small handheld screens that if you move slightly a different image would appear. It was as if he had to project confidence to the residents, yet preserving humbleness in front of the chairman. Sure, the chairman's words were warm, even effusive, but he's got to be wondering if Newhouse's fiefdom will continue to expand and swallow up all of pediatrics.

For all his admiration for Newhouse, Egan did wonder at times how he kept it all going. Every so often, Egan would catch a look of surprise in his eyes, sort of a deer caught in headlights expression, as if he was momentarily confused about which facet he should be revealing at that particular moment. A consummate politician, he thought, able to project just the right feeling at just the right time. Newhouse, gazing about the room, now seemed to pause as he made eye contact with Egan, giving him a penetrating albeit brief look that discomfited him for an instant, and he wondered somewhat irrationally if Newhouse knew exactly what he was thinking.

The evening wound down as yawns increased and one resident even nodded off over his dessert, his face falling on top of his crème brulee. This briefly energized the group, only to quickly sink back into a communal torpor.

Dr. Newhouse surveyed the scene and laughed. "One would think we worked you too hard. Anyway, it's late, egads, almost 8:30!" he exclaimed with mock astonishment.

Chapter Thirteen

Fall 2005

He sat at his desk, staring at a long column of figures on the computer screen in front of him. Occasionally, he would glance at a screen above him where a series of stock, bond and commodity prices were parading across. "Okay, now's the time," he muttered to himself. He began to make rapid keystrokes and when he finished, he sat back in his chair with a sigh, and reached for a tall mug of coffee perched at the edge of his desk. He swiveled his chair away from his desk toward a large window which commanded an excellent view of the East river and Roosevelt Island. He took a large sip from his coffee while he watched the Roosevelt Island trolley swaying slightly while making its way slowly over the river.

A voice from the intercom caused him to turn back to his desk. "Mr. Maitland, Rod Smith on two."

"Thanks, Thelma." He picked up the phone eagerly. "Hey, Rod, what's going on?"

"John, that's quite a bet you placed on oil futures. I'd be quaking in my boots."

Maitland let out a loud laugh. "Rod, my man, this is the big leagues. Chicken shit moves just won't make it around here."

"Okay, hope you can sleep tonight."

"I will sleep like a baby tonight, though only after making passionate love to my wife."

He heard a spasm of laughter and then, "I'll say one thing, you've got nerve. I've never seen you ruffled about anything, except maybe when the Knicks are down twenty in the fourth quarter. By the way, you enjoying married life, not cramping your style?"

"I'm enjoying it immensely. Rod, I highly recommend it. Sure beats the parade of bimbos I see you out with."

"Ah, you're just jealous. Remember variety is the spice of life."

"Oh, don't you worry, I have variety. My bride is a regular Scheherazade, something different every night."

"Jesus, John, do you lead a charmed life or what."

Maitland leaned forward in his chair, to peer closer at the screen and grinned. "Hey, Rod, speaking of which, check out oil futures."

"Jesus fuck. Up three bucks. How the hell do you do it? By the way, any bambinos on the way?"

"No, but we're in no hurry. It will happen when it's meant to happen. Joyce and I are enjoying ourselves, and we're both working hard."

"Okay, my man, later."

"Later."

Maitland hung up the phone and then quickly picked it up again and pressed speed dial. He got a voice mail. "This is Joyce Maitland, and I'm away from my desk." He pressed pound, heard the buzz.

"Hello, Joyce Maitland, this is your loving husband who scored big time today on the oil market and am hoping to score big time on the marital bed tonight. Love ya. I'll be home at six."

Before hanging up, he pressed intercom. "Thelma, hold all my calls."

With a smile on his face, he began to type rapidly while taking occasional looks at the screen. His smile slowly faded as he continued to work and his lips became pursed in concentration as he worked on a memo.

"Mr. Maitland."

"Thelma, I thought I told you to hold all my calls."

"I'm sorry, Mr. Maitland. It's not a call, it's a visitor." She paused before continuing. "Your dad."

"Oh, Christ," he murmured. "Okay, Thelma, show him in."

Sixty-year-old John Maitland, Jr., was a tall man with an erect patrician bearing. His dark suit was perfectly pressed and red tie firmly knotted. He extended his hand as he entered the room.

Maitland took it. "Dad, this is a surprise."

"Son, sorry to barge in on you. I'm sure you're busy, but you are a hard man to get on the phone."

"I'm sorry, Dad, it has been crazy around here."

The older man looked around the spacious office and then walked to the window. "Quite an office you have here."

"Thank you; here, take a seat." He walked over to his desk. "Dad, you want coffee?"

"Sure, thanks."

"Thelma, can you bring in two coffees?"

"Right away, Mr. Maitland."

Maitland sat down behind his desk, and eyed his father sitting, but maintaining his posture. They were both silent for some minutes until Thelma, a matronly woman in her mid sixties, brought in coffee. After she left, the two men continued to look at each other. Finally, the elder cleared his throat.

"You're probably wondering why I'm here."

"Well, that thought did cross my mind."

"Listen, son, I know things have been tense between us. I just thought we should have a chat."

"Okay," answered John simply "Why don't you start?"

"First off, I owe you an apology."

John's eyebrows lifted in surprise.

"You can spare me the facial expressions. This isn't easy for me."

"Sorry, Dad. I'm all ears."

"I know I gave you a hard time about marrying Joyce, but I really only had your best interests at heart. No, wait, hear me out. I know you think I am some sort of unreconstructed bigot, but I merely was of the opinion that marriage is tough enough without adding the burden of being of different religions. But, I have come to see what a wonderful person Joyce is and think in the end you made a good choice."

"Well, dad, I don't know what to say. Your muted enthusiasm was the imperfection on what was otherwise a perfect wedding day."

"I know, son. I just hope you will forgive me."

Maitland got to his feet. "Dad, of course, I forgive you."

His father also stood and the two men approached each other. Maitland extended his hand, but to his surprise, his father sidestepped the proffered arm and embraced his son. In accented Spanish, he said, "Un abrazo es major, mi hijo."

Father released his son. "Now, how about returning to the family business?"

Maitland turned from him and walked to a large window and gazed out. "I don't know, Dad," he began while still facing the window. "As you can see, I'm not doing too badly here."

"Now, son, hear me out. I know I've been stubborn about turning over the reins of Maitland Energy, but I promise you that will change. The company needs someone with your ability and your vision. I'd hate to have someone else run it after I'm gone. And son, I can see you have been a smashing success on your own. I'm so proud of you."

He turned to face his father, a faint smile on his lips. "Dad, an apology, an admission of stubbornness, and an expression of filial pride all in one day? What have you been smoking?"

"The peace pipe, son. You'll understand some day. You get to an age when you finally realize what's really important. I'm getting older. The future belongs to you. I want more than anything for you, my son, to step into your rightful position as president of Maitland Energy."

He stared at his father for a long minute. "I really think you mean it. But, Dad, run means run. I've got to do it my way. The future is not in oil, it's in solar, wind, geothermal—we've got to make that transition."

"Son, you have my word. Some day you'll be in my shoes and you'll remember this day and hopefully, you will handle it better than I have. By the way, anything on the way?"

"Dad, we're taking our time. Joyce has her career and we're in no hurry. What was that about letting me run the show?"

"Sorry, son, I know, it's just that it would be so wonderful to have a John Maitland the fourth."

"Dad, you are getting way ahead of yourself. First of all, what if we have only girls and secondly, who says if I have a son, I'll name him John. I may just name him Moon Beam or Ishmael."

"Oh, son," said the older man putting his head in his hands in mock despair.

Chapter Fourteen
August 21, 2008 11:00 PM

The lights in the Pediatric Intensive Care Unit were dimmed at 11 PM as they always were at this hour. The director of the PICU, Dr. Jack Newhouse, had implemented this policy the previous year in an effort to create consistent light/dark cycles, important in preserving the circadian rhythms of his young patients. He had met with resistance from some of the older staffers, who questioned whether this would have any effect upon medical outcomes and could potentially negatively affect the ability to carefully observe patients during the dark phase.

Newhouse had patiently but firmly pushed the notion by carefully compiling the relevant research and arguing that with modern monitoring equipment, a nurse sitting at a central console could see at a glance not only a patient's real time vital signs, but also blood oxygen saturation, and end expiratory CO_2. Indeed, in the year since changing the policy, Newhouse had data from his own ICU that suggested a definite salutary effect, not only on the psychological states, but on the medical outcomes of his patients as well.

This was just one of dozens of changes he had implemented since he had taken over as director, having been lured, with promises of complete autonomy and generous funding for his research, from an Ivy League institution in Boston. He brought with him a whole cadre of doctors and nurses. His energy was legendary, and it was not uncommon for him to be in the PICU at all hours of the night. He also spent long hours in his lab where his special interest was the blood brain barrier, a complex membrane made up of a variety lipoproteins that while serving to protect the central nervous system from toxins and pathogens, impeded the delivery of medicines to the brain.

Newhouse leaned over the chart of the Gold baby who had been admitted some thirty-six hours earlier. He was a large man, well over six feet with broad shoulders and huge hands with thick fingers that were astonishingly dexterous. One of those fingers was pointed at a section of the chart. "There, you see, that's where the first signs of septic shock developed," he said, turning toward the two male nurses who were with him. They were both heavily muscled, their blue scrubs fitting tightly around massive deltoids and pectorals and gaudy tattoos peeked out from their sleeves. Bob and Ray had followed Newhouse from Boston, and both, despite an appearance that bespoke more of mercenary soldiers of fortune, had earned considerable respect for their clinical abilities.

"It looks like Egan was right on top of things," commented Bob. "Placing that intraosseous needle was gutsy, but it looks like it turned the tide."

"Yes, there is no question that Egan is smart," answered Newhouse. "Let's go in and see the baby."

They went into a small isolation room where patients with contagious diseases were housed. Besides the intraosseus, the baby now had large IVs going into the groin and the neck and an arterial catheter in the wrist. In addition to being used to deliver fluid and medications, one of the IVs resided in one of the large veins of the body which allowed a continuous measurement of central venous pressure, which was crucial in determining the current status of the baby's shock. Newhouse looked at a large monitor that showed tracings of heart rate, respiratory rate, EKG, and arterial blood pressure. An endotracheal tube was in place in the mouth and a nasogastric tube went into the nose to the stomach. Yet another tube penetrated his urethral meatus into his bladder.

"It looks like we've turned the corner. Blood pressure is fine." He pinched one of the fingertips. "Good capillary refill, good perfusion." He looked over at the two nurses. "Well, I think things are under control here."

Chapter Fifteen
Fall 2006

The two men stood at a window that looked out over a large courtyard. Below, three girls in traditional flowing Saudi robes and veils were playing a spirited game of tag. The oldest, a girl of twelve, was running backwards as her youngest sister of 6 attempted to catch her. The middle sister stepped behind the older and impeded her backward progress just enough to allow the youngest to catch her.

"Hey, not fair!" she shouted while the two younger girls burst into laughter and sprinted to the far end of the courtyard with the oldest in pursuit.

One of the men turned to the other. "Fasi, they are quite lovely. Each one more pretty than the next."

Fasi continued to watch the cavorting of his daughters for a minute before turning his head to the man next to him. "Yes, Abdul, there is no question about that. I do adore them."

"And, Farah, she has recovered?"

"Yes, thank you, though she is indisposed this afternoon. She told me to send you her regrets."

"I understand. I sure it is not easy for her."

The two men were silent for a moment and turned their attention back to the courtyard.

Abdul spoke again, this time not turning his head. "It was her third miscarriage, yes? Such a pity. Would it have been a ... ?"

Fasi cut him off, "Please, Abdul. I don't want to talk about it."

"Fasi, as your brother, I have to talk to you about it. Don't you realize what is happening? Do you want to be a third-rate official the rest of your life?"

"I'm perfectly happy with what I have."

"No, you're not. This is Abdul you're talking to. I see the frustration in your face at family meetings. Don't you see how this looks? Every one of your brothers has sons."

"Stop it!" shouted Fasi. "I can't listen to this."

"Fasi, listen to me, take another wife. Do the sensible thing. Look at me. I now have ten sons."

"I can't do that, Abdul."

"Why not? It's Farah, isn't it? I don't understand you, brother. Are you afraid of her, a woman? Just tell her firmly, this is the situation and this is the solution."

"I can't, I said."

"She really has you wrapped around her little finger. Be a man, Fasi, and you will have sons."

Fasi turned to Abdul, his face contorted and red with anger. "Out!" he shouted. "I've had enough."

Abdul took two steps back, momentarily nonplussed, but then stood his ground and a faint smile, almost a smirk appeared on his face. "Okay, my brother, but I warn you, no sons, no cabinet position."

"Out, I said!" Fasi took a step toward his brother holding an outstretched arm pointing to the door.

Abdul, smirk still in place, shook his head from side to side while he walked to the door and left without a backward glance.

Fasi watched him leave, his eyes blazing and continued to look at the closed door as he clenched and unclenched his fists. There was a fresh burst of laughter from the courtyard and he looked back to the window, leaning forward with his hands on the pane. The two younger girls had ganged up on the eldest and had her trapped in a corner tickling her.

He felt gentle pressure on the back of his shoulders. He took his hands from the window pane and reached back behind his neck, finding fingers, and gave them a squeeze. "Oh, Farah, look at our daughters." Still holding her hands he turned lifting one of her arms over his head and faced her.

"Farah, you look pale. You should be lying down."

"I heard shouts. Were you fighting with Abdul again?"

"It was nothing. Really, Farah, you need your rest."

"Fasi, I heard everything. You can take another wife. My cousin, Nela, is young, pretty, and I'm sure will give you lots of sons."

"Farah, what are you talking about? You need your rest. We will talk about it later."

He tried to lead her toward the bedroom.

"No, I don't want to rest. I want you to have sons."

"Farah, you've never said this before. Remember at our oasis, you had me swear that I would marry you and only you? That I laughed and you got so angry and then I saw that you meant it, that you wanted to be a modern woman. And I loved you for it, and I agreed and took an oath."

"I release you from that oath."

"Farah, you are talking nonsense. You are the only woman I want. I couldn't live the way Abdul does, all his wives fawning over him."

"But, Fasi, I know you. Don't you think I know how you feel in your ridiculous position at the ministry? You are smart and ambitious. You should take your rightful position. You can only do that if you have sons."

"Farah, Farah, I confess to you, when I made that oath, I thought you would change your mind and did not take it seriously at first. And, honestly, I thought, as any man might, that it would be fun to have several wives. But my love for you has grown and I respect your strength. And look at those three." He gestured toward the window. "Three beautiful daughters, I couldn't love them more. And Farah, I want them to grow up and be just like you, to take a single man as their husband."

She looked at him and began to cry, and he took her in his arms and they embraced for a long minute. "Oh, Fasi," she said her voice muffled by his tunic. "I always loved you, but I never imagined the man you would become. I love you so. Know that, when I tell you,

you must take another wife. You will grow old and bitter, and I can't stand to see that."

"Farah, listen to me. There must be another way. I swear to you that I will find another way. Now, you need to sleep and rest."

They began to walk toward the bedroom. "Fasi, I've let you down, I feel so ashamed. No sons, one miscarriage after another."

"Farah, you talk nonsense. Now get some rest."

Chapter Sixteen
August 22, 2008 10:00 AM

"Are you sure?" Egan asked, barely hiding his exasperation.

"Doc, look for yourself," answered the record room clerk while turning the computer screen so that Egan could look at it.

Egan peered at the screen. Jamie Reed—no records found—check spelling. "Maybe it's R-e-a-d."

"Doc, I already checked every conceivable spelling. It's not in our system."

"How come he's listed in the peds ER log?"

"I don't know what to tell you. Wait, let me check one other thing."

He made some rapid keystrokes and leaned in close to the screen. "Okay, that explains it; it's listed under access block."

"Access block?"

"It's a designation for certain sensitive files, like when there's pending litigation and that sort of thing."

"Is there pending litigation in this case?"

"Even if I knew, I couldn't tell you."

Egan continued to stare first at the screen and then at the clerk, a polite young man of Haitian descent who had obviously been at the job long enough to deal with a variety of physician personalities without fluster.

Finally Egan looked away. "I'm sorry. I shouldn't give you a hard time. Thanks for your time."

"No problem, doctor, anytime."

Egan left medical records and had not taken two steps before his cell went off. Sure that it was a call from one of the ward nurses with yet another chore, he snapped it open irritably. "Dr. Egan."

There was silence at the other end and then a soft female voice. "Eric?"

"Oh, sorry, this is Eric."

"It's Gail, the med student, remember? Is this a bad time?"

"No, as good time as any. What's up?"

"I wanted to find out how the baby with meningitis is doing. Remember that I was thinking of doing my senior research project on meningitis?"

"Of course I remember."

Egan couldn't help but smile. "Sure, I'll do what I can. Actually, I'm heading over to the ICU right now. Do you want to meet me there?"

"That would be awesome. I'll be there in ten minutes."

"That sounds like my ETA." Egan noticed just in time a gurney right in front of him and managed to dodge it.

"Well, let's not waste any time. We covered meningitis in my infectious disease course, but a few things that aren't totally clear to me. Can I pick your brain as we walk?"

"Sure, but you might find it to be slim pickings."

"I doubt that. First, just how does a baby get meningitis?"

"Good question. It's believed that bacteria in the blood, or bacteremia, is the primary event. It's very common. Usually, though, it is transient and the immune system is incredibly efficient at repelling the invaders. In rare cases, for reasons that are not completely understood, bacteria will settle into a particular organ or tissue and will establish a beachhead, as it were. This applies, incidentally, to any number of infections in the heart, the bone, the kidney, etcetera. What's interesting about the brain is that the bacteria have to traverse the blood brain barrier in order to cause an infection. Why that happens one time out of a million episodes of bacteremia is the big question."

"That sounds very interesting. What is the blood brain barrier on the cellular level?"

"Another good question. The vessels in the brain have especially tight junctures where endothelial cells meet. Therefore large things like bacteria can't pass into the brain."

"Wow, that's really interesting."

"By the way, have you been to the peds ICU before?"

"No, but I've heard that it is a top-notch facility."

"Right you are about that. Jack Newhouse is a brilliant, energetic director, and he's built that place into a real state of the art ICU, arguably the best on the East Coast. He is innovative and fanatically dedicated to patient care and he has ruffled more than a few feathers in the medical center with his uncompromising opinions. If we have time, I'll show you around. Among other things, Newhouse is quite interested in transplant medicine and many people attribute the excellent survival rate among pediatric organ transplants here at the medical center not just to the skill of the surgeons, but to the incredible post-op care they get in the peds ICU."

Egan rounded a corner, almost colliding with Gail who was coming out of an elevator, each with cell phones pressed to their ears and smiles on their faces. They stood there staring at each other for several seconds. "Oh, hi," said Gail with a laugh.

"Going my way?" Egan managed to sputter out, though with none of the savoir faire he was hoping to affect.

They walked together to the ICU, which was at the end of the corridor. The pediatric ICU was a very large single room with twelve occupied beds surrounded by a stunning array of equipment. A cacophony of beeps and alarms filled the air. Off to one side were two smaller windowed rooms with closed doors. One had a sign that read "Respiratory Isolation—Gown, Masks and Gloves Required," and it was to this room that Egan went. They both donned gowns, masks and gloves and went in. In the small room were already several gowned figures. Egan recognized Dr. Newhouse, the director of the Pediatric ICU. With him were the two male nurses, Ray and Bob, and a second-year resident.

"Dr. Egan! Recovered from your night in the ER and last night libations? Not quite, I see. You do look a bit bleary-eyed," said Dr. Newhouse.

"Good morning, Dr. Newhouse. So are you saying, I should go home and get some sleep?"

Newhouse laughed. "Ah, good response. In my day, we wore our fatigue like a badge of honor."

"Dr. Newhouse, as much as I love hearing tales of the days of the giants, I am rather anxious to find out about the Gold baby."

Newhouse laughed again and turning to Gail said, "Ah, the irreverence of today's residents. In my day, we treated our attendings with deference."

He turned back to Egan. "Anyway, I have to say, that was a hell of a good pickup. He is one sick puppy now, but we have a good shot. That intraosseous you performed was bold and probably saved him because once you get too far along with septic shock, it becomes an irreversible cascade."

Newhouse turned again to Gail and, as always, anxious as always to express his ideas, launched into a discussion of the complex biochemical and microbiologic underpinnings of septic shock. While listening, Egan looked at the baby and was startled to see how ill the baby appeared; pale and limp, with numerous red purple blotches that indicated bleeding into the skin, an ominous sign that meant the baby had most likely entered into DIC or disseminated intravascular coagulation, a dreaded consequence of sepsis. Egan thought sadly about the parents. The next two days were crucial. "If anyone can save this baby, it's Newhouse," thought Egan as they left the isolation room.

Egan and Gail slowly removed the isolation gowns, masks and gloves, both silent, sobered by the appearance of the desperately ill infant. They headed toward the ICU exit.

"Eric, what's wrong with that baby over there?" asked Gail pointing to a young infant.

Egan found the chart and quickly scanned it. "A six day old baby with jaundice", he read out loud. "Seems routine enough. Bilirubin is 18, not too bad, could use some phototherapy." Then he read the neuro exam and looked up with a start. "Gosh, this baby has kernicterus. Boy, that's unusual these days and with a bilirubin of only 18."

They walked over to the bedside where a young infant laid, skin a bright yellow color. The baby let out a shrill, high-pitched cry, with his head twisted to one side. Both arms were stretched outward with tight fists and a slight tremor was evident. They gazed at the baby, sad expressions on their faces, transfixed by the obviously abnormal cry and posture of the baby.

"Gail, are you familiar with kernicterus?"

"Not really."

"It's a form of damage that comes with deposition of bilirubin in the brain. It's pretty rare these days, but fifty years ago it was common. When a baby has a different blood type from the mother, it can result in the formation of antibodies against the baby's red blood cells. They get destroyed and the hemoglobin is broken down into bilirubin. At very high levels, it begins to seep into the brain. We rarely see it now because we have all sorts of ways of preventing the rise of bilirubin in the blood." Egan continued to stare at the baby quizzically. He leaned over to take a closer look.

"Eric, what are you wondering about now?"

"Oh, just that kernicterus is in and of itself quite rare, but it is extraordinarily rare with a bilirubin of only 18."

"Why is that?"

"Well, in order for bilirubin to do its damage, it has to traverse the blood brain barrier. There is a threshold level that must be exceeded in order for the bilirubin to penetrate. There are certain conditions such as infection or prematurity that can be associated with an altered blood brain barrier, but this baby looks like he must have been a full-term baby. Let's take a look at the chart"

They opened the chart. Gail began to summarize aloud as she ran her finger down the first page of the chart. "The baby was born at full term, mother's first pregnancy, via in vitro fertilization, that's sad. Had regular prenatal care, ultrasounds at twelve, twenty, and twenty-four weeks were completely normal. Entered spontaneous labor on the morning of August first and delivered thirty-six hours later—bit long, but the apgars were nine/nine which is almost perfect."

Egan had scanned ahead of her and now pointed at the bottom of the page. "The baby's blood type is 0+ just like the mother's, which would make a bilirubin problem—at least from red cell breakdown—really unlikely."

They looked again at the baby who let out another high-pitched cry, his neck writhing to the left while both arms stretched to the right in full spasm.

Chapter Seventeen
August 22, 2008 12:04 PM

Egan had been summoned back to the pediatric floor to attend to yet another recalcitrant IV that had evaded the best efforts of three interns. Gail remained in the ICU, studying the Gold chart for the second time, her face in pursed concentration. After finally getting the IV restarted, he glanced at his watch and saw that he had a rare half-hour hole in his schedule and decided to bolt for the library.

In the medical library, he tensed for a moment when he heard a cell go off and relaxed when he realized it was not his own. He strode into the stacks with the ease of a man in his own living room intimately familiar with its artifacts and decorations. He had spent many happy hours here especially during his two year stint working on his doctoral dissertation. Now as a resident, he rarely had the time and therefore all the more relished his brief escapes here.

He often liked to linger at different shelves; more in the manner of a bookstore browser for his interests and reading were eclectic. He paused before the title Paroxysmal Neurophysiologic Events and began to take it, but then stopped himself, muttering "No time for that now." He went deeper into the stacks and began to gather books and bound journals and finally went to find an old favorite: Feigin and Cherry's Pediatric Infectious Disease, a massive three-volume work that was a compendium of all the known medical knowledge in this complex field. Feigin and Cherry were missing from their familiar spot, leaving an impressive gap in the shelves.

"Damn," said Egan out loud.

He was startled to hear a voice behind him. "I'm surprised that a man of your erudition needs to consult a book. Don't you already know Feigin and Cherry cover to cover?"

Egan turned to find Gail comfortably settled in one of the stack cubicles with her own pile of books and journals including all three volumes of Feigin and Cherry.

"Of course I do, I'm just doing my daily check to see if any of my medical students are actually doing any reading. What are you reading anyway?" He stepped forward and saw that she was reading the section on meningitis. "Very good, you definitely earned some brownie points." He leaned down closer to read the section she was on. His shoulder brushed lightly against hers.

Each looked at the other and both simultaneously averted their gazes and turned back to the text book.

"Let's take a look at what you have read. Good, you're reading on the pathogenesis. That's key, in my opinion. I'm big on basic science."

"Well, glad you approve. This stuff is actually pretty interesting."

Another look up and quick return of four eyes to the text.

"Let's see what you've learned. Fill me in on, for example, why is meningitis potentially such a devastating illness?"

Gail paused, knitted her brow and leaned forward slightly to get a better look at the page. A lock of hair fell forward over her cheek and she brushed it back. Egan found himself staring at this rather than the page before them. She looked up, and he shifted his gaze back to Feigen and Cherry.

A brief smile, one more attempt to secure the recalcitrant lock, and then, "It's actually ironic."

Egan's eyebrows shot up in mock astonishment. "Irony in medicine? Better not let Johnson hear you say that. He'll have you up before the medical irony board."

"No, really, according to this a lot of the damage inflicted is the result of the wholesale slaughter of the bacteria by massive doses of antibiotics. This battleground of dead and dying bacteria releases a whole alphabet soup of chemicals that seem to be potent stimulants of the body's immune and inflammatory mechanisms, which in turn causes brain damage or death."

"Bravo, I'm impressed. That's an important, subtle point. Ideally our therapy should be directed toward a controlled elimination of the bacteria without the secondary effects of the dying bacteria." Egan stood up, paused for a moment with hand on his chin reflectively, and continued. "Quite frankly, our current treatment of meningitis is like using a grenade to open up the abdomen in order to remove an inflamed appendix. Obviously, based on our current knowledge, we have no choice. Bacterial meningitis left to its own devices is rapidly fatal 60 to 70 percent of the time.

"But, you'll see, the thrust of research these days is to develop modulators of inflammation that will lessen the secondary effects of killing all the bacteria. Giving corticosteroids before the first dose of antibiotics is a crude attempt to accomplish this. Treating meningitis is like bringing down an airplane with only the crudest of instruments, which results in a lot of crash landings. So we end up with a pyrrhic victory; the patient survives, but with the brain turned to mush."

Gail had listened to all this attentively and appeared reflective for a moment and then stood up, stretched for a moment and leaned forward and kissed him lightly on the lips. Egan, startled, took a step back. They gazed at each other, her eyes flitting back and forth between his eyes and his lips and finally slowly moved in for another kiss. Egan pulled back and they stood staring at each other for a long moment until Gail broke into a smile and began to laugh.

"What's so funny?"

"I was just thinking—your mouth has the minty taste of Scope."

"So you heard that story too." Egan began to laugh as well.

They kissed again, then stood staring at each other until Egan glanced at other books on the desk. "What else are you reading about?"

"Kernicterus, of course, I was especially intrigued by your statement that the bilirubin was theoretically too low to cross the blood brain barrier. Listen, Eric, this could be totally wacky but I couldn't help but think about the two babies in the ICU, both of whom are suffering from the consequences of something crossing the blood brain barrier, in one a bacterium, in the other a molecule. Can they possibly be connected?"

"Seems pretty farfetched." But Egan paused to consider it. Having always had a tendency to make strange and quirky connections, he was loathe to dismiss this out of hand. "Well, let's see, I must say that nothing comes to mind. I assume these babies are not distant cousins or something. If you're postulating some sort of genetic problem, it would be an extraordinary coincidence to find two babies in one ICU with the same very rare underlying problem."

"Maybe you're right. I was thinking that it would be a very interesting honors research project."

"Well, you can look into it, but I'm dubious at this point. I would stick with something more basic like looking for other cases of meningitis."

"I guess you're right. So, are you still willing to help me out? I promise you I won't throw myself at you again."

"Oh, in that case, no help from me!"

"You'd said yesterday that you'd be willing to lend me your pass code so I can do a med record search. Is that offer still good?"

"Absolutely. Let me write it down for you." He took a pad from his lab coat pocket, wrote a series of numbers and handed it to her.

"Now come here." Said Egan with a smile and he took her in his arms.

"Well, excuse me."

They jumped apart, startled at the interruption. It was Doug Barrett.

"I'm glad to see that things are so under control on the pediatric floor that you have time to linger in the library, though I must say the expression I saw on Joan Richter's face," Barrett paused to look at his watch, "not fifteen minutes ago said to me that there is probably a lot to do."

"Yeah, Doug, but you know Joan, even if there is nothing to do, she finds something. Anyway, we're actually doing a bit of reading."

"Oh, yeah, I'm sure you got a lot done here."

Egan ignored the sarcasm, holding his gaze evenly. "So, Doug, what are you doing here?"

"My boy, do you think you are the only erudite one among us? I was merely coming to feast upon the wisdom of the ages, hoping that the knowledge I glean from this sojourn will enable me to apply it to saving a life or just bettering mankind in general.

"By the way, I now know why you dash off to the library with such alacrity and I must say I can't blame you," said Barrett as he turned his eyes to Gail with an appraising, appreciative look.

"Well, Doug, it's fun chatting with you, but we had better get back to work."

"Well, okay, but I'd try to wrap it up and get back to the floor." And with that Barrett strode off.

Egan watched him as he disappeared into the adjoining stacks. "Jesus, I could do with a little less Doug Barrett in my life." He looked back at Gail. "I'd better get back to the floor. Give me a call once you've gathered the data. I was actually down at medical records looking for a previous case that the ER nurse told me about, a Jamie Reed and there was an access block on the record. I'd be curious to see what you find."

Chapter Eighteen
Spring 2006

It was a spring evening, not long after John Maitland had left Goldman Sachs to take the position of president of Maitland Energy Enterprises. He and Joyce were seated across from each other by a window in a small French bistro on the Upper East Side. They held hands across the table while sipping chardonnay and gazing out the window at people walking on the sidewalk. A young couple walked by pushing a baby carriage. The man was holding a little girl's hand. They watched them make their slow way up the avenue and simultaneously looked at each other. Joyce broke the silence. "Kids, I think it's time."

"Honey, I'm game if you are, but we probably better wait until we get back to our apartment," John said with a laugh.

"No, John, I'm serious. I don't want to do the typical yuppie thing, wait and wait until we're in our forties."

"You're serious, aren't you?"

"Yes, I'm afraid I am. Hope I'm not scaring you, but I know it sounds crazy, but I worry about waiting. Everything has gone so well, that I am almost superstitious that the thing I want most will never happen."

"Quite honestly, it's what I want most, too. I won't admit it to my father, but I was daydreaming the other day of my child taking over the business someday."

* * *

For several months their lovemaking was spontaneous, following the dictates of their desire. But each month brought increasing disappointment with the start of her menses. After eight months had gone by, Joyce, in characteristic style, raided the library and the Internet to learn all she could about reproduction. She began to take daily temperatures to determine her time of ovulation. John gave up his weekend bike rides and switched from briefs to boxers to ensure that his testicles never strayed above the 96 degrees optimal for sperm production.

Sex became a calendar event, waiting until two days before her anticipated ovum release and they embarked on lovemaking marathons. It was during one of those sessions that John heaved himself off of her and lay out of breath from his exertions while Joyce stayed absolutely still, legs and hips elevated on pillows to allow a downstream swim for the millions of sperm, flagella beating in their salmon like quest to fertilize.

"Jesus," panted John, "if that doesn't do it, then I don't know what will. That was definitely my best shot."

Joyce turned her head toward him, keeping the rest of her body rigidly still and offered a wan smile. "Yes, darling, you were wonderful. Maybe this will be the time."

John turned and patted her stomach. "I feel a lot of action in there."

Joyce's smile faded and tears began to roll down her cheeks.

"Oh, darling," began John and reached to embrace her.

"No, John, I can't move now." She pushed him away with her arms and began to cry more audibly. "I'm just so discouraged." She managed to choke out between sobs. "What is wrong with me, what is wrong with us? Why can't I get pregnant?"

"But Joyce, it has only been—"

"Two years," interrupted Joyce, "two whole years. Do you know what I have been going through? Not an hour passes that I don't think about conceiving. It's always there, whether I'm on day one of my cycle or day fourteen. When I see mothers loaded with groceries and with kids trailing, my heart breaks. I picture myself at sixty, with no kids, nothing."

They were quiet for a moment. John continued to gently stroke her stomach and reached with a tissue to dry her tears.

"Joyce, we are going to get there. We just may need a little help, that's all. I know you think I'm a typical oblivious male blob, but I tell you, I've been obsessing a bit myself. In fact, I have found the name of the top infertility person in the city and we are going to call him."

"Oh, darling," began Joyce excitedly and turned to give her husband an embrace.

"Wait; remember you have to stay perfectly still."

"Oh shit, yeah," and she resumed her former position now laughing.

"Hey, laughing has got to help, jollying those sperms to their appointed mission."

She stopped laughing and tears once again began to form at the corner of her eyes. "Oh, John, I don't know. I do appreciate it, but the whole fertility thing, I'm not sure I'm ready for that. It seems unnatural."

"Joyce, there is nothing wrong in just talking with someone. Review our options."

"Okay, let me think about it. By the way, what is this doctor's name?

"Dr. George, Dr. Blake George."

Chapter Nineteen
August 22, 2008 1:05 PM

Egan and Gail were leaving the library when the overhead speaker blasted: "Stat! Pediatrics to the delivery room!" At the same time, Egan's cell went off.

"Oh, shit," muttered Egan "I've got the delivery room call today."

"Can I come too?" asked Gail.

"Sure, I may need a hand. Let's go."

They took off down the corridor. They arrived at the delivery suite, winded and sweating.

"Which room?" Egan asked the nurse's aide. She pointed to room two. Once in the room, he was relieved to see that the baby had not been born yet. In the labor chair was an exhausted appearing young woman with legs up in stirrups. Seated on a small stool in the delivery position at the base of a birthing chair was the obstetrician, gowned, gloved, and masked.

"Peds here," said Egan a bit more loudly than he intended still catching his breath.

The obstetrician looked up and in spite of the mask, Egan recognized that it was Dr. Blake George. Remarkably, despite all the blood and other secretions that make deliveries a pretty messy business, Dr. George appeared neat and unspotted. Like a famous chef who never gets any sauce on his apron, thought Egan. "Ah, Doctor Egan, working up a bit of a sweat I see".

"Sir, I was called stat."

"Oh, yes, very much appreciate your prompt response. We have a spot of trouble, here. Take a look at this tracing."

Egan looked quickly at the tracing of the fetal monitor that showed a continuous reading of the fetal heart rate. "No question about these late decelerations; this is clear-cut fetal distress."

George's mask did little to conceal the wave of displeasure on his face as he looked sharply at Egan. "Well, perhaps, but I'd say you're overstating it. I'll have this baby out in a jiffy. The main reason I called you is that we have some thick meconium."

Oh great, thought Egan, *a depressed baby with thick meconium.*

"What is meconium?" whispered Gail.

Egan leaned toward her and spoke softly. "In short, it's fetal shit. Thick, black, and tarry. Its only saving grace is that it doesn't smell. Usually it stays in the intestines until after birth. When it is expelled before birth, it is a sign of fetal distress. The kicker is that meconium gets into the baby's mouth and trachea and makes it real difficult to breath. Up shit's creek as it were. What we have to do is, quick as we can, get a tube into the trachea and suction that stuff out before the baby takes his first breath, before he has a chance to suck all that meconium into his lungs."

"Hey, is everything okay?" asked the father from the head of the birthing chair who was eyeing Egan's urgent low tones with increasing concern.

Dr. George's reply was immediate and soothing. "Nothing at all to worry about. Purely routine to have the pediatrician here. I believe in taking every precaution."

"Okay, doc, you're the boss." He turned his attention back to his wife. "Honey, you're doing fine. Keep pushing."

Egan was not so easily soothed and turned away from the father to hide his worried expression and kept busy preparing his equipment. He had taken another look at the tracing and been startled to see that the fetal distress had started two hours ago. Why hadn't he done a Cesarean section? He knew that Dr. George had a reputation for natural deliveries, but this was a little too close to the edge. His patients loved him though. He was charming, imperturbable, and inspired confidence.

"O2 on, ambu bag working, suction working, endotracheal tubes available," Egan said out loud for Gail's benefit as he went down his checklist. "A meconium baby requires that all equipment be instantly available."

He turned back to wait for the baby to be born, an agonizing few minutes as he wondered just what kind of shape this baby would be in. Finally, he could see the top of the head emerge. Dr. George had kept up an almost continuous chatter praising the mother for her pushing, commenting on the miracle of childbirth. "Mary, here she comes," Dr. George said in an excited voice, not betraying any worry about the condition of the baby. "Just one or two more pushes."

Egan looked closely for any early clues on how the baby was. Suddenly with one more push the baby was out, covered with thick black meconium and quite limp. "Okay, Mary, the baby's out. It's a boy! Stop pushing, take some easy breaths." *Not good,* thought Egan, itching to get his hands on the baby. Dr. George, though, did not immediately hand the baby over, but held him up to show the parents.

"Oh," cried the mother, "let me hold him for a second." Dr. George looked as if he was about to hand him to the mother, but this was too much for Egan who stepped forward and took the baby from George's hands and hurried over to the infant resuscitation table. Dr. George looked momentarily startled, but quickly recovered his poise and told the parents, "All routine. We have to let the pediatrician check the baby quickly and then you can hold him."

Egan wiped the tarry meconium off the baby's face and grabbed the laryngoscope and placed it inside the infant's mouth, inserting the blade to the base of the tongue and lifted slightly. He quickly suctioned out the black lava-like muck from the mouth and finally was able to visualize the vocal cords. He placed an endotracheal tube through the vocal cords and into the trachea and suctioned out copious amounts of meconium. The baby remained utterly limp and unresponsive during this procedure, which in fact made Egan's intubation and suctioning much easier.

"This is good. I got all this stuff out before the baby took a first breath. Gail, check the baby's heart rate."

"It's about 60."

"Too low for a newborn. Hand me that ambu bag and keep track of the heart rate, in fact, tap it out for me."

Gail continued to listen to the baby with her stethoscope and tapped the rhythm with her index finger against the edge of the radiant infant warmer.

He positioned the ambu bag over the baby's mouth and nose with one hand and began to rhythmically squeeze the bag with the other, pushing a high concentration of oxygen into the baby's lungs. Egan waited to see if this intervention would do the trick or whether he would have to get more aggressive.

"Come on, baby, let's go. You can do it," urged Egan in a barely audible whisper.

Suddenly the baby roared into life with a cry and began to move his extremities.

Egan broke into a grin. "All right!" Kind of like trying to start a car on a cold morning, the whine of the starter turning over and over but not quite catching until finally the engine roars into life, he thought.

"Heart rate is over a hundred."

"Okay, great, you can stop tapping now. Let's do a quick exam."

With relief, Egan did a careful exam of the baby, and once he was convinced the baby was okay, wrapped him up and carried him over for the parents to see. He completed some paperwork and after a word with the parents, they left the delivery room.

"Dr. Egan, can you hold on for a second?" Egan turned around to see Dr. George hurrying after him. Now his surgical mask was off revealing his handsome face with a meticulously groomed beard. "I didn't appreciate your grandstanding in there. You got the parents pretty worried."

"Grandstanding?" asked Egan incredulously. "That baby was born two hours after signs of fetal distress limp like a rag doll with some of the thickest meconium I've ever seen. Luckily, I was able to intubate that baby quickly and get all that stuff out."

Dr. George seemed unmoved by his words and broke in with a faint smile. "Oh, I see, with your vast experience you came and saved the day! That baby revived quickly with a bit of O2. Why don't you just admit that you panicked in there? I don't blame you, that's how you learn, but your pseudo heroics are most alarming to parents."

With that, Dr. George turned and walked back to the delivery suite leaving Egan standing in stunned silence in the corridor. He was not totally unaccustomed to this sort of conflict. He realized that there was, coupled with the natural alliance of purpose of obstetrics and pediatrics, also a natural antipathy that occurs whenever more than one body shares responsibility. The delivery itself represented a sharp demarcation of responsibility with the sudden shift from obstetrician to pediatrician, and there is a pull and tug between the two professions as to who is to blame for a bad or near bad outcome.

Egan continued to review the events that had just transpired and he became increasingly convinced that the level of his concern and intervention were justified, yet George's criticism continued to gnaw at him.

"Shit, Gail, am I crazy or was that one depressed baby in there?"

Before Gail could answer his cell went off and this time it was a welcome distraction from his unpleasant reverie.

Chapter Twenty

August 22, 2008 5:00 PM

Egan signed out to the on-call resident. He took the elevator to the ground floor and after exiting he stood for a moment. He was eager to get home, especially since he was on call the next day, Saturday, but the mystery of Jamie Reed was rattling around in his head. He found himself turning right toward the Peds ER, rather than left toward the hospital exit.

The ER was quiet and after waving at the attending and residents who were lounging in the doctor's station, he made his way to the back. Tina was bent over the trauma cart taking advantage of the inactivity to go over the equipment. Egan watched her for a moment, impressed with her industry. Tina never sits still, he thought.

"Hey, Tina."

Tina turned. "Why, Eric, what are you doing here?"

"Just dropping by to say hello to my favorite nurse."

"Sure, you think I believe that jive? You want something."

"As usual, you see right through me. More evidence that you are also the most perceptive and smart nurse I know."

Tina laughed. "Okay, okay, Eric, just tell me what you want."

"Do you remember that other baby with meningitis that you told me about? Jamie Reed?"

"Sure."

"I checked medical records and for some reason there is an access lock on his records."

"Access lock?"

"They do that sometimes if a case is under litigation, for example. Was there anything unusual about this, I mean, did everything go smoothly?"

"As far as I remember, it was pretty routine. The baby came in with fever, just like your case, but it was a bit more clear-cut. The fever was over a hundred and three and the baby appeared ill. This was during the day, so there was plenty of staff. The baby was tapped, IVed, and sent upstairs—all within an hour."

"Do you remember anything else like how long the baby had been sick, the birth history, that sort of thing?"

Tina pursed her lips in concentration. "I wasn't directly involved at the beginning; it was busy that day. The parents were older, early forties or so. They were obviously quite upset, and I spent a few minutes with them while the spinal tap was being done. It was their first baby."

"Anything else?"

"I'm sorry, Eric. I was really just trying to comfort them. And it was a few months ago. Wait, I do remember one thing: The baby was an in vitro pregnancy."

Chapter Twenty-One
August 24, 2008 9:00 PM

Egan emerged into the bright morning sun. He paused and blinked trying to adjust his eyes accustomed to indoor light for the previous 24 hours of his on-call shift. He took out a piece of paper and squinted at an address. He began to walk, not in the direction of his apartment, but instead toward Greenwich Village. The streets were Sunday morning quiet. Soon he found himself before a West Village townhouse. He double-checked the number, went up the stoop and rang the bell.

As he waited, he looked up and down the tree lined street. He was staring off in the distance when the door suddenly opened and he started. The woman at the door was tall and angular with black hair tied neatly back. "Dr. Egan?" Her tone was formal and her expression fixed.

"Yes."

"Please come in."

He followed her down a corridor lined with stained oak panels and they entered a room with a large domed ceiling and ornate wood carvings.

"Please, have a seat." She gestured toward a leather chair while she sat on an adjoining couch. "Can I offer you some coffee or tea?"

"Coffee would be wonderful, if it isn't too much trouble."

"Not at all. I'll be right back."

Egan watched her walk out, her gait refined and posture erect. He looked around at the room, which had been meticulously restored to its late nineteenth-century glory. He felt suddenly uncomfortable and out of place, and was tempted to get up and leave.

The woman returned with a tray of two china cups, an urn, a silver pitcher, and matching sugar bowl. She carefully placed the items on the table and poured coffee for each of them. She looked at him expectantly.

"Mrs. Reed, thank you so much for agreeing to meet with me."

She looked at him silently for a moment, and took a refined sip from her porcelain cup. "I am puzzled that you wanted to see me. I don't recall that you were one of the doctors involved in Jamie's care. It brings up painful memories that are still quite fresh so this isn't easy for me." She paused. She dabbed the corner of her eye with the edge of her napkin. She drew herself to an even more erect position.

"But curiosity got the better of me. I thought to myself, why would a pediatric resident want to come all the way to the other side of town to talk with me? I could barely get a word out of you fellows in the hospital, scurrying around like mice loaded down with vials of blood." Her tone had hardened and she stared directly at Egan.

"As I think I mentioned on the phone I took care of a baby that has a very similar illness to your baby, and I wondered if there was any connection."

"Meningitis is so rare?"

"Meningitis per se is not rare. However, the type of bacteria that caused meningitis in your baby and in the baby I took care of, is quite unusual in an infant less than eight weeks old."

"I see; so you are conducting a little investigation for the betterment of mankind. For goodness sakes, couldn't you just look at the records and not bother a grieving mother? Dr. Egan, do you have any idea what I'm going through?"

Egan leaned forward. "No, I don't. I don't have kids, at least not yet."

Her gaze hardened. "At least you're honest. All I hear is I understand how you feel and I want to scream—you don't understand—never in a million years could you understand." Her facial musculature, held so rigidly for so long, suddenly cracked into a sea of folds and wrinkles and an animal-like howl emitted from her mouth.

Egan sat shock-still as she sobbed uncontrollably, wanting to comfort her, but sensing that someone with her patrician bearing would not welcome soothing words or a comforting hand. He kept his gaze fixed on her and finally she lifted her head from her hands and looked at Egan. "I'm sorry, I just couldn't hold it in any longer. The last six months have been utter hell. Family and friends rushing in at the beginning, but not knowing what to say and I could see the awkward discomfort in their faces. Now hardly anyone calls, probably saying to themselves, 'I don't want to disturb her.' Even my husband, he's at work right now—on a Sunday."

Egan continued to sit silently, leaning forward slightly.

"How did you learn to listen like that? A male and a doctor to boot."

Egan smiled faintly. "My mother needed someone to listen to her. My dad wasn't too good at it."

She looked at him for a long moment. "I guess I'm not the only one with losses. Dr. Egan, I thank you. You wanted to find out about Jamie's illness.

"Well, yes, but only if you are feeling up to it."

She paused to take a tissue, dried her face and blew her nose. "Once again, I'm sorry for that explosion." She had brought herself back to an erect bearing. "I went through so much to have Jamie. You can see I'm no spring chicken. In my twenties and thirties for some reason the urge to have kids never hit me. Ticking biologic clock? I had no idea what people were talking about. I had my career, my friends, and my interests."

"In what field is your career?"

"Oh, I'm an art historian. Post Renaissance drawings. I work as a curator at the Met. Anyway, I was totally involved in my work, so it really took me by surprise when I began to think about a baby. And it hit hard. I found myself wandering over to the medieval section of the Met and staring at cherubs in those religious paintings. My husband, a Wall Street lawyer as consumed with his work as I am with mine, didn't know what to make of me. He never had wanted kids either and I thought how lucky we were to be so similar and compatible. He went along with it, but I think he secretly hoped it would be a temporary passion. But no, the desire just got stronger.

"Poor man; I made him give up biking because I read that it affects sperm counts. But I couldn't get pregnant. So we went to an in vitro clinic here in the West Village. Spent God knows how much money, went through cycle after cycle, but nothing. Finally we went to the clinic at your hospital, and we succeeded on the first try. We were ecstatic. My pregnancy and delivery went without a hitch. Dr. George, who did the in vitro personally, delivered Jamie."

She paused and dabbed her eyes. "Jamie got sick on a Tuesday. He was only six weeks old. I took him to the ER. They told me he had meningitis and he went to the intensive care unit." She began to cry, softly this time and she seemed for a couple of moments transported back to that time. Finally she composed herself. "On the second day of his hospitalization, he had some sort of crisis and they told me he was brain dead. They asked me if I would consider donating his organs and I agreed. So Jamie's organs are scattered around the world now."

Chapter Twenty-Two
August 25, 2008 3:00 PM

Egan strode rapidly toward the outpatient department where he was scheduled to spend the afternoon seeing emergency room patients who had follow-up appointments. The waiting room was packed with mothers, wailing infants, bandaged toddlers, and tattooed teenagers. He tried to avoid their glances as he picked his way through the throng and entered a small corridor behind the exam rooms.

Each room had a back door to this corridor so that the doctor could move from room to room without running into waiting room patients who had a tendency to try to collar any doctor they saw with a question. All six exam rooms had a chart sitting in a rack on the door indicating that besides the crowd he had seen on his way in, he had an additional six patients.

Egan spotted Tina bent over a tray of instruments.

"Tina, sorry! I'm here.

"Man, you are late, even for you. Did you think that this was evening clinic, rather than afternoon?"

"Please, Tina, spare me. I'm already stressed to the max. Just point me in the right direction and give me a push."

"That I will do. Better put your roller skates on. Room two is first—a suture removal—here's your kit." She handed him a small tray with fine tweezers and scissors.

He took with one hand, while reaching with the other for the chart sitting in the rack and barged into the room.

"Dr. Egan, what a pleasure to see you again."

It was the blond, sitting on the examining table, with her daughter in her lap. Last time she had been in workout clothes and had had on little makeup. Now she was dressed with a chartreuse chiffon blouse and black leather skin tight pants. What was her name again? He looked at the chart, nonplussed and feeling awkward. There, Brookfield.

"Hello, Mrs. Brookfield."

"Oh, please, call me Chelsea. I feel like we're almost old friends."

"Okay, uh, Chelsea. How's your little girl?"

"Wait until you see. According to my unprofessional eye, the boo-boo has healed beautifully. Let me take the bandage off. Elizabeth, don't cry; this won't hurt."

The girl began sobbing and pushed her face into her mother's low-cut blouse. Egan stepped forward to help pry her away so that Chelsea could remove the band aid.

"No, no!" screamed the girl, but Egan kept a firm grip on her arms and her mother leaned forward. Her blouse opened and Egan could not help but see two milky white breasts below her tan line. She removed the bandage with one swift motion and looked up at Egan with a smile. He averted his eyes.

The door opened. "Hey, do you need a hand?"

"Yeah, thanks, Tina. If you could try to hold her head still, while Mrs. Brookfield holds her in her lap, I think I can probably get these out fairly quickly."

"It's Chelsea."

"Okay, Chelsea, hold on tight." He leaned forward with scissors with a beveled tip and was able to quickly get under each suture and cut it. He then took the tweezers and pulled each one out.

"We're done."

Tina released her hold. "Dr. Egan, if you don't need me in here anymore, I'll go get the next patient ready."

Egan looked up. "No, I'm fine." They locked eyes and Tina with a frown, tapped her watch and gestured with a shake of her head toward the waiting room. Egan winked at her as she rolled her eyes and scurried out.

Egan sat back, happy that it had gone smoothly and was quite pleased at how well the laceration had healed.

Elizabeth had stopped crying and was hugging her mother. "It's okay, Elizabeth, you're fine. It's all over. Here, let the doctor take a look." She repositioned her daughter in her lap so now she was facing Egan. Egan leaned forward taking a close look at the forming scar.

"I think it's going to heal with very little scarring. Put on a little vitamin E cream every day. Also, this is very important; put some zinc oxide over it before going out into the sun. If you do all that, I think this will be invisible in three months or so."

"Thank you so much, Dr. Egan. You did a marvelous job."

"Call me, Eric, it's only fair."

"Fair enough, Eric. By the way, Eric, when do you get off work?"

Egan looked up with a start.

"I'm sorry, am I being too forward?"

"No, no, uh, Chelsea. It's quite all right. Actually, by the looks of the waiting room, it won't be until 7 or so."

"How about if I meet you in front of the hospital at say 7:30? It'll give you a chance to change out of your scrubs. They're some nice bars I know, and I'd like to buy you a drink for all you've done."

"Well, Chelsea, that's very kind of you, but you really don't have to go to all that trouble ...."

"It's really no trouble. But if you don't want ...."

"No, it's not that. Having a drink with you, to be perfectly honest, seems heavenly. But I'm just not sure about the propriety. Going out with a patient and all."

"Elizabeth is your patient, not me."

Egan smiled and rubbed his bearded chin thoughtfully. "Not a bad loophole. You sell real estate, as I recall. I bet you're good at it."

"As a matter of fact I am, though I do have other talents."

Egan opened his mouth to reply but was interrupted by a quick knock, and Tina poked her head in. "Dr. Egan, I'm sure your patient appreciates your meticulous instructions, but please, you've got a packed clinic."

"Uh, sorry." Egan jumped to his feet. "Okay, remember to keep it out of the sun."

Chelsea smiled and mouthed the words, "Seven-thirty." He gave a barely perceptible nod before following Tina out the door. Once in the back corridor, Tina, arms akimbo, gave him a hard look. "What was that all about?"

"No time, remember?" he answered, as he escaped into the next examining room.

When he left the hospital at 7:20, it was still light out, a fact that cheered him considerably. He had always felt demoralized during the winter months when he arrived in the dark and left in the dark, a whole sunlit day missed entirely and gone forever. He looked up and down the avenue and spotted Chelsea at the end of the block walking toward him. She hadn't seen him yet, so he watched her as she made her unhurried way down the block. Her gait was casual though confident, her posture erect and her arms describing wide arcs balancing her long legged graceful steps. What am I getting myself into, he thought as he began to walk toward her.

Soon they were seated in the back terrace of an East Village French bistro. The sommelier held the bottle of wine so the label faced Egan. Egan peered at it, which read Chateauneuf Du Pape Blanc 2000. He nodded solemnly. The sommelier poured a small amount into his glass. Egan lifted it to the light, swirled the glass and sniffed. He took a sip. He held it in the front of his mouth and closed his eyes while he inhaled through pursed lips. "Wow, this is lush, with hints of mango, pineapple, peach and" he paused and took a second sip and repeated the process "and yes, honeysuckle, definitely all backed by a pleasant hint of bitter almond."

Chelsea laughed. "Does that mean you like it?"

The sommelier stood patiently, face with a fixed solemn expression. Egan looked at him and nodded. "This is excellent."

The sommelier broke into a smile for the first time. "Very good, sir. And I must say, you do know your wines."

Chelsea stared at Egan, mouth agape. "Was that for real? I was sure you were doing a mocking imitation of a wine connoisseur."

Egan laughed, "The truth is that I'm not really a wine expert. If you had me taste a wine blindly, I couldn't tell what the year was and what chateau it was from and all that."

"You could have fooled me. Wait a minute, did you set this up in advance? But, no, that's not possible. I picked this place. Eric, you got to tell me how you did it."

Egan looked at her with a smile, enjoying keeping her in suspense. Finally, "All right, here's the truth. As I said, I don't know wines, but I do know how to taste them. In other words, I don't have it here," he said tapping the side of his head, "but I do have it here." He touched the side of his nose.

"What on earth do you mean?"

"I'm what you could call an olfactory savant. You've heard of those people with autism who are able to do rapid computations in their head, the so called idiot savants. I just happened to be born with a schnoz that can distinguish very small differences in tastes and odors. Mozart could write sonatas when he was four. I have always been able to detect minute quantities of ingredients in food or drink. In some ways it's a curse, because it has made me somewhat particular about what I eat. I mean, if it isn't absolutely fresh, I can tell."

"That is absolutely amazing. Are you sure the sommelier wasn't just being polite? I mean, probably guys are coming in here all the time waxing eloquent over wine to impress their lady friends."

"You can put me to the test, if you want."

"Nah, that's Okay. It's too incredible not to be true. Anyway, rather than just talk about wine, let's drink some." She lifted her glass to his. "Here's to the skilled surgeon who sewed up my daughter's face."

"I'm hardly a surgeon and it wasn't exactly brain surgery I was performing. She's a really cute kid. Where is she tonight, with her father?"

"No, she's with a babysitter." She took a long sip of her wine and swirled it around in her mouth. "Honeysuckle, huh? You know, think I can taste it, very faintly." She finally swallowed it and leaned forward. "She doesn't really have a father, not in the normal sense.

I mean, of course, she has a biological father—we all do obviously. She was, I mean, my pregnancy, was the result of in vitro fertilization with an anonymous sperm donor. I just decided that I wasn't going to sit around and wait for the right man to come along. I wanted to have my own child so badly. For all that, I had trouble getting pregnant so I ended up going to the in vitro fertilization clinic at Malloy. It's the best thing I've ever done. Christ, why am I telling you all this?"

Egan, who hadn't taken his eyes off her during the whole of her recitation, reached forward and took her hand. "I'm glad you told me. That makes Elizabeth a very special child."

* * *

It was two hours later. They had started with fois gras, which they shared, and then she had quail and he had sole in a béarnaise sauce. Two more bottles of Chateauneuf Du Pape blanc 2000 had found their way to their table by the time they started digging into the best crème brulee Egan had ever eaten. Now they were on the sidewalk just outside the bistro.

Chelsea looked at him. He looked back at her. The dim light from a nearby street light created shadows on her face that only enhanced her beauty. I want her, he thought. They continued to stare at each other, the question hanging in the air between them. He swayed under the influence of the fine French wine, traversing easily across his blood brain barrier, bathing the neurons of his frontal lobes and wreaking havoc. Frantic neuronal impulses from his amygdala threatened to overwhelm his higher centers. He thought of Gail.

"Chelsea," he finally said as he felt himself pulling back from the vertiginous edge of the precipice, "I have to get up really early tomorrow. I'm on call and after all that wine I'm going to need all the shuteye I can get."

She looked down at the sidewalk and up again at Egan, a faint smile curling the edges of her lips.

'I understand."

"Thank you so much. I had a wonderful time. And say hello to Elizabeth."

He walked toward the hospital figuring he would just crash in one of the on call room beds rather than go all the way to his apartment. Damn, my friend Michael would have been all over her.

Chapter Twenty-Three

Spring 2007

Farah and Fasi strode into the opulent waiting room. One whole wall was taken up by a huge fish tank brimming with an array of brightly colored tropical fish. Fasi recognized a huge lionfish, a Red Sea denizen he was familiar with, bedecked with beautiful, but deadly spikes and fins, making a languid turn around the tank, which was in contrast to the more skittish movements of fish not so fiercely armored. The room was almost full with couples, some reading magazines, others fidgeting restlessly in their chairs and a couple of the husbands were pacing in front of the fish tank. Fasi looked around for a place to sit, but before he had spotted one, they were summoned by the receptionist who beckoned them into the consultation room. One glance backward and Fasi saw a sea of resentful faces watching them disappear behind the broad oak door.

"Prince Fasi and Princess Farah, it is truly a pleasure to meet you," said Dr. Blake George as he maneuvered around his desk to greet them. "Please, make yourselves comfortable. Would you like some tea perhaps?"

"Dr. George, the pleasure is all ours. Thank you so much for seeing us on such short notice. Farah and I were getting quite anxious about our, uh, situation. And yes, tea would be wonderful. We only just landed some two hours ago. It was a bumpy flight over the Atlantic and we hardly slept."

"I'm so sorry to hear that. Tea is on its way."

Once Fasi and Farah were comfortably settled in two large leather chairs, George returned to his seat behind his desk. He picked up a thick sheaf of papers and began to leaf through them.

"Let's see here. I have had the opportunity to review all your gynecological and obstetrical records that you so kindly furnished me with. I note that you have had three healthy girls and also have suffered three miscarriages." He looked up to give a sympathetic look at the couple. "I know how that hurts." After a pause, he continued. "But, let's look to the future. I can definitely help you."

You have our full confidence, Dr. George," said the prince. "I'm well aware of your international reputation."

"Thank you, thank you, you are too kind. Okay, let's get down to brass tacks."

The prince looked confused. "Brass tacks? Is that a fertility device?"

George laughed. "Oh, goodness no. My dear, prince, I apologize for the use of an idiom. Your English, of course, is excellent, but I can hardly expect you to know this Americanism. It means, let's get down to business."

Fasi exchanged a brief smile with Farah before leaning forward and exclaiming, "By all means, bring on the brass tacks."

"Now," continued George, "your letter indicated a strong desire to have another baby and specifically, a baby boy, is that right?"

"Yes," nodded Fasi, "you understand I love my daughters, but …."

George extended a preemptory hand. "Of course. I completely understand. A very natural desire to round out the family. Okay, let's continue. We have two problems—the first is your tendency, Princess, to have miscarriages. I have carefully reviewed your medical records that pertain to your miscarriages and I believe with a few simple changes in your obstetrical care, the odds of caring a baby to term would be quite high. The second problem is a bit trickier: making sure that you have a boy. You would think that with each pregnancy the odds of having a boy versus a girl would be fifty-fifty, but actually that is not the case. The fact, my dear Prince, that you have three girls indicates the possibility that you have a genetic predisposition toward fathering girls. For example, some men produce sperm that are 80 percent female."

The prince appeared momentarily nonplussed. "Doctor, do you think—?" he began.

George cut him off again. "Don't worry, it's just an example and has nothing to do with your masculinity. I'm just pointing out that leaving things to nature in this case may not produce the desired results."

"Well," said the prince after looking at his wife again, "we want the next one to be a boy, definitely."

"You have come to the right place. In all modesty, our statistics in sex selection approach 98 percent, the best in the world."

"Yes, doctor, that is exactly why we are here. How do you do it?"

"Let me explain the major methods we use. The first is sperm selection or as it is known in the industry, microsort. Because the X chromosome is much bigger than the Y chromosome, the female sperm contains 2.8 percent more DNA than the male sperm. A dye that is taken up by DNA is put into the semen sample. The male and female will have different shades of blue and thus can be manually separated with micropipettes wielded by our cadre of painstakingly careful lab techs. But even with meticulous care, it is possible only to enrich the spermatozoa to about 90 percent of a single gender. So we carry it further by combining this method with a new, quite elegant technique known as Preimplantation Genetic Diagnosis or PGD. Here's what we do: We microsort and use the enriched male spermatozoa to do in vitro fertilization. We generate a number of embryos. Presumably, most, but not all, will be male. But before we implant, we take a single cell from the embryo and check for the presence of a Y chromosome. We implant and voila, a male fetus."

The prince had been leaning forward, brow furrowed in concentration as he listened with an excited gleam in his eyes. He turned to Farah and smiled. His smile faded as he looked at her, slumped back in her seat, with a crestfallen expression on her face.

"Farah, what's wrong?"

"Oh, Fasi, it just seems so, so unnatural. And what about those other embryos? It feels like going against the will of Allah."

Fasi's face constricted briefly, but then softened and he took her hand. "Farah, there is nothing unnatural about wanting a son. I have prayed for this for years and I am convinced that Dr. George is the answer to my prayers to Allah." He extended his hand to her chin and lifted it. "Have I ever misled you? Farah, trust me on this."

Farah stared into his eyes and he held her gaze until she finally lowered her gaze and nodded while murmuring, "I trust you, Fasi."

Fasi turned back to George who had been implacably watching them.

"We are in your hands."

"Wonderful. Let me introduce you to some of my staff that will be involved in this process. And you should know that these techniques are cutting edge and quite expensive and—"

Now it was Fasi's turn to cut him off. "My dear Dr. George, please have no worries on that account."

Chapter Twenty-Four
Summer 2006

"The doctor will see you now."

John and Joyce Maitland struggled up from the plush, over-stuffed couch each heaving well-thumbed magazines to the ornate cherry wood coffee table in front of them.

"About time," muttered John to his wife as they followed the nurse into the inner sanctum.

"Just make yourself comfortable," said the nurse, an attractive blond who appeared to be in her early twenties as she gestured toward two large leather chairs facing a massive oaken desk covered with family photographs, papers, and an anatomical model of the uterus and fallopian tubes. They sank down into the chairs.

"The doctor will be right in."

"Yeah, I'll bet," said John after the nurse had left. "Let's see, two hours in the waiting room and I'm willing to guess that we'll be in here for another half-hour. We should bill him for our time."

"Oh, John, just simmer down. He is well worth the wait. Did you read his statistics for in vitro? They're really impressive."

"In vitro? I don't think we are at that stage yet. Let's see what he has to say about the fertility workup."

John got up and restlessly paced the ample room, pausing at one end to look at the wall plastered with framed degrees and certificates and then to the opposite side with a window that had a commanding view of the East River. A tugboat was hauling a barge downstream, while a medium-sized sailboat appeared to be struggling upstream in a light wind.

The door opened and a smiling figure strode in. "Joyce and John, how very nice to see you again," reaching first to Joyce pumping her hand energetically and then to John. John took his extended hand impressed as he had been on their first meeting with the meticulously groomed appearance of the doctor. His jet black thick hair was combed straight back and his grey tinged beard was closely cropped. His dark blue suit fit perfectly over a trim well-proportioned body. A faint scent of expensive cologne wafted off of him.

"Dr. George, nice to see you as well," answered John.

"Please, sit down," urged Dr. George as he made his way behind the desk and sat as well.

"Nice view you have here," said John gesturing toward the window.

"Oh, yes. I noticed you taking it in as I came in. That's an attractive sailboat. I would say that's an Alden Challenger, a seaworthy vessel, though it appears to be struggling a bit at the moment. Do you sail?"

"Well, no. We're anxious to know our test results," said Joyce speaking for the first time.

"Oh, yes, of course, I do apologize. That view never fails to distract me."

He opened the chart on his desk. "Let's see what we have here. John, let's start with you. Anatomically, you are quite adequate, no problem there."

"Well, gee, thanks a lot."

Dr. George looked up and laughed. "My goodness, John, I'm not referring to your, eh, external anatomy, but your vas deferens, spermatic ducts, that sort of thing."

"Don't worry, John," said Joyce patting his arm. "You are more than adequate."

"Anyway," continued Dr. George. "Your sperm count is fine, robust actually. It's really a marvelous sight under the scope, like Times Square at New Years, flagella flapping like mad."

"So, what you're saying is that John is perfectly fertile, so does that mean I'm the problem?"

"Joyce, wait. This isn't a finger pointing exercise. Let me finish. In a nutshell, though that is probably a poor choice of words," added

Dr. George with another laugh, "John, within the scope of our ability to determine by current state of the art of medical technology, is completely fertile. Joyce, let me finish. Your workup, in essence, is also totally normal. Your salpingogram, which in simple terms, is a detailed picture of the inner lining of your uterus and fallopian tubes, is a thing of beauty, pristine and unscarred. You are ovulatory and every indication is that your ova are of excellent quality. On paper, the two of you should be breeding like rabbits."

John and Joyce looked at each other.

"So," began Joyce, "we should be breeding like rabbits, yet we're not. I'm confused."

"It is confusing. Bear with me a moment and I'll try to explain. The reproductive system is an incredibly complicated, nuanced process. I sometimes marvel that anyone ever gets pregnant. Despite our much vaunted medical progress, we are still fumbling in the dark so to speak and there are doubtless many subtleties of the male and female reproductive systems that we simply do not understand.

"Here is what we do know: There are times when two particular people with normal reproductive systems have trouble conceiving with each other. In other words, John, your sperm may have no problem impregnating a different woman than Joyce. By the same token, Joyce, sperm from a different man may result in immediate fertilization. There is some factor that we don't understand that makes certain pairings incompatible as far as reproduction is concerned."

Joyce looked at John again and tears began to form in the corners of her eyes.

"Are you saying that Joyce and I have to split up and find different partners in order to have a baby?"

"No, of course not. We have a situation I have termed 'incompatibility X syndrome' which so happens is an area I have done a lot of research in. We are just going to have to resort to a little bit of biochemical trickery to get you pregnant."

Dr. George stood up and came around the desk, took Joyce's hand and patted it. "Now, my lady, dry those tears. We will get you pregnant, I mean to say," Dr. George paused to chuckle and gestured toward John, "John will get you pregnant with a little sideline help from me. I promise you." Dr. George held her gaze until a smile began to lift the corners of her mouth.

Chapter Twenty-Five
August 26, 2008 11:00 AM

Egan was seated at a small cubicle next to the nurse's station, bent over a to-do list that seemed to be growing exponentially as passing nurses alerted him to various problems on the floor. A clank of clogs on linoleum caused him to look up. It was Gail and he felt a thrill. Gail regarded him with an amused smile. "You look like you are up to your eyeballs in work and desperately need an extra pair of hands."

"I'm deep in it all right, in fact, I'm downright desperate."

"How can I help?"

"Thanks, but I'll manage."

Her smile faded and she turned to leave.

"Gail, wait. What am I saying? I could really use your help."

"Okay, I know I'm only a third-year med student, but—"

"No, that's not it. I'm sorry, I'm just being a macho resident—you know, the 'I can handle everything myself' syndrome. I'd love if you would help. Anyway, let's get organized. Consider this part two of my series on the savvy resident."

"Oh, God," said Gail emitting a low groan. "Okay. Proceed, uber resident."

"You'll be happy someday that you had me teach you this stuff."

"I know, I know."

Egan broke in with a grin. "Do you know that there are always one or two residents who are bright enough, but with appalling organization skills and find themselves constantly retracing steps? These poor souls frequently miss lunch and are often toiling late in the evening post call trying to wrap everything up and finally get home."

"So that's what it's all about: getting out early?"

"Hell, Gail, I'm as dedicated as the next guy, but I see no reason to spend any extra time in the hospital spinning my wheels. I take a Machiavellian approach, organizing my interns, students, and nurses for a massive assault upon ward duties."

"But, pray tell, how is it that a lengthy discourse on the utter efficiency of your organization does not constitute spinning your wheels? Just think what we could have accomplished during the time you took to say all that."

"Ah," said Egan while he stretched his arms above him and began to grin again. "You have, with your usual perspicacity, hit upon the fatal flaw. The beauty of my organization is so sublime that I frequently stop to admire it, thus wasting time."

At that moment, one of the nurses stopped before them to inquire if he remembered that "the post op appendicitis in room four needs a new IV" and they got to their feet and walked down the hall.

Two hours later, Egan had the satisfaction of crossing out the last item on his list. Gail had left a half-hour earlier for another of the lectures that punctuate a third year medical student's day. Egan headed upstairs to the hospital cafeteria, a place that always reminded him of where he had eaten during elementary school. The only difference, he thought, is the cell phones going off—though I imagine today every school kid these days carries a cell. He grabbed a plastic tray and placed a container of yogurt and a cellophane wrapped sandwich with some sort of generic luncheon meat inside upon it. He scanned the room and saw a small group of his fellow residents, which included his friend Michael, and he moved to join them.

"Hey, Eric," exclaimed one of the residents, "haven't seen you in a dog's age. Come sit here and catch me up on your latest exploits."

"Everybody, nice to see all of you". Egan nodded at the group. "You know me, I've been low profiling it just trying to stay out of trouble."

The group laughed knowing Egan's penchant for getting into fracases with his superiors.

"Eric," said Michael, "Did you hear the latest? They just nabbed a young man who has been impersonating a resident. This guy wore scrubs, stethoscope, the works and would wander the corridors aimlessly...."

"Sounds like he would fit right in. Can I have him for my team?"

"Wait, Eric, get this. He would wait until he heard an overhead page for gyn to the emergency room and then he would race down there and get his jollies examining the female patients. He apparently did this a number of times without exciting suspicion. He even wrote notes and orders."

"Sounds awful. How did he get caught?"

"One of the nurses got suspicious—he kept showing up within twenty minutes of the page, and nobody could recall a gyn resident responding to an ER page in under two hours. Plus his courteous demeanor toward the patients and nurses was a dead giveaway."

"It is kind of creepy," broke in Maggie, one of two female residents across the table. "Security is incredibly lax here. Anybody can put on scrubs and have instant access. I've occasionally seen strange people up on the twelfth floor near the on call rooms. I don't even like to go up there to sleep."

"Well, in their wisdom," replied Egan, "the administration has handled that problem by making sure you are so busy, that there is no way you are going to get close to the twelfth floor when you are on call!"

They all laughed, but it was an uneasy one. The hospital was huge and old and had numerous nooks and crannies. There had been rumors for years of homeless people who had inhabited various areas of the hospital and in fact exhausted residents often bore close resemblance to the homeless, shuffling along, never quite sure when their next meal or sleep would be. It's no wonder that the homeless would seek protective coloring in a city hospital, thought Egan.

"What's this afternoon's conference?" asked Maggie.

"I believe it's Newhouse talking about some of his latest research," replied Egan.

Two cells went off at once and lunch was suddenly over.

Chapter Twenty-Six
August 26, 2008 1:30 PM

Egan arrived at the nearly full eighth floor conference room chewing on a Reese's peanut butter cup. Newhouse, a dynamic teacher, was always a big draw. Egan scanned the room, noting the numerous tired, slouching residents, some actually catnapping, punctuated by occasional rested, suited professorial types who were the attendings. Cells would intermittently go off so there was frequent movement of residents going to or returning from the outside corridor. There was a constant hum of conversation. It reminded Egan of a beehive with worker bees flying in and out. A group of residents were standing around Newhouse jockeying for position. He's the queen bee, thought Egan. The analogy captivated him briefly, and he began to ponder the many astonishing similarities between an insect social caste and a medical center.

Dr. Newhouse strode to the lectern and the room silenced. He smiled and began to speak.

"Today, I'll be reviewing current concepts about the blood brain barrier, what we know about the anatomical and physiological aspects, what its many functions are and I hope to put it into the context of clinical medicine. Some of this may strike some of you as just so much esoterica and in the interests of full disclosure I will admit that much of what you hear will not be on the boards that you're studying for, but I think this topic has wide ranging applications."

A muted boo emerged from one of the residents and Newhouse laughed.

"Okay, okay, I'll make a deal with you—if I put any of you to sleep, I'll ring my beeper every time I mention something that may be on the boards."

Many in the room chuckled, though Newhouse's assessment of their interest was closer to the truth than they cared to admit. Egan, on the other hand, came to full attention, always interested in obscure topics.

"Now," Newhouse continued, "I'd like to start with a bit of basic biology and consider in a general sense the role of barriers. Biologic organisms are rife with barriers. First of all, barriers really define an organism and separate the organism from its environment and maintain its integrity. Evolution is really a story of refinement of these barriers that allow for ever more complex adaptations to allow selective intake of useful things in the environment and to exclude the useless or even dangerous things. All of this is because of the creation of barriers, whether it be a multilayered outer integument of a mammal or reptile or the membrane that lines a nerve axon which creates electrolyte gradients that allow for nervous transmission.

"Barriers, by the way, also protect the integrity of a species, in part by preventing a different species sperm from penetrating a foreign egg. The barrier I am going to focus on today is the blood brain barrier."

Newhouse continued, outlining the key anatomic and physiologic aspects of a barrier that defined the protected area which is the central nervous system. Several seats over, Egan noticed Barrett nodding off, and he made a mental note to try to bring up blood brain barrier at the next chief of service rounds and watch the chief resident fry in his own ignorance.

"Now, I want to get into some of the research that has been going on here at the medical center in my lab." Egan leaned forward in his seat and began to listen more attentively. "We have recently been looking into a protein that appears to be a modulator of blood brain permeability. We have termed this protein F. Barrier is really a misnomer when applied to most living biological systems as it is in this case. Barrier implies a simple mechanical impediment like a stone wall. In this case we are talking about a complex system of modulators and regulator's which dynamically change depending upon the situation. Protein F is an important part of this story, how important we don't know yet since research in this area is in its nascence." Newhouse went on to explain protein F's role in altering membrane permeability upon stimulation of its receptor site.

"In essence, protein F is a gatekeeper." Newhouse paused and scanned his audience. "Dr. Barrett, what do you suppose the clinical implications of this are?"

It was now Barrett's turn to snap to attention, though this was a more subtle-appearing transformation since Barrett through years of schooling had perfected the technique of appearing intently interested, even rapt, while half asleep.

"Well, the implications are many and varied and one can only speculate ..."

"Thank you, Dr. Barrett," said Newhouse cutting him off with a chuckle. "The bullshit meter I always carry with me is becoming fully activated."

"Dr. Egan, what do you think?"

"The first thing that strikes me is that once these receptor sites are further delineated, drugs could be designed to stimulate these sites and thus penetrate the blood brain barrier. Antibiotics and chemotherapeutic agents for example."

"Excellent," exclaimed Newhouse. He looked at his watch. "That's all we have time for. Sorry, Dr. Barrett, but your naptime is over."

Barrett looked over trying to remain impassive, but a sour expression was hard to conceal.

The lecture over, the residents and medical students began to file out.

"Eric." He turned to see Gail hurrying over to him. "Hey, are you okay?"

"Yeah, just tired."

"Were you on-call last night?"

"Actually, no, but, the truth is I have been tired since the beginning of my internship."

"Too bad. Hey, that was a good answer you gave in there. Pretty good for a guy as tired as you look. And your friend Doug Barrett seemed none too pleased."

Egan smiled. "Yup, pretty sweet. How'd you like the lecture?"

"Really interesting stuff. Newhouse is pretty amazing. What did you think?"

"Awesome. I was particularly interested in that stuff about protein F, something I know something about, but not in connection with the blood brain barrier. I did some research a couple of years back on the biology of embryo implantation. Didn't go too far and soon I got diverted into transplant immunology, but I did enough to learn that protein F is involved in that process as well."

"That is really fascinating. I'll have to read up on that. By the way, you have a little time now?"

"Actually, I do. The ward is pretty quiet."

"Do you have time to look over some of the data I gathered?"

"You've got data?"

"Yeah, I used your code. I found twenty other cases of pneumoccocal meningitis in the last year."

"You've got to be kidding."

"I'm not."

"I still don't believe it."

"Well, not all of them were young babies."

"How many?"

"I didn't really look at it too closely. Let's go someplace where we can sit down."

They walked into a small resident's work area. Gail pulled out a spread sheet and they sat down together. Egan studied it. Down the left side was a list of numbers and in columns to the left demographic data was neatly recorded. Egan knew that his research code allowed gathering of data, but did not reveal actual names. He looked at Gail.

"Are these in chronologic order?"

"Yes. The first case was almost a year ago. A six-month-old, hospitalized for two weeks and discharged."

Egan scanned down the page to the bottom. The last entry was of a six-week-old, date of admission: July 12, 2008. Hospitalized four days and then expired.

"Gail," he said putting his finger on that entry. "That must be Jamie Reed."

"Jamie who?"

"Jamie Reed was the name of the baby that Tina showed me in the ER log book. I went to the record room and there was an access block."

Egan looked at the spread sheet again and ran down the column that gave the patient's ages. He paused four times, each time mouthing a number.

"Gail, there are four cases over the last year of babies under six weeks with pneumococcal meningitis. Not including the Gold baby."

"Four doesn't seem like that many. I'm not sure that's enough to study."

"Don't worry about your study—you can write up all the other cases."

"I'm relieved to hear that."

"It is extraordinary that there were four cases in the last year. Pneumococcus just doesn't occur that often at this age."

Egan looked back at the page.

"Gail, was this all the information that was available?"

"There was other info on there, but I figured at first pass I would just get the basics. Why do you ask?"

"Well it's just that I don't see much here about birth history, except for birth weight and Apgar scores. It would be nice to know some other things like how long the membranes had been ruptured and something about the pregnancy."

"Hey, I'm only a third-year med student."

"I'm not putting you down. Tell you what, let's go to a computer terminal and we'll look together."

Soon they were seated before one of the hospital computers and Egan began to rapidly stroke the keyboard. "Okay, I'm into the hospital patient record site. Can you read me the first medical record number?"

Egan peered intently at the screen. "Looks like this baby is a six-week-old who presented with a two-day history of fever."

For the next ten minutes, Egan's eyes were glued to the screen as he searched out each clinical item while Gail made careful entries into her notebook.

She was entering the data from the last case, when the shrill sound of his cell startled both of them.

"Gail, it's a code, in the ER. Let's go."

They quickly picked up their notebooks and were in the ER within two minutes.

"What's going on?" asked Egan as he entered the ER. One of the nurses replied, "In the code room, a six-week-old baby in full arrest. It happened while they were doing a spinal tap." Egan and Gail hurried in to find a scene of controlled chaos that typically accompanies a dire emergency. The room was already full of medical personnel.

Egan pulled gently on Gail's arm and whispered. "Looks like they've got a full complement of people. We should just watch and standby to relieve somebody if needed.

"Too often in arrest situations too many people trying to do too many things at once. That's the ER director, Dr. Young, in charge."

The baby had two IV lines and an endotracheal tube. One of the residents had an ambu bag attached to the tube and was rhythmically pumping air into the baby's lungs. Another was doing chest compressions. Dr. Young stood impassively, but periodically in urgent but even tones would give directives. "Jim, lighten up a bit on the ambu bag, you don't want to blow a pneumo. Sarah, good compressions, but speed them up to eighty per minute. Now, let's give .06 of epi, followed by 6 of bicarb."

Egan could not help but admire Young's cool efficiency, having been involved in many arrest situations that bordered on being fiascoes. In this case, Young had assigned one person to each vital area—one resident to handle the airway, one to do the compressions, a third to handle vascular access. Young merely stood there taking in the whole situation, like a captain on the bridge of a burning ship, delivering crisp orders.

Egan looked around the room. He saw an open spinal tray, with a used spinal needle. He moved closer to it and folded back a flap of the paper wrapping that was obscuring three quarters of the tray and found three capped test tubes, with cloudy fluid in them. He picked it up, uncapped the tube and took a sniff. An odor emanated, and his mind flashed to the Gold baby. Not fishy, like the Gold baby.

The doctors continued to work for another 30 minutes, despite the dismal outlook simply because it was hard to conceive that a young previously healthy baby should die. Finally, Dr. Young said softly, "I think we're going to have to call it." Sarah, an intern, looked up from her chest compressions. "Not yet, let's try another round of meds." Sarah looked almost distraught. Egan gazed at her with understanding, remembering similar times in his first year.

Dr. Young gently put his hands on hers and began to tug gently. "No, Sarah, we have done all we can do." She resisted briefly but then allowed herself to be pulled away. The rest of the team stood there in stunned silence. Dr. Young looked at all of them. "There's nothing worse than this, but you did an incredible job trying to save this baby. Now, Sarah, you and I have to go talk to the mother."

Egan was impressed with Young again, knowing that some attendings would have sent the intern by herself to talk to the mother. Egan watched them leave the room, the intern already composed and ready. A moment later heart rending screams could be heard echoing throughout the ER.

Chapter Twenty-Seven
Summer 2007

John Maitland waited impatiently outside the medical center, pacing, looking at his watch repeatedly. Finally he spotted his wife walking briskly in his direction as rapidly as her high heels would allow her. As always, John was struck by her slender elegance and his irritation at her tardiness melted away.

"I'm sorry," said Joyce as she got within earshot. "I got stuck in a meeting, and then my cab got caught in cross town traffic and—"

John leaned forward and silenced her with a kiss. "It's okay, you're here. Anyway, I don't know why I'm getting so bent out of shape. Ten to one, our esteemed Dr. George will have us cooling our heels in his opulent waiting room for at least another hour."

"Now, John, it's not so bad. Think of it as an opportunity to sit and talk with your wife. With our schedules all we do is work or make love."

They made their way into the medical center and took the elevator to the 6th floor. Soon they were seated on a couch in the waiting room facing the large tank of tropical fish having been informed by the receptionist that Dr. George was running "a little behind".

"Simmer down, John. Let's go through our stuff here and make sure that we have everything. Let's see, temperature chart, intercourse diary, record of lupron injections. Yes, it's all here."

"You are a model of efficiency, Joyce."

John gave her hand a squeeze and they were gazing at each other when the receptionist called their names. "A miracle," whispered John as they were led in to the office.

Soon they were seated in Dr. George's office, admiring the river view. Dr. George entered and greeted them with his customary bonhomie.

"John and Joyce, how very nice to see both of you. No, don't get up."

"Let's see what we have here." He opened their chart and peered at it for a moment. He looked up.

"Do you have your charts? Oh good." He spent another moment looking them over. He took off his glasses and looked out the window for some thirty seconds before swiveling his chair to face the Maitlands.

"You've done an excellent job. You have followed my instructions precisely and your notes and graphs are models of organization. John, you mastered the PIO injections more quickly than most medical professionals."

"Dr. George," John broke in, "enough flattery and believe me if there is one thing both of us are good at, it's getting our homework done. Let's cut to the chase. I know Joyce is not pregnant, at least according to this morning's urine test. What are our prospects at this stage?"

"Okay, you both deserve my honest professional opinion. As I told you both before, each of you individually has absolutely nothing demonstrable by current medical techniques that indicate any problem with fertility. However, in your case as a couple, some sort of physiologic incompatibility is at work that quite honestly has resisted every medical trick that I have thrown at it. Certainly, if you wish to get a second opinion, you have my full blessing, though frankly speaking what I do here is pretty much state of the art."

John and Joyce were now holding hands and looked at each other.

"No," began Joyce, "I don't think we want a second opinion. As John mentioned, we are good at doing homework and according to our homework, you're the best. You have our full confidence. But we need to know; where do we go from here?"

"Thank you for those kind words. To answer your question, I think we are at the stage of seriously considering in vitro fertilization."

John drew Joyce a little closer to him. "We anticipated that in vitro was probably our next step. We actually have a list of questions."

John leaned forward and unlatched a large brief case and pulled out a yellow legal pad and a stack of stapled sets of papers.

John held up the papers. "As you can see, we've been reading."

"Just how many pages of questions do you have there?"

"Just three," answered Joyce with a sheepish grin. "Hope we are not overwhelming you."

"My goodness no. I am fully prepared to answer all your questions. But let me give a brief overview which may answer some of them. Since Edwards and Steptoe performed the first successful in vitro fertilization in 1978—you may remember baby Louise. Anyway since then there have been more than 20,000 such births worldwide. The success rate has risen steadily through the years so that today on the average 25 percent of individual IVF attempts result in a viable pregnancy and delivery."

John interrupted, "But I thought—"

Dr. George held up his hand. "I know what you are going to say, that our center here recently reported 74 percent, that's true, but this is somewhat preliminary and while I'd like to think that some refinements unique to our center have resulted in this gratifyingly high pregnancy rate, actually the highest reported by any center in the world, but time will tell, as it could be, as they say, a statistical anomaly."

"You're too modest," said John holding up his stack of articles. "These beg to differ with you."

"Okay, okay, enough of that, you embarrass me. Anyway, where was I? I think I was about to outline the whole procedure. First we stimulate your ovaries, Joyce. What I like to use is synthetic FSH, follicle stimulating hormone. We monitor your cycle very carefully and when we see via ultrasound that your follicles have matured, we give you a dash of HCG, human chorionic gonadotropin, to induce ovulation. Next step is oocyte retrieval, that, is your eggs." He said with a smile nodding at Joyce. "The way we do that is with what is known as transvaginal ultrasound guided follicular puncture or in other words we locate the follicle on ultrasound and after using a bit of local anesthesia we insert a needle through the lateral wall of your vagina and by watching the advancement of the needle on the ultrasound screen, we guide it into the follicle and aspirate gently."

"Dr. George, excuse me, a question. Does this, uh, egg retrieval have the potential to damage my ovaries?"

"Good question. Actually believe it or not, there is no evidence at all that it causes any damage to the ovaries. In fact, there are some reports of spontaneous pregnancies occurring after follicular puncture. Any other questions before I continue? Okay good. Well then the oocytes are immediately examined and put into media. Next, we prepare the spermatozoa which, John, you will be so good to provide us with. Then quite simply we put the spermatozoa and oocytes together in a Petri dish and watch carefully for signs of fertilization. Once fertilization has occurred, we allow what we now term a nascent embryo to develop to the four cell stage and then we place them via the cervix into the uterine cavity. At that point, we hold our collective breaths and watch carefully for signs of implantation, that is, attachment of the embryo to the uterine wall and if that occurs then, voila, you're pregnant."

John and Joyce listened with rapt attention and seemed transported by George's enthusiastic description as if she was already pregnant. They both continued to sit quietly with half smiles and dreamy expressions while George also smiling looked from one face to the other as he waited patiently.

"Wow," said Joyce finally breaking the silence. "Pregnant, I could be pregnant, what an amazing thought."

"Yes, amazing." said John who thought for another moment and then added, "Excuse me for this unsophisticated question, but it seems all so cook bookish. Add this, add that, then mix, and into the oven."

"I know what you mean. I suppose what I do is quite similar to what a chef does. Surrounded by a state of the art apparatus and a devoted experienced staff I stand over say, a Hollandaise sauce making subtle adjustments in heat, stirring. There is a French restaurant on the Upper Eastside that I favor, and I can tell almost from the first bite if the head chef is on a night off. You see, it is meticulous attention to very fine precise details that enhance our success rate, from the purity of the water, to the fine microforging of the glass pipettes, to the careful calibration of pH and temperature.

"We just try very very hard here. I will tell you there is one area where we have a leg up on some of the other clinics—that is in the implantation process where as a result of research here at the medical center, mine and others, we have delineated some of the biochemical and physiologic mechanisms involved and" George paused and lowered his voice into an almost conspiratorial whisper "this is yet unpublished, but we believe we have found a key substance known as protein F that is involved. The manipulation of this protein is what has really sent our statistics through the roof."

The intercom buzzed. "Dr. George, pick up please."

"Excuse me," said Dr. George as he picked up the phone and turned his head to the window as he talked. "Yes, I see, okay, okay. I'm almost finished."

Dr. George hung up the phone and turned back to the Maitlands. "My goodness, time is once again getting away from me. My nurse informs me that the natives are getting restless out in the waiting room and as we speak are organizing a party to batter down the door to my office. To make matters worse, I have a delivery I have to rush to which means that their wait will be even longer. Anyway, we will have to continue this discussion next time. It will give you time to think things over—if you have more questions, my nurse is available or you can email me or check my website. In the meantime, let me give you some paperwork to look over with some of the mundane financial details. As you can imagine, this is all fairly expensive. Let me know what you decide. I'm not rushing you, mind you."

Dr. George rose from his seat and extended his hand. "Joyce and John, as always, an absolute pleasure to chat with you."

"My nurse will show you out." He added as he rushed out the side door.

"Wow, he wasn't kidding when he said it was expensive," said John, lifting his eyes from the dossier of paperwork breaking the silence that had ensued after Dr. George's departure and had continued between them out to the avenue and a three blocks stroll. Joyce was silent a moment longer, walking slowly her gaze fixed upon the pavement in front of her. She stopped and turned to John and took both of his hands and faced him. "John, how can you think of money at a time like this? I want to do it."

Chapter Twenty-Eight
August 26, 2008 3:00 PM

Egan was alone heading toward the peds psych ward to do a consult. Gail had headed back to the pediatric floor to finish writing up an admission. As Egan strode through the long cavernous corridors, he consciously tried to avoid thinking about the death in the ER. Any death was tragic, but the larger implications of this death weighed upon him and he purposely focused on his consult in the psych ward. The unit was physically housed in a separate building which was connected to the main hospital via a series of dilapidated tunnels. This long trek was not a popular one among the pediatric residents, often the call coming on the busiest of days.

Many of the problems presented seemed less than serious and often prompted the comment "Don't those psych residents know anything?" not considering their own ignorance of psychiatric problems. As Egan continued on his way, his footsteps echoing off the dark, dank walls, he went over in his mind the facts presented to him over the phone from the psychiatric resident. A ten-year-old girl had been admitted to the eating disorder ward with a diagnosis of bulimia. She had been on the floor for two days and had been vomiting intermittently since then and now appeared dehydrated.

He arrived at the elevator, and while waiting bent forward to rub his calf which had cramped up during his long trek. The elevator arrived after a seemingly interminable time and Egan waited impatiently for the doors to open. Another long pause and then with a creak and a groan the elevator began almost imperceptibly to rise. Another five minutes was spent at the entrance of the locked ward until an attendant arrived to open the door. "Jesus," he muttered to himself as he followed the attendant, "this could take all day."

They passed the "quiet room" where a seven-year-old child was screaming and hitting the walls while a large, lethargic attendant watched impassively. Another child came running over to him and engaged him in rapid-fire conversation. A third sat in a corner repetitively rocking and muttering.

Egan, as always, felt sad when entering this world of child psychosis, a seeming oxymoron. He thought of the chaotic family situations that some of these kids must have come from and wondered if a locked ward with other psychiatric patients, bored, indifferent attendants, harried psychiatry residents, and occasional visits from the attendings was any more therapeutic than the milieus they left behind. It struck him suddenly that it was quite similar to the neonatal ICU, where incubators, IVs, respirators, and the other equipment that provide a very poor substitute for womb and placenta. These thoughts quickly left his mind as he confronted the problem at hand, mindful of all his other responsibilities back on the floor.

In the examination room, he found a thin but quite alert prepubertal girl. He read her name on her chart: Jane Orlofsky. He could see from her parched lips and doughy skin that she was dehydrated and so after a quick introduction and explanation, he started an IV and began to infuse normal saline. "Jane, I know this hurts a bit, but these fluids will have you feeling better soon. Now tell me, what's a nice girl like you doing in a place like this?"

"Well," she started looking suspiciously at Egan's bearded visage that was set in a relaxed grin and seemed to get solace from it, "I've been vomiting and the thing is everybody is telling me that I'm doing it on purpose. This doctor, who was in this morning, wanted to convince me that I don't like my body, wanted to know about when I got toilet trained and whether my parents yell at me when I get bad grades. All this while I'm vomiting. Finally, he must have gotten sick of it, because he stomped out saying he'd return when I was ready to cooperate." She paused to lean forward and retched into a basin next to the bed, briefly wiped her face and continued. "I swear to you that I can't help myself."

"Tell me, Jane, when did this all start?"

"About two months ago, all of a sudden, I got sick to my stomach, and it went on for more than a day and then it went away. Then a few weeks later, it started again, but this time it went on for three days and I had to go to the emergency room. They gave me an IV and eventually sent me home. I was fine for another week and then boom, it started all over again. Back to the emergency room, though this time a psychiatrist came down and talked to me. Didn't listen to me, though. Next thing I knew I was here in the loony bin."

Egan smiled. "Does anything else hurt besides your stomach?"

"My head is killing me."

"It sounds like the vomiting starts and then stops sort of suddenly. Is that right?"

"Yes, you're right."

"And do you get a headache each time that goes away when the vomiting stops?"

"Yes."

"One more question: Do either of your parents get migraine headaches?"

"Are you kidding me? My mom gets the worst headaches and has to stay in her room for a whole day! Dad gets them too, but not quite so bad."

"Jane, I might be able to spring you from this joint. I'm going to give you some medicine. If it stops your vomiting, we'll be able send you home after we give you enough fluid in a day or so."

Egan gave her hand a squeeze and strode purposefully out to the ward nursing station, wrote his note and orders and as he was finishing looked up to find Dr. Finkelstein, the ward attending before him.

"Ah, Dr. Egan, thank you so much for coming to see young Jane and starting an IV. A classic case of bulimia. A stubborn case, but I'm convinced after a thorough analysis of the underlying psychodynamic factors, we should be able to help this disturbed young lady. Did you know that she was nearly four before becoming toilet trained?"

"Fascinating, but I believe she suffers from abdominal migraines, also known as cyclical vomiting. She has a strong family history of migraines. Oh, didn't know that? Anyway, I've ordered periactin, which the nurse is probably administering as we speak which I hoping will abort this attack. You will find an interesting reference in Pediatrics, June 1998. Gosh, there goes my beeper, I'd better get back to my floor."

Dr. Finkelstein became red in the face and appeared close to apoplexy as he listened to Egan and he sputtered in effort to reply, but by the time he found his voice Egan was halfway down the hall. "Of all the arrogance. Who does he think he is?"

Chapter Twenty-Nine
August 27, 2008 11:00 AM

"Come in" barked the voice from inside the office where Egan had just knocked. He had been summoned to his advisor, Dr. Newhouse, by overhead page. Not a good sign, thought Egan. He had never heard of a resident being paged in order to receive praise for a job well done.

Dr. Newhouse smiled broadly. "Have a seat, Eric. How are you doing?"

"Doing okay. I think," Egan responded with a hesitant smile.

"Good. Listen, I'll get right to the point. You've been rattling quite a few cages. Just recently I got two rather substantial complaints about you. Dr. George gave me a long rant about your behavior in the delivery room, and Dr. Finkelstein, who is, by the way chief of psychiatry, just finished with some choice words that had my ears ringing. Where shall I start: arrogance, rudeness, no respect for authority, etcetera. Can't you get out your aggressions like everyone else around here by picking on people below you on the pecking order?"

"Dr. Newhouse, I can explain."

"Eric, don't even start. Look, you know I have been a fan of yours all along. Beneath that sleepy demeanor lurks a first-class mind. Also, between you and me, Dr. George is a bit full of himself and can skate close to the edge clinically at times and Dr. Finkelstein is quite frankly a pompous ass."

Egan's smile began to return.

"But, before you get too happy, let me tell you the following: You've offended some powerful people and you are certainly not doing your career any good by getting into these conflicts. Do you have some sort of problem with authority figures or something?"

"Well, actually I had a great deal of difficulty with toilet training. I was the only frosh on my dorm floor still in diapers."

Newhouse suppressed a smile and went on. "It is just that sort of irreverence that gets you into trouble. Let me spell it out for you. Either you start doing a bit of old-fashioned groveling, or you may find yourself completely out of the running for the O'Neil fellowship."

"For God's sake," Egan exploded, "doesn't patient care count for anything around here? Do you think I antagonize people for the hell of it?"

"Now calm down, Eric. Believe me you are not too different from the way I was, and I know you are quick, but you've got to learn to not rub people's noses in their mistakes."

"Okay, okay, I'll try."

"Good, now can I count on you to apologize to George and Finkelstein?"

Egan looked around the room, up at the ceiling for a moment and finally at the floor, while Newhouse maintained a steady gaze. "Okay. Yes, sir."

"That's my man!" exclaimed Newhouse rising from his chair.

"Wait a second. I have something on a completely different matter I need to discuss with you and need your advice on how to handle it." He paused, hovering half out of his chair for a moment and then sank back down with a sigh.

"Okay, Eric, spill it, but somehow I don't think I'm going to like it."

"Well, it started with the Gold baby, you know the baby with meningitis."

"Of course I know, that baby is in my unit, and once again compliments on a great diagnosis."

"That case disturbed me for a couple of reasons; the kid got sick so quickly and with an unusual organism for a baby of that age. I'm wondering about the kid's immune system."

"Good thoughts, but there is no evidence of an immune problem. I ordered the tests, which I got back just today, that demonstrate a normal immune system. Eric, unusual doesn't mean never. Sometimes, tragically, things turn for the worse despite our best efforts. I do applaud your curiosity and I wish more of the residents were like you, but let's face it, you are still wet behind the ears and experience trumps genius most of the time. This is just what I was talking about before, keep asking the questions, but learn to defer to people who not only have your smarts, but years of time under their belt. Now Eric, if you will excuse me I've got quite a bit to do."

Egan made no motion to get up and leave but instead sat, appearing deep in thought, and rubbing his chin, while Newhouse's facial musculature labored under the strain of suppressing signs of annoyance. He was thinking about the blood brain barrier and remembering Gail's conjecture and suddenly it didn't seemed so farfetched.

Newhouse gave him a long look, concern etched into his forehead above his raised eyebrows.

"Look," Egan continued, "what if that baby got sick so quickly because the bacteria had a free pass into his cerebral spinal fluid? I mean, what if there is something wrong with the baby's blood brain barrier?"

Newhouse emitted a short staccato laugh.

"Eric, Eric, once again I commend you, but you are wandering into an area in which I have considerable expertise. I saw you at my lecture on this very topic, so I know you know. An imperforate blood brain barrier to the degree that would allow a bacterium to pass is extremely rare."

"Well, you just said, rare does not mean never. And you have also in your unit a baby with kernicterus who has none of the usual risk factors. And a baby just died in the ER after arresting during a spinal tap. The spinal fluid looked cloudy."

"Yes, I heard about that. A real tragedy. I've been in this business for a long time and it never gets easier."

"I know it sounds farfetched, but I'd like to look into it, see if any of those babies have anything in common."

"Eric, I wish more of my residents had your original turn of mind. I predict a very bright future for you. What I'm suggesting, however, is that at your stage of training, you need to keep your head down and acquire some more seasoning. Remember, you've got a full load of patients to take care of. You wouldn't want your patients to suffer from lack of attention because you're distracted by what may be a wild goose chase."

Egan tried again to break in but Newhouse silenced him with an outstretched arm.

"Look, do you think I feel good about that kernicterus case in my ICU right now? As far as the Gold baby, I'm quite optimistic. We caught it early, thanks to you. Now, don't be discouraged. Take care of your patients and learn all you can. There will be plenty of time for exploration of esoteric theories in the future."

Chapter Thirty
Spring 2007

"Slow down, Farah, I mean it!" shouted the Prince while grabbing the reins of her horse.

"But, Fasi my dear, if I go any slower, I will be going backwards."

"I should not have agreed to go riding. There, that's better." The two horses had slowed from a brisk walk to a more sedate gait. "Farah, remember your condition."

"Fasi, how can I possibly forget my condition with you constantly at my side reminding me? I swear, you are worse than my brother Habib, who made guarding my virtue his full time occupation. Anyway, Dr. George said I could ride as long as I don't go beyond a trot."

"Okay, I'll try to relax. Here we are, our spot." He leaped off his horse and then helped Farah off of hers and they strolled hand in hand to the oasis which now contained a small one room dwelling, a sumptuously outfitted tent, an Arabian retreat.

Farah smiled at her husband, because in truth she enjoyed his constant attention and worrying, so different from her sister's husband or for that matter different from any other husbands she knew. He had not been that way the first pregnancy or even during the second. But after three daughters and four miscarriages over a ten-year period, he had become increasingly solicitous, even obsessional about her care. It didn't help that his brother had already sired five sons and was relentless about teasing Fasi about it. She would sometimes catch him staring at his nephews frolicking with a wistful expression on his face. Not that he gave short shrift to his daughters—indeed he doted on them and was fiercely protective of them. But the feeling of this void had always hung over him like a shroud.

"You shall have your son, she whispered softly to herself as she watched Fasi scurry around the tent as he gathered pillows and began to arrange them on her settee.

Chapter Thirty-One
August 29, 2008 3:00 PM

The ward was fraught with the typical Friday afternoon "before a holiday weekend" type of problems. Attending physicians, anxious to get off for the weekend, barraged the residents with orders. Some, already Hampton bound, were unreachable for clarification. The ER was bustling with the worried well seeking reassurance before the long weekend, but nevertheless, as Egan knew, a busy ER inevitably created pressure to admit as frantic ER physicians anxious to clear their department, knew of only two ways either up (to the floor) or out.

The interns who had the weekend off were depressed and worried about getting everything ready for the all important weekend sign-out. The interns who had the weekend on were depressed and worried about how busy and crazy their weekend was going to be. The nurses usually possessed of the implacability of shift workers, could not help get caught up in the mood and irritably scurried around, snapping at the interns.

Egan arrived and quickly became the focal point of everyone's frustration. Interns and nurses fought for his attention to their particular problems. He felt like a fencer in eighteenth century France confronted by multiple foes, but he thrust and parried with energy and skill and was able to send off each in turn with a suggestion, information or encouragement. Soon he had the satisfaction of noting a palpable change in the mood of the ward as the afternoon wound down as inevitably as a sunset and the interns began to sense that this day would eventually end; for some of them with an exhausted trudge home and a blissful collapse onto their beds. The others, who were on call, had already gone through the predictable stages of anger, denial, and bargaining, and had reached the stage of acceptance of their fate for the weekend and now prowled the wards more calmly, expressions of grim resolve on their faces.

Egan signed out to the second-year resident on call, turned off his beeper and for a moment just sat there savoring the sheer delight of being off call. He got up and didn't tarry any longer, knowing that off call or not, it would be very easy to get sucked back into the maelstrom of patient care. He took quick steps to the ward exit, tensing his shoulders, expectant of being called by a nurse or intern with "one more question," but joyfully, there was none and he breathed a sigh of relief once he had cleared the exit.

* * *

Early the next morning, Egan was driving a borrowed convertible with the top down, on the upper level of the George Washington Bridge. He gazed at the vast expanse of the Hudson shiny in the early morning light and at the cliffs on the west bank, the top third brightly illuminated by the sun rays from the East. "Ah, what a day," he exclaimed while stretching one arm high above him, reveling in the cool breeze washing over him.

"And goodbye to all that," he added with a brief over the shoulder glance at the Manhattan skyline. He turned north on the Palisades Parkway paralleling the Hudson. He dug into his jeans pocket and pulled out a half torn envelope and peered at it. "Exit 14" he muttered to himself.

He exited the turnpike and after several wrong turns, he eventually found himself climbing a small dirt road that switched backed its way up a small mountain. He arrived at a closed automatic gate which opened after a push on the intercom and proceeded up a curving forest shaded driveway for a quarter of a mile until he emerged into sunlight. With a spectacular view on either side of him came the realization that he had reached the summit. Before him was a large house of a style reminiscent of a French chateau with ornamental tower-shaped porches gracing each side of the roof with a larger one in the center.

He was greeted by Dr. Newhouse.

"Welcome, welcome."

They strolled around the back of the house where ornate terraced garden plots had been carved out of the side of the hill at whose crest the house was situated. The French style of the house abruptly ended at the garden which had the boxed pruned hedges and square plots of an English country garden. The bottom of the garden was bordered by a thick New England forest. To the left was an American style swimming pool and tennis court. The three of them stood for a moment at a terrace that commanded the garden below as well as a broad view of a forested valley.

"This is just gorgeous. What a beautiful view."

"Well, yes, Eric, it certainly is. And what a clear day to enjoy it. Isn't it just the tonic to dispel the tensions of a hard week at the hospital? Anyway, before I get too relaxed, there are a few things I have to do to get things organized for today. You are welcome to wander around or take a swim. The only other arrival so far is Blake George who is down on the tennis court practicing his serves. Actually he is itching for a game. I'm too busy to accommodate him at present. Do you, perchance, play, Eric?"

"I used to play a bit in college. For some strange reason, I don't seem to have time to play these days," answered Egan with a laugh.

"Well then, my boy, here is your perfect opportunity. Plus a chance to get better acquainted with the estimable Dr. George."

Egan walked down from the circular driveway to the swimming pool and tennis court. He saw that George was there, at the base line on the far end of the court, in mid-serve, the ball arching up from the outstretched fingers of his tossing hand to at least four feet above his head. His serving arm whipped forward with cobra-like speed. His racquet face made contact with the ball at the apex of his swing with a loud thwack and sent it hurdling at a speed of at least 70 miles per hour Egan judged. The ball cleared the net by inches and took a topspin engineered dive to the court skidding just inside the left outside corner of the service box, and seemed to defy the laws of physics and accelerate as it took a low leftward arching trajectory finally landing inches from Egan's feet.

"Holy Jesus" thought Egan.

"Why, Dr. Egan," George said, walking over to him smiling. "How are you?"

"I'm fine, Dr. George."

"How about a quick game or two?"

"Are you kidding me? I would have to be crazy to volunteer to be on the receiving end of your serve. I'm sure I wouldn't have been able to even land my racquet on that last one."

"Oh nonsense, I'm sure you'll be able to hold up your end quite admirably. Come on, a friendly game."

Egan looked at George, craned his neck to the sky while rubbing it. "Okay, okay, I'll play. Let me go change."

Soon he was back and spent a moment selecting a racquet from a large rack at one end of the court and after swinging a few he picked one and turned back to see George bent forward stripping off his warm ups.

Egan trudged over to the baseline to start the first game. He tossed the ball and managed to make solid contact and the ball landed on the backhand side of the service box. George stepped neatly around the ball which had taken a high bounce and delivered a hard forehand deep to Egan's backhand. Egan took three quick backward steps and lunged to his right and was able to make just enough contact to send it back in an easy arc. George in the meantime had charged to the net and had his feet planted and racket at the ready. His eyes followed the ball and he took three backward steps and crushed the ball with an overhead winner to the forehand corner.

Two points later, and George had won the first game. They changed sides and Egan positioned himself at least three feet beyond the baseline and shuffled his feet and twirled his racquet nervously as he waited for George's first serve. He didn't have to wait long as it seemed to appear suddenly in one corner of the service box like a scud missile. Egan moved to his right an instant too late and only managed to nick the ball with the edge of his racquet frame. George sent shots that sent Egan scurrying first to the backhand corner, then the forehand corner. Three more games ensued, long rallies punctuated by sharp winners. Egan managed in most instances to give as good as he got, but somehow always seemed to falter at crucial points, sending an easy overhead into the net to give George game four, just missed a lob to give up game five and finally misjudged a drop shot to lose game six.

In only 15 minutes, George had amassed a 5-0 lead and stood at the baseline impatiently bouncing the ball, as Egan limped slowly to his receiving position. He took several deep breaths as he tried to recover from the last rally that had sent him on a frantic tour of all four corners and ended with a lunge, just short, at a beautifully executed drop shot.

Egan settled into his receiving crouch and peered across the net and tried to decipher some clues as to where the next serve may go. George stood like a picador ready to deliver the coup de grace. He tossed the ball lower than usual sending a fast flat serve straight to Egan's body. Egan was surprised by the speedy delivery, but was able to lift his racket to block it, sending the ball just over the net. Egan became energized and won the next three points to take the game. Egan capitalized on his momentum and won the next game with four straight serves that landed just where he had intended.

The next three games were hard fought on both sides. George lifted his level of play and long rallies ensued with each hitting straight at the other with full bore. They were like Ali and Frazier in Manilla exchanging punches, each giving as good as he got. Their world shrank to a 40 by 60 square foot clay court. Egan managed to produce enough winners to eek out close victories in each of the three.

Finally, Egan stood at the service line for his first set point opportunity. High toss, hard swing, into the net. Another long pause, peered hard across the net, another high toss and Egan went for broke swinging hard which caught George sneaking toward the service line. Game and match to Egan.

"Hey, nice game. That last set could have gone either way." Egan extended his hand. George gripped it briefly.

"Your style is unorthodox, to say the least. I hope you grant me a rematch. Now, if you'll excuse me." Dr. George turned heel and strode off the court.

Egan watched him go until he felt a hand on his neck. He spun around to find Gail grinning. "Way to go, champ."

"Gail! What are doing here?"

"I won last year's Bowman Prize, you know for second-year research, so one of the perks is to get an invite to this weekend."

"That's awesome. Really glad to see you. Bowman prize, huh? You really are the academic whiz kid."

"Hey, I'm a nerd, I admit it."

"Most attractive nerd I've ever seen."

"You're embarrassing me."

"By the way, how much of the match did you see?"

"Most of the set. Quite a comeback you had."

"Thanks." Egan toweled off the sweat off his face and scalp. "Gail, do you think I totally blew my chances for an O'Neil?"

"Well, I hate to say it, but maybe. Dr. George was anything but a happy camper. But to my mind it was worth sacrificing an O'Neal to give that cheat his comeuppance."

"Cheat?" asked Egan in astonishment.

"Oh, yes. I had quite a good view of the proceedings and there were at least three of your deep shots that caught the line that he called out."

Chapter Thirty-Two
Fall 2007

Joyce lay on the examining table, draped with sterile linens, her legs elevated in stirrups. She stared at the ceiling; her eyelids drooped, half asleep from the tranquilizing medicine that had entered her left antecubital vein via the thin venous catheter that had been inserted there 15 minutes before. Her eyes drifted over to John who was seated on a stool at the head of the examining table. He smiled at her and gave her hand a squeeze. She gave a half smile back and turned slightly to gaze at the large ultrasound machine that was situated next to her.

She looked across the room at a masked and hooded figure that stood hunched over a small table covered with a green sterile drape and ordered rows of instruments and fluid-filled Petri dishes. She watched as the figure carefully examined each item on the table. That must be Dr. George, she thought, getting everything ready. A twinge of anxiety crossed her brow, but was quickly overcome by patrolling molecules of diazepam. A baby, I'm going to have a baby. Everyone's here, my ovaries, my sperm donor. She looked at John again with a spacey smile and he returned her smile with another squeeze, "Honey, you're doing fine."

"My egg, his sperm, all in the same room, but yet so far apart. We need all of this and Dr. George to bring them together to produce our baby. She smiled again and murmured "our baby, our baby, our baby."

The hooded figure finished his meticulous preparations at the table, straightened up and walked over and stood next to the stirrups. "Joyce, it's me, Dr. George. How are you feeling?"

"We're having a baby," she whispered with a smile.

"Of course we are. John, how are you doing? Are you comfortable?"

"I'm fine. A bit nervous I suppose." He looked over at Joyce who was still whispering with a beatific smile. "You sure she's okay? How much medicine did you give her?"

"Oh, don't worry. I gave her quite a modest amount. Never can tell how one will react. Important thing is that she is relaxed. Anyway, isn't the reproductive process supposed to be pleasurable?"

John took another look at her and she beamed back at him. "I don't think I have ever driven her to this level of ecstasy. How about a hit for me?"

Dr. George laughed. "I would if I could. Let's get started, shall we?"

He turned to Joyce and more loudly said, "Joyce, are we ready to begin?"

"Yes, I will, yes, a baby."

"You're going to be fine." Dr. George took a seat on a small stool between her legs. "Okay, a little pressure." He inserted a lubricated speculum and gently squeezed the handles to open the vaginal vault. After a brief inspection, he withdrew the speculum. He reached for the microphone like appendage of the ultrasound machine, the ultrasound probe, and put a generous amount of green lubricating ointment onto the end of it and inserted it slowly into her vagina. He gently rotated the probe while he peered intently at a large screen which showed shifting, vague black-and-white images.

"John, take a look. Let me orient you. Up top here is a white solid area, that's the abdominal wall, now over here is her uterus, all this black stuff is parts of air-filled intestine. Okay, let's move a little lower. There's her bladder. Let's hunt a bit. Good, good, see, do you see? There is her right ovary."

John stared at the seemingly patternless black and white images and strained to comprehend. "No, I don't." But then suddenly a pattern emerged, like looking at a hologram. "Yes, I do see it," he said excitedly. "Look, Joyce, your ovary, a perfect oval, it's beautiful."

"Okay, ready for the next step. This is the tricky part. John, you see here on the side of the probe this small opening. This is where I'm going to insert the needle. It connects to the other end of the probe." He reached around behind him while maintaining visual contact with the ultrasound screen and his groping hand found a syringe with a long needle. He inserted the needle point into the small opening and slowly advanced it.

"Okay, any minute now. There, look, John, see that white pointed thing at the lower left-hand corner of the screen, that's the needle."

John was transfixed as he watched the needle, submarine-like gliding inexorably millimeter by millimeter to the ovary. The needle tip paused at the verge and pierced the ovarian wall. Another miniscule advance and the needle tip was in one of the follicles. The needle tip stopped and he noticed a barely perceptible perturbation inside the follicle. At the same time, Joyce emitted a low moan.

In another moment the ultrasound probe was removed along with the needle and Dr. George had turned to the tray and carefully discharged the follicular fluid onto one of the Petri dishes. He picked up the Petri dish and with quick steps crossed the room where a large microscope sat. He positioned the dish on the viewing platform and quickly and expertly turned the focusing knobs as he peered into the lens. "Beautiful, beautiful. John and Joyce, we have several wonderful cumulus-oocyte complexes. Our timing was impeccable."

"We have what?"

"I'll explain the details later. To put it simply, your wife's eggs are perfect, just perfect. Now I must leave you because time is of the essence if we are to have a successful fertilization."

Chapter Thirty-Three
August 30, 2008 6:30 PM

"My dear Dr. Egan, don't dally. The rest of us are gathered here for predinner drinks."

Egan had just reached the bottom of the stairs and was looking uncertainly around until Newhouse's booming voice directed him. He made his way out a double door onto the terrace at the back of the house where the group was assembled. Doug Barrett was at the hors d'oeuvres table lifting a smoked mussel and after stuffing it into his mouth gave him a little wave. Blake George was at a small bar ministering over what appeared to be the makings of a martini. John Oden, on the other side of the room, gave him a big wave and a smile.

The three other finalists were standing with glasses of red wine admiring the view with Michael.

"Eric, please get yourself a drink. Our multitalented Dr. George is doing the honors at the bar. As soon as he has finished mixing mine, I'm sure he'll outfit you with the cocktail of your choice."

On hearing his name, George looked up and gave Egan a tight smile of greeting. After fifteen minutes of mingling and socializing, the group gradually coalesced around Newhouse and Egan, attracted by the increasing intensity of the discussion they were engaged in.

"Eric, medicine has always involved a tradeoff, the greatest good for the greatest number. If you treat enough sore throats with penicillin, you're eventually going to get a death from penicillin allergy. You are in essence sacrificing one life to treat a million cases of strep throat, the great majority of whom would have recovered without any antibiotics. But you would prevent a thousand cases of rheumatic fever with its various complications. How would you explain that to

161

the mother of the child who died of penicillin allergy? 'Your child died so others will live?' Sounds cruel, but virtually every medical decision carries just this sort of weighing risks and benefits."

Egan stood, drink in hand, aware of the silent group that had gathered around them, considered this, wanting to choose his words carefully before answering. All eyes were upon him when he finally took a breath and began to speak.

"Yes, I understand that sure, there are imperfections in the real world of medicine; that decisions are based on incomplete data, without absolute certainty as to the outcome and that some of those decisions may have unintended effects on others. I guess my point is that it's a brave new world, advances are continuing apace; stem cell research, the genome project for example. The medical research complex is a juggernaut. We sometimes have to pause and consider the long term effects, ethical and otherwise."

George, who's face had begun to redden as he listened, now broke in, his voice rising. "Naiveté! That's what I call it. We can't make an omelet without breaking some eggs. Take the genome project. What an incredible achievement that is and what bounty we will harvest from it. Soon we will, with a simple blood test, be able to precisely predict an individual's response to a particular drug. Penicillin, for example. Medical research is per force, the sharp edge of the plow, cutting abruptly into the unscarred earth, turning soil, in a messy chaotic assault, but in short months fated to be a neat orderly, productive field of amber grain."

George stopped and gazed aggressively at Egan who felt like he was back on the tennis court on the receiving end of a searing top-spin serve. All eyes shifted back to him.

"I don't dispute that. But, speaking of the genome project, I think that all sorts of philosophical questions are raised by the increasing amounts of self-knowledge that will become available; do we all really want to know exactly what our medical future holds via a detailed analysis of our individual genomes?'

"Of course we do," George rejoined. "Isn't that the whole point of medicine? To know our medical future? Come on, man!"

"I know, I know. The ancient Greeks believed—"

George broke in again. "The ancient Greeks? Now really."

Egan held out his hands. "Now wait, hear me out. This is relevant. They believed that man's fate was preordained and that even Zeus could not alter it. Today we are positing that fate lies in the genes, but we are not only predicting, we are also intervening. Even more troubling is the area of genetic surgery in which individual genes can be altered. This would certainly be a boon for people with specific genetic disorders such as cystic fibrosis, but it raises the specter of humans directing their own evolution."

Several heads nodded thoughtfully as he spoke which seemed to infuriate George who was almost sputtering when he answered.

"I just don't get you, a talented aspiring researcher. Are you also against using animals for research purposes? Should we set loose all the fruit flies that are subjugated for research purposes? You should care so much for your patients."

Egan almost recoiled physically from this rejoinder and he opened his mouth to respond when he felt Newhouse's hand grip him at the elbow.

"Okay," Newhouse said, "let's all calm down a bit. I'm beginning to hear the alcohol talking. Anyway, I believe dinner is served."

Egan again opened his mouth, but Newhouse's tightening grip, which was beginning to steer him out of the room, effectively silenced him.

Later after dinner, Egan stepped outside for a stroll, feeling a need to be alone with his thoughts. The moon was nearly full, and the sounds of the night were dominated by a cacophony of cicadas. He walked for several minutes down a grassy lane bordered on one side by a stone wall and the other by a tall manicured hedge. He emerged from the lane to find himself in a large meadow bordered by an impenetrable tangle of vines. He stopped to look again at the moon. *I can kiss the O'Neil goodbye at this point. Christ, the way the other finalists sucked up to George during dinner. Oh what the hell, what will be, will be.* He heard a rustle to his left and he jerked his head in that direction. He could see the glow of a lit cigar tip moving toward him out of the shadow of a large oak. Into the moon light emerged a large figure.

"Eric, it's me, John Oden. Sorry I didn't mean to startle you."

Egan breathed a sigh of relief. "Not to worry. I just figured you were a large man-eating bear. Us city folk are not used to such a natural setting."

Oden laughed and took a puff of his cigar and blew out a large plume of smoke. "If you're such a city boy, what are you doing wandering around out here?"

"Well, to tell you the truth, after dinner I felt this overwhelming need for solitude. I'm figuring that my chances for an O'Neil are pretty low after my disagreement with Dr. George."

"Hey, buck up. He's not the only member of the selection committee. Newhouse seems to be on your side, from what I hear. Jesus, George can be such a blowhard. I came out here myself just to get away from all the hot air he was spewing during dinner."

Egan laughed and they stood together for a moment while Oden took a couple of thoughtful puffs on his cigar.

"Eric, I remember you telling me about that baby with meningitis. How is that baby doing?"

"In the ICU, pretty sick still, but with a fairly good prognosis."

"That must make you feel good. I think you told me there was a similar case?"

"Yes. I actually visited the mother of that child. I was planning to look for other cases."

"Did you say 'was'?"

"I discussed it with Dr. Newhouse, and he in a nice way told me to back off and not engage in, as he put it, 'exploration of esoteric theories.' Though, I have to admit, I'm torn because something just doesn't sit right with me. There are too many unusual cases: meningitis with an unusual organism and a case of kernicterus."

"Well, Eric, Newhouse and George are a bit up there in the hierarchy and that rarified atmosphere makes one a bit intolerant of young blood. Take it from me, I know. Just curious, do you have any theories as to what links these cases, short of coincidence?"

"I do, but I hesitate to mention it, since it seems so farfetched. Actually, it was first suggested to me by a med student, even lower on the totem pole than me: that all these babies could have a problem with the functioning of their blood brain barrier. I thought it absurd when I first considered it, but as I think about it, I don't see any more plausible explanations emerging. As Sherlock Holmes told Watson, once you have eliminated the impossible, what remains, however improbable, must be the truth."

Egan could not see Oden's facial expression as he talked, but was relieved not to hear a derisive guffaw. Oden's cigar tip glowed bright briefly lighting up his face.

"Well, you're right to describe it as improbable, though it is an interesting idea. Look, I don't want to discourage you. I'm on your side. But be careful. Look into this if you must, but be discreet. You've got a bright future. In the meantime, keep in touch with me and let me know what you're finding, but perhaps for now you shouldn't be sharing this with Newhouse or anyone else for that matter. At least, until you have the O'Neil under your belt!"

Returning to the house, they found Newhouse alone in a study just off the front entrance, sipping brandy in semi darkness, illuminated only by moonlight shining in through a bay window. He waved them in. "Enjoying the night air? It is beautiful out there, so peaceful. Please, have a seat. I'm going to pour myself another brandy. Can I get you one as well?"

"Sure," answered Egan.

"Thanks, Jack, but I'll take a rain check. I'm ready to turn in." Oden clapped Egan on the back. "Nice chatting with you, Eric. See you all in the morning."

Egan sat down on the edge of a small couch, brandy in hand while Newhouse resettled into a large leather chair.

"Eric, I sense that you are a bit discouraged about your prospects. Let me reassure you, that you are very much in the running. If it were just up to me, it would be no contest. But you have to understand something. We really demand loyalty from our fellows. Our research is cutting edge and easily prone to misinterpretation. Hence, the outburst before dinner. We have to have your most fervent promises that you will be a one hundred per cent loyal member of the team and in addition, at least in the beginning in a subordinate role. Am I being clear?" Newhouse leaned forward his gaze like a laser locked onto Egan's face, causing Egan to involuntarily avert his eyes for an instant, but then resumed eye contact and after a pause said, "Yes, sir."

"So can I count on you to take Dr. George aside sometime before the weekend is over and reassure him on these points?"

"Yes, sir. I want you to know that I really want this fellowship."

"Good, and for goodness' sake, if you find yourself on a tennis court with him again, have the good sense not to win!"

Chapter Thirty-Four
August 31, 2008 5:30 PM

Early the next morning Egan opened his eyes, woken by the bright light at the window. He glanced at his watch and was amazed to see that it was only 5:30. He lay there for a moment, luxuriating in the knowledge that he didn't have to get up. There were no patients, nurses, or lab techs clamoring him with needs or notions. He thought of Gail and how throughout the evening he tried to get some time with her, but she was always surrounded. Finally he had given up and gone up to bed.

The normal urban cacophony that Egan was so used to was completely absent and it was too early for the country din of insects and birds. It was almost eerily quiet. He became aware as he lay there of a faint buzz, not produced by the countryside, but instead generated by his own brain unaccustomed to so little auditory stimulation. He got out of bed and stood by the large window that commanded the manicured grounds of the rear garden and the tangled unplanned thicket of forest beyond. The sun had just risen above a hill far off to the east and its oblique rays were beginning to heat the dew laden grasses, producing a mist that hung over the whole of the garden like a shroud. He looked, transfixed, at the almost hypnotically calm natural scene before them.

He dressed, tiptoed downstairs, went outside and wandered down the terraced garden until he stood on the verge of the forest. Egan cupped his hand around his ear and leaned forward slightly. He could hear the faint sound of running water. Curious, he plunged into the thicket through a very small break in a tangle of wild grape vines. The sound of water became louder and soon he was upon it. The stream was no more than 20 feet wide and was a series of gentle rapids punctuated by still pools of varied sizes. In one pool, Egan spotted a large trout suspended in the water a foot or so below the surface, pointed upstream, his fins moving just enough to counter the gentle downstream current. Suddenly, the fish lunged for the surface and sucked in a hapless katydid that had had the misfortune to fall in from an overhanging tree upstream. The fish returned to his spot, chasing away a smaller trout that had attempted to usurp this prime position.

He heard a sound of something moving and wondered if a deer or some other large animal was making its way through the brush. He felt a brief shiver of fear as the sound got closer, wondering if this time it really was a bear. Seconds later, Gail emerged from the thicket.

"Gail, what are you doing here? You gave me a bit of a start."

Gail laughed. "Same thing you're doing, I imagine, exploring a bit. It's so beautiful here."

"You can say that again. Gail, do you see that large trout?"

They stood a moment looking at the trout, its bright rainbow colors illuminated by a thin shaft of sunlight that had managed to penetrate the canopy above. Finally, Egan lifted his eyes and peered upstream.

"I wonder where this leads?"

"Only one way to find out."

They began to make their way upstream and the going got rougher, the vegetation producing at times an almost impenetrable barrier and they were forced to detour deep into the woods to circumvent particularly thorny brambles, using the babble of the stream to guide them back. But they gave no thought to turning back, consumed by the desire to explore, to plunge deeper into what was wild. Finally, they reached a waterfall. After a rather formidable climb over an adjoining boulder strewn embankment, they knew they had reached their goal. It was a large beaver pond surrounded on three sides by woods. On the fourth side rose abruptly a rocky prominence. They stood at the edge of the pond, breathing hard, sweat dripping down their faces.

"I don't know about you, but I'm going for a swim." She startled him by stripping off her clothes and plunging into the cool tannin-stained water. Her head popped up seconds later, her mouth set in a wide grin.

"Come on. What are you waiting for? The water's great."

Egan hesitated, but slowly at first and then more rapidly removed his clothes. They swam together to the middle. Gail turned over and floated on her back taking in the sky and the canopy of trees reflected in the pond. Egan treaded water resisting the urge to stare at her nipples just breaching the surface of the water, like emerging twin volcanic islands rising from the sea. Nonplussed, he dove under the water, searching for the bottom. Egan had always felt comfortable in the water. He loved the feeling of buoyancy, of floating, and in moving water, the feeling of being transported by a force more powerful than himself.

After college and before medical school, he had traveled by himself to Mexico and Central America, either hitchhiking or sharing third-class buses with chickens, market-laden natives, and once even a small burro, sort of a last undirected hurrah before the grind of med school. He had come across a stretch of nearly deserted beach on the West Coast with waves that were as big and perfectly shaped as any he had ever seen. He spent a full two weeks there, silently pitting himself against the surf. He would position himself at the crest of a breaking wave and from the pinnacle would hurl himself down the glassy smooth front of the wave. Sometimes he would be able to look up and see the curling top of the wave begin to encircle him before completely engulfing him in a watery embrace.

At that point as he had learned it was pointless to struggle against the force of the wave and instead would give himself up to it and he would find himself pinned on the bottom under a seemingly endless torrent of water. He learned to control the panicky feeling of being trapped and to adopt a passive, oxygen-sparing attitude until finally the wave's energy was dissipated. At times, a solitary Mexican man would watch him, shaking his head and muttering, "*Muy peligroso.*"

Now he remembered that time as he dove under water and explored the bottom until his brain screamed for oxygen, and he rapidly ascended to the surface light, feeling the sudden warm layer of the last two feet or so before emerging and taking a deep breath. He repeated this maneuver several times, bringing up first a fresh water mussel, then some representative vegetation and finally small wriggling crawfish.

Gail at first just observed this otter-like behavior but soon joined him in his cavorting. They explored the muddy bottom together and chased each other, finally shooting up to the surface.

"Eric, you really are a water creature."

"I admit I am. After all this is where we all came from. I view it as sort of a return. Some theorize that early man had an evolutionary stage that was temporarily water bound. Just like whales, which started as land animals, I can imagine a group of primitives living next to a body of water, using it for refuge, for sustenance." He looked at Gail for a long moment and she added, "And even for lovemaking."

They embraced in a long kiss and drifted downward, separating finally when the urge for oxygen exceeded their sexual desire. Their attempts at coupling were awkward initially, but with the persistence of youth in pursuit of pleasure, they kept at it, though still breaking from time to time to surface, to take a breath and then frantic resumption. Their progress toward climax warred with their need for oxygen which prolonged the experience but also intensified it. Finally, with sexual desire and the urge to breathe equalized, they both convulsed with pleasure, before once again frantically seeking the surface and taking deep breaths that were equally pleasurable.

They floated on their backs staring at the sky, but their post coital reverie was abruptly shattered by the crack of a rifle shot. Egan and Gail, startled, looked around frantically and within seconds there was another discharge. For an instant, Egan thought that it was hunters in the woods nearby, but a splash not two feet from his head alerted him to the fact that they were the ones being hunted.

"Gail, dive!"

They both plunged under water. Egan groped for Gail's hand and they swam 30 feet. Now the twin sensations of oxygen deprivation and terror assaulted them. They surfaced as quietly as they could.

Breathing hard, trying to catch his breath, Egan said, "Gail, I have an idea. Dive and follow me."

Two more shots resounded and they dove. Egan felt a sting in his left calf. Under water again, Egan swam with long even strokes and the rhythm of the swimming began to calm him slightly. He could feel Gail just behind him. He had already learned that her oxygen carrying capacity at least equaled his own, so he knew they could continue underwater until he reached his absolute limit. They came upon an area of thick underwater debris and vegetation. Egan led them both through a small opening, which he had discovered during his previous underwater explorations. They surfaced, sucking air in deep frantic gasps. They were inside a dark enclosure.

"Eric! Where the hell are we?"

Egan breathing hard tried to choke out some words, but only sputtered and choked. Finally his breathing slowed enough and he began.

"Gail, believe it or not, we are inside a beaver dam."

Chapter Thirty-Five
Fall 2007

Prince Fasi paced quickly up and down the small room. Finally, he stopped before a large arched window decorated with ornate gypsum carvings and stared out. He could see the dim glow on the horizon that was just beginning to cast a hazy light upon the massive walls of the Masmak fortress on the outskirts of Riyadh. He was dressed in surgical scrubs. His facial expression, calm appearing in the dimly lit room, belied the fact that he was quite excited. In his left hand he had a lit cigarette, which he would periodically lift to his mouth for a deep drag, the end glowing in the semi-dark. He blew the smoke out through pursed lips while his dark eyes remained fixed on a distant point. Allahu Akhbar, Allahu Akhbar!

Abruptly, he whirled around and resumed his energetic walking. "Please, please, oh Allah, if it be thy will, grant me a healthy son." Finally, he sank down into an overstuffed chair. He leaned forward crushing his half-smoked cigarette into a marble tray already over-flowing with butts and placed his head into his hands.

After some minutes he lifted his head. He stood and walked slowly to the window, his expression was now calmer and his face assumed an almost meditative cast as he looked once again at the coming of the dawn.

He heard the faint sound of footsteps approaching and he jerked his head away from the window and raced toward the door. He pulled the door open and there was another man in scrubs covered with a red stain.

"Yes, yes?" said the Prince with a large smile on his face.

"It's a boy," answered the man with a smile that was not as effusive as the prince's, but rather tense and guarded.

"Oh, praise be to Allah, what joy, what rapture!" cried the Prince. "This is truly the start of a new day." He lifted his head and extended his arms toward the ceiling and stood this way for a few seconds as he took in this news. After all this time, he had his boy. He could now hold his head high among his legion of brothers and half-brothers in the court and would not have to endure the whispers, the imputations evident in every glance. He had his heir, his legacy was secure.

He brought his arms back to his sides. "Doctor, when can I see my son?" He smiled again at the words and repeated "my son," reveling in the way it felt to move his tongue and lips to produce that glorious sound.

"Soon, Prince. There is a slight problem."

The prince looked hard at the man. "A problem? What kind of problem?" His voice raised into almost a shout.

The doctor was quiet an instant longer, his eyes darting from the prince's face to the floor.

"Doctor," screamed the prince, now placing his hands on the man's shoulders as if to shake the words out of him. "What is the problem?"

Chapter Thirty-Six
August 31, 2008 Afternoon

They remained inside, shivering from cold and terror. Gradually, the terror of the outside became replaced by terror engendered by the pitch darkness of their enclosed space and their wondering about the possible reaction of beavers to the abrupt invasion of their woody abode. It was a trifecta of terror: claustrophobia, rodentia-phobia, and nyctophobia. They huddled together and Gail could not suppress a sob.

"Oh God, I'm so scared. The thought of a beaver biting me is freaking me out. Oh shit, get me out of here." Gail suddenly jerk-ed trying to get out of Egan's restraining arms, which tightened in response to her struggle.

"Gail, Gail, you have to listen. We don't know what's out there. Try to calm down, just a few minutes longer."

She stopped her struggling and felt limp in his arms, and he willed himself to breath quietly, listening intently for any sound that would indicate that the rifleman was still lurking. Total quiet reigned except for the pounding of his heart and their raspy breaths. Gail had gone limp and he wondered if she had fainted out of sheer fright. He could feel a calming of their shivering and he knew that it was a sign of advancing hypothermia. His legs that had ached with cold now began to feel warm and for a brief instance he wanted to succumb, to slide peacefully into the rapture of the depths, but he caught himself.

"Gail, now's the time. We got to get out of here. Come on." He shook her to no avail until finally he squeezed the skin over her ster-num, a painful stimulus used to evaluate the depth of coma and she was roused from her stupor.

"Hey, that hurts."

"Listen! We've got to get out of here, but easy does it. We swim out and we come to the surface gently and quietly."

"Okay," she answered groggily.

Egan took her hand and together they submerged and groped their way out and surfaced as quietly as possible. The pond was completely still and the sun was beginning to sink behind the rocky west bank. They slowly swam toward shore, breaststroking quietly looking around constantly, but there was no one except for a deer at the far side of the pond taking a drink. Their manner was cautious; the memory of rifle shots echoing off the distant hills was fresh. They ventured onto the bank and stood shivering for a few moments, preferring to air dry in order to keep their clothes dry.

Egan suddenly became aware of a throb in his left calf and he leaned over to examine it. A small area of flesh was missing as if a surgeon had neatly cut out a grape-sized piece out of the back of his calf.

"Eric, you're bleeding!"

Gail ripped a piece of her shirt to use as a bandage. She examined it carefully.

"I don't think it needs to be cleaned or debrided. Soaking in that pond water took care of that. From the appearance I'd judge that the bullet grazed you, taking a small piece of you, but not really penetrating. By the way, have you had a recent tetanus shot?"

"Tetanus shot? I have no idea. I'm just a doctor. Do you think I keep track of that stuff?"

"Well, as soon as we get back to town, I'll give you one personally. We probably should put you on antibiotics prophylactically. Are you allergic to anything?"

Egan smiled slightly despite his pain, amused by her officious tending to his wound. "Ah, Gail, there is no more secure feeling than being wounded deep in the wilderness with a third-year medical student."

Gail ignored him and finished bandaging his leg. "Let's see if you can get up."

He rose tentatively and took a few steps. He shook each leg in turn trying to restore circulation. A sharp stab of pain in his calf caused him to topple to the ground.

"Come on, try to get up. Let me help you get dressed. You can lean on me and let's try to get back before it gets dark."

Their progress was slow but steady. The dusk turned by slow degrees into pitch darkness and they were forced to grope through the underbrush, their faces and forearms were continually assaulted by thorns and swinging branches. Small flies attracted by the warm sweat and blood relentlessly bothered them. With the darkness came a chill and their shivering returned. Their only comfort was the sound of the stream nearby, guiding them and soothing them on their seemingly interminable trek.

"Who do you think it was?" Gail began after ten minutes of silence.

"I didn't see anybody, but I had the impression that the shots were coming from the direction of the rocky heights on the west side of the pond. That would have meant that whoever was shooting was a good 200 yards away. Do you suppose it could have been a passing hunter unable to resist taking some shots at two naked people making love in the middle of a beaver pond? Hell, that's an opportunity that doesn't present itself too often."

"Eric, how can you joke about this?"

"I'm sorry, Gail. I guess I'm whistling past the graveyard. But I'm not completely joking. I can't think of this as anything more than some sort of random act of violence."

They emerged from the woods and paused at the verge. The lights of the house shone at the other end of the garden. They made their way up the terraces and steps at what was for Egan a maddeningly slow pace. As they neared the house, they heard a shout, "There they are!" And all of the house's inhabitants poured out to help them. Within fifteen minutes, both were situated in front of a fireplace that had been hastily assembled and lit, wrapped in blankets and were sipping on steaming mugs of hot cider. Egan's face and left leg were the only parts of his body uncovered and it was over his leg that Newhouse was engaged in a minute inspection. "This is going to hurt." And Egan winced as Newhouse probed and debrided the wound. Finally, one last probe sent an electric bolt of pain up his leg and caused Egan to cry out for the first time. Newhouse pulled out a metal fragment and dropped it into a small dish. He swabbed the area with betadine and wrapped his calf with sterile gauze. He stood up and peered down at his patient.

"It's really just a flesh wound. It should heal up fine, though it will leave a fairly impressive scar." Newhouse picked up the metal fragment and held it up. "This looks like a piece of shot, the type favored by local hunters. I feel that I was remiss in not telling you that the woods are full of hunters this time of year, though my land is strictly posted against any hunting. Where were you exactly?"

"Well, we followed this small stream until we got to a beaver pond and we went for a swim. That's when the shots came."

"Yes, I know that pond. Unfortunately, it is outside of my property. That is a popular spot for hunters. They wait there for deer to come to the pond to drink."

Chapter Thirty-Seven
December 2007

"Today's the day. Oh God, I'm so nervous."

"Relax, Joyce, everything will be fine."

"How do you know everything will be fine? Do you have some special powers to predict the future or something? Tell me, will we have a daughter or a son? Will our child be athletic or a klutz, brainy or merely average intelligence, social or shy? Tell me."

As Joyce talked she paced around their bedroom, opening drawers. "Where the hell is my lucky bracelet?" she asked while slamming shut the top drawer.

"Jesus, just calm down. Getting all bent out of shape can't be good for getting your uterus into a receptive state."

"Shit, you're right. Okay, be calm, deep cleansing breaths. Oh, John, hold me please."

John wrapped his arms around her. "I do have special powers, it's going to be a girl with dark hair just like you, except with some curls that will bounce up and down as she skips into the house after school yelling 'Mom, Mom.'"

Joyce wriggled out of his arms and looked at John, her eyes now laden with tears. "Do you really think so?"

"Of course, I do. Look at the time; we've got to get a move on."

They left their apartment and rather than wait for the elevator, raced down ten flights of stairs. They were in luck; a Yellow Cab homed in on them from across the avenue like a heat-seeking missile just as they were rushing out the door, arms outstretched.

The downtown cab ride was uneventful except for the shocked look on the turbaned Sikh cab driver's face when Joyce cheerfully announced to him that they were on their way to make a baby.

Soon they were sitting in Dr. George's office.

"So here we are," began Dr. George who was sitting with both elbows on the desk, his head supported by his clasped hands as his eyes darted from Joyce to John and back again. "As I've said previously, today should be a piece of cake compared to the egg retrieval. No anesthesia required and you'll be on your way in a jiffy. Any questions so far? John, you look like you have a question".

John hesitated for a moment. "Um, how long before, um..."

Dr. George smiled. "You can have intercourse in two to three weeks."

"Think you can last that long?" asked Joyce with a smile.

"Actually I was thinking about you."

"Anyway, I'm sure that both of you will find three weeks of abstinence extremely trying, but look at the bright side. What an opportunity for spiritual growth?" Dr. George looked at them with an amused smile and continued. "Okay, here is what will happen. In a moment we will go into the examination room. I am going to have you get into a knee chest position on your stomach. Remember when we did the mock embryo transfer with radiopaque dye, we determined that with the shape of your uterus, that position would optimize the retention of your embryo. Once you are in position, I will thread a small catheter through the cervical canal and transfer the embryo."

"Did you say embryo, not embryos?" asked John. "Isn't it customary to place several embryos?"

"Yes, you are right. As usual I'm impressed with what a quick study you are. It's true, the more embryos placed, the more likely a pregnancy will result. However, the more embryos, the greater the likelihood of a multiple pregnancy. Many centers, quite honestly, place far too many embryos to enhance their statistics. It's a competitive world out there. Let me explain. Joyce; you are young, your uterus is in prime shape, which makes you an ideal recipient. Added to that, as I think I mentioned, we have refined the transport media with a protein that greatly increases the implantation success. Also, there is some evidence that placing multiple embryos increases the possibility of congenital defects. For all those reasons, I am going to place one embryo. By the way, your other embryos are safely tucked away in our cryovault. Okay, John and Joyce, are you ready?"

Soon they were in the examining room and Joyce had assumed the knee-chest position.

"Are you okay?"

"I'm fine, except for total loss of dignity," Joyce answered.

Two weeks later John was in front of the bedroom mirror straightening his tie when from the bathroom came a scream. "It's positive!"

Damn, that man is a magician, thought John as he raced into the bathroom.

Chapter Thirty-Eight
Fall 2007

The doctor led his highness Prince Fasi into the Neonatal Intensive Care Unit. The prince looked around, overwhelmed by all the equipment; monitors, wires, IV solutions, and large radiant warmers. He could see that each baby was a nidus for its own collection of equipment. Some of the babies were so tiny that he felt he could have held two of them in his palm. His eye fell on one of the smallest, a scrawny rat-like creature wriggling under the glare of the radiant warmer. How could my baby possibly belong in here? he thought frantically.

"Please, your highness," said the doctor in a gentle, subservient tone.

The prince felt the pressure of the doctor's hand on his elbow and looked up from the small baby that held his gaze and allowed him to be led forward. Finally, they stopped in front of a warmer where a full-sized baby lay. The baby was perfectly formed, but its young body had already been invaded by a startling array of tubes. In one hand he could see an IV. The baby's umbilical cord had two different clear tubes protruding from it, in one of which he could see blood pulsating near the point where it entered the baby's body. From his penis emerged yet another, thicker, clear tube. Finally, into his mouth was the largest tube, as thick as one of the baby's digits and it was attached to a large hissing machine.

The Prince was transfixed by what he saw and stared mutely, though with such intensity that the doctor did not dare break the silence. Finally, he let out a cry, a primal scream of such pure animal agony, that the doctor felt a shiver go down his back. The Prince put his face in his hands and sobbed. "My son, my son, my sweet son."

The doctor, unsure of what to do, laid a tentative, comforting hand on the prince's shoulder which seemed to have no effect. After a moment, the prince lifted his head, glancing at the doctor. "None of this is to be spoken of, you understand."

"Of course, your highness."

He walked over to the window which had a commanding view of Riyadh and in the distance the desert and then mountains. He stood shock still as he stared. He put his head back into his hands.

After many minutes, the prince lifted his face from his hands and the doctor was startled by the transformation. Instead of grief, his face showed a steely resolve, with the slight reddening of his eyes being the only remaining evidence of his prostrate grief of a moment ago. His mouth opened and his voice was firm, controlled.

"Doctor, tell me now, what is wrong with my son?"

Chapter Thirty-Nine
September 1, 2008 11:00 AM

Egan limped slowly down the hospital corridor toward the pediatric floor. He paused to rub his calf and winced. He resumed his painful gait and opened his cell phone and began to scroll down a list of messages that he had chosen to ignore. He shut his phone with a sigh. It promptly chirped yet again. He resisted the urge to fling it out the nearest window, along with every other technologic advance of the computer age. He peered at the screen. It was Gail.

"Eric, where are you?"

"I'm limping toward the peds floor to help the interns."

"Come up to your on call room, its important."

"Gail, I already told them I on my way."

"You're a wounded man. Milk it. Call the floor and tell them you had to lie down or something. Please get up here."

"Okay, will do."

He spotted an open elevator door, and hurried his pace, grimacing with pain.

He got off on the 12th floor and went to his on call room. Gail was sitting at a small desk with papers scattered in front of her. Her face was shining with excitement.

"Eric, take a look." She pointed to a sheet of paper. Down the left side of the page were written in neat regular handwriting each medical record number with the gender and age listed. Egan leaned his head down to get a better look and read across the top: Bacterial type, white blood cell count, cerebral spinal fluid protein, cell count, glucose, birth history. "Wow, very nice. Looks like you have included everything of importance." Egan continued to peer at the page and finally looked up. "Jeez, why is it that girls can write so neatly? How are you going to learn to be a doctor with that kind of handwriting? Look at that, each i with its dot exactly above it. Just amazing."

"Damn it, Eric. Forget the handwriting. Look again and tell me what you see."

Egan, chastised, looked again and now concentrated on the content. Gail watched him, with a half-smile under tense control.

Suddenly, he jerked his head up. "Christ, all but one of the cases are from the in vitro clinic!"

His cell went off. He looked at the digital message: "Come to my office, immediately. Dr. Newhouse."

"Oh shit, what does he want? I'm sorry, Gail. This is really interesting. Good work. Let's meet later today."

"Okay, who knows, maybe Newhouse is summoning you to tell you that you got the O'Neil."

Twenty minutes later he was seated in an all too familiar chair across from Dr. Newhouse. "Eric, I'm not sure I know what to do about you. I got a call this morning from one of the IT people. It seems that you have been gathering data on kids with meningitis. Didn't I expressly tell you to leave it alone?"

Egan turned pale. "How did they…?"

"Seems that you are not always as smart as you think you are. In today's environment of HIPPA and patient confidentiality, access to patient records is carefully monitored."

"I'm a PhD candidate, so what I did is totally legitimate."

"So I can assume that you filed an application with the research board of the medical center? No? I didn't think so."

Egan sat staring at Newhouse who was holding his gaze mongoose-like. His mind raced but he could think of nothing to say. Finally, Newhouse broke the silence, his voice taking on a more sympathetic tone. "Eric, you are young with a long career ahead of you. Get some experience under your belt. Use your time here to learn undistracted. You will have plenty of time in the future to pursue your ideas."

"Dr. Newhouse, I know, I'm sorry. You're right, I should have gotten authorization, but this whole thing is really bugging me."

Egan stopped, looked up at the ceiling while rubbing his neck. Still looking up, he thought of Oden's admonition to be cautious, but he felt compelled to continue. "Do you know what all three of these babies have in common?"

"I'm not sure I want to hear this."

"In vitro conception from Dr. George's clinic."

Newhouse rose from his chair, face reddening, all pretense of equanimity vanishing.

"Listen, young man; you are a second-year resident and your job is to learn how to be a pediatrician by taking care of patients and learning from those who know more than you, of which this medical center is chock full of. You are not, I repeat, not to engage in fanciful speculations in areas that require far greater sophistication than you currently are in possession of. As far as the in vitro, do not say a word about this to anyone. Last thing we need is for years of Dr. George's research to become victim of innuendo. Do I make myself clear?"

"But Dr. Newhouse—" Egan broke in almost with a shout.

"Eric, Eric, you calm down and let me finish. What I'm suggesting is that if this gets out and hits the rumor mill before it can be substantiated, grievous harm will be done to several people's reputation as well as tarnishing the medical center. You know better than most residents that in general these kinds of suggestive early findings usually don't pan out."

Egan held his gaze as he talked. "Shouldn't we at least talk to Dr. George?"

"Damnit, Eric, don't you ever back down? How the hell do you think Dr. George will react if you come to him and in your typically subtle fashion say to him: 'I've uncovered some cases that not only will destroy your career and reputation but will leave you wide open for lawsuits that will make the silicone breast implant verdicts look like chump change and so by this time next year you'll be lucky to be cleaning bed pans in north central Nebraska.' Actually the silicone implant debacle is a good cautionary tale here. Pseudo-science ruled the day and by the time the real scientific facts emerged, the lawyers of the land had already feasted like so many prehistoric beasts upon billions. Let me handle this and not a word to anyone. Am I being clear?" Newhouse stared at him red-faced.

"Yessir," was all Egan could muster.

Chapter Forty
September 1, 2008 1:00 PM

Egan retreated to his on-call room to mull over his conversation with Newhouse. His cell went off.

He wrenched it from his belt and with a shout flung it at the far wall. At that moment the door opened and Gail came in.

"Boy, when you quiet types blow, you really blow."

Egan looked at her, a vision of loveliness in blue scrubs and clogs, and he could feel his anger and frustration drain out of him. Gail moved over to the on call room bed and sat down next to him and began to massage his shoulders. Egan was silent with his eyes half shut for several minutes and then looked up and smiled wanly.

"I erupt like that regularly like Old Faithful—though it only happens every five years or so."

"That's okay, it was a sight to behold. Now tell me your tale of woe."

"Well, it looks like my much vaunted career is in tatters. It appears that I have a rare talent in being able to push the wrong buttons of every powerful person I meet in the medical center. Newhouse read me the riot act and intimated that my current path is a slippery slope to oblivion. I came back here to lick my wounds and that damn cell went off for probably the gazillionth time today."

Gail drew him close and rubbed his head. "Why was he so upset at you?"

"He learned from the IT people that I was pulling data using my research code."

"You mean we were pulling data," Gail corrected gently.

"I know, I know, but it's my code and my responsibility. I saw no reason to drag you into this. Anyway, it started out as a gentle remonstration—you're young, inexperienced, here to learn, don't want this to distract you from your purpose here, etcetera, etcetera, but then degenerated into a full-throated, ego-stomping dressing down after I told him that most of the cases were from George's in vitro clinic."

Gail stared at him. "Maybe you should have kept that under your hat."

"Duh, you think so?" asked Egan with a rueful smile.

Gail didn't smile back at him but knotted her brow. "Eric, what was that protein you were telling me about after Newhouse's lecture?"

"Protein F?"

"Yeah, that's the one. Tell me more."

Egan looked at her for a long moment and suddenly a look of recognition suffused his face. "Do you think ...?"

"Tell me about your research with it," broke in Gail impatiently.

"My initial research project before dealt with studying the processes involved in fertilization and implantation. It proved to be devilishly elusive, and I gave it up to do a more doable project in transplant immunology. But I had dabbled enough to learn that protein F, along with a whole other alphabet soup of molecules, is involved in some way as a modulator in the breaking down of the outer membrane of the ovum and has a similar role in the implantation process, though the details are quite sketchy. You can imagine the jolt I got when Newhouse mentioned protein F in reference to the blood brain barrier."

He looked at Gail who could barely conceal her excitement. "That could be the connection, between in vitro and the meningitis cases." Egan's facial expression echoed Gail's and belied his previous anxiety.

"It's very possible that protein F is a ubiquitous protein throughout the body having some role in modulating permeability in a number of membranes. Let's think this through. Suppose that George's method involves some sort of manipulation of protein F, perhaps a chemical that has an affinity for one of its receptor sites that facilitates fertilization and/or implantation. Let's further suppose that this chemical is tightly bound so that it remains in the fetus and binds to nascent protein F throughout the fetus including the blood brain barrier, thus permanently altering its function."

"But if that's the case," broke in Gail, "why aren't all the babies from the in vitro clinic being affected?"

"Well," mused Egan, "like everything else in biology it functions over a backdrop of variability. In other words, each individual is uniquely coded with a complex array of DNA and any small change is going to have a variable effect dependent on the particular genome of that individual. A similar phenomenon is the different graded effects that we see using the same medication in different individuals—some who react beautifully on one extreme and those who don't respond to the drug at all on the other."

Egan's cell sounded from the floor on the far side of the room.

"Impressive cell craftsmanship. I am amazed that thing still works after what you did to it."

"Oh my God, I forgot to answer that last page."

Egan picked up his cell. After a short exchange, he hung up.

"The day continues to get better. I have three admissions waiting down in the ER and a consult on the surgical floor."

"Buck up, Eric, I'll help you. Look, I'll go down to the ER and get started. You do the surgical consult and then meet me in the ER. Hopefully, I'll have the write-ups ready for your review by the time you get there." Egan smiled and gave her hand a squeeze.

Chapter Forty-One
September 1, 2008 3:00 PM

Things were hopping down in the ER and Egan and Gail worked for several hours, writing up admissions, doing blood work, taking histories, and trying to remain in control of the seemingly endless numbers of small details and duties that constitute medical care.

"Okay, that should do it," said Egan, putting his pen down. "All we have to do now is get through evening rounds and with any luck be able to get some shuteye afterwards."

"Sounds good. What time do rounds start?"

"Usually about this time, though it's at the discretion of the on-call third-year resident."

"Who's the third year on tonight?"

"Good question. It's been so hectic that I didn't even check the on call schedule."

Egan pulled out his palm. "Oh, shit, it's Richter. Rounds will take forever. It was bad enough when she spent her days on the pediatric floor, but now she's on a peds ICU rotation."

"Why will that make a difference?"

"She won't be familiar with any of the patients and she'll want a detailed description of each case. You know the expression 'can't see the forest for the trees'? Well, she takes it to a whole new level: She can't even see the trees for the twigs. You know what? A little preemptive action is called for. Let's get the interns together and prep them a bit."

Half an hour later, Egan and Gail were standing with the rest of the on call team. Joan Richter, face set in grim relief, listened to an intern presenting a case. She thrust her hand out, like a policeman directing traffic. "Stop. I don't want to hear that the sodium was normal; I want to know the actual sodium level." Richter followed this statement with a hard look at the intern who was shuffling through his papers.

Egan broke in. "Joan, the sodium was 138, well within normal range and in fact it has not been an issue for this patient for about three days."

"Eric, I don't care; I want the interns to know the exact numbers. I can't tell you how many times I have heard 'normal' and found by digging in the chart that it was not normal. Speaking of which, let me dig into this chart and see what I can find."

Egan groaned inaudibly. "Looks like Joan's in a mood tonight. We're in for some rough sailing." he whispered to Gail.

Joan looked up from the chart. "Dr. Egan, why don't you present the next case?"

"This child was admitted two weeks ago with a history of recurrent episodes of diarrhea and dehydration." Egan glanced at Gail, remembering this was the same boy that when the team had been in the room on rounds, he had spoken to Gail for the first time. She winked at him. Egan went on. "Today there was a rather startling development. His mother was caught on videocam administering something to the boy. A subsequent search of the room uncovered enough laxatives to keep an elephant running for many a moon. Mom was confronted, banned from the premises, and our young lad here had his first formed stool in ages just this afternoon."

"Very interesting," said Joan. "Any of the students know what the diagnosis is and can explain what it is?"

There were no volunteers, so Joan nodded to Gail. "How about you?"

"Well, it sounds like Munchhausen's by proxy. In this, which is really a psychiatric disorder, a parent either creates fictitious symptoms or actually inflicts harm on their kids like partially asphyxiating their baby to mimic a near miss sudden infant death syndrome or as in this case feed their kid laxatives in order to create diarrhea. These parents seem to get a sort of strange sustenance from all the kind concern that is generated by their child's illness."

They were all silent for a moment as they contemplated this rather strange disorder. Egan thought back to some twelve hours earlier when the mother was confronted and how her whole façade had crumbled. Prior to that she had been a ward favorite, outgoing, vivacious, and she constantly visited other parents in order to dispense understanding and sympathy. She even provided food for the residents. After a short conversation with the ward attending, she had collapsed crying and was finally led from the ward stone faced and staring at the floor.

Rounds picked up again and finally at past midnight they were over, but not before Joan had extracted every last piece of ignorance from the students and interns and laid it out for all to see. She had briefly probed Egan's knowledge base, but had been discouraged by his quick lucid answers so she redirected her laser beam back to weaker quarry.

Egan spent the next two hours directing his interns and students in completing extra tests that Joan felt were absolutely vital. Finally, Egan realized that the work was all done and no new cases had appeared in the ER. He looked at his watch. It was 2:30. He looked up at Gail.

"We're done."

Arms around each other, they walked into the on-call room and onto the bed, falling asleep instantly.

Chapter Forty-Two
September 2, 2008 5:00 AM

A dull ache woke up Egan. He reached down to massage the area around his wound. Gail stirred and then awoke.

"Are you okay?"

"Just hurting a bit. I'll just pop a couple Advils."

"Do you want me to massage it for you?"

"That would be great. I'm getting muscle cramps around the wound. But don't you want to get a bit more sleep?"

"No, I'm wide awake. I've hardly slept this whole time. Eric, what are we going to do?"

"I don't know. I'm afraid to go to Newhouse."

"How about Oden?"

"Oden. That's a good idea. I think I can trust him, but I don't know enough of what's going on. Lot of it just seems crazy when I try to explain it."

"Well, something is going on. I mean look at your leg. Dr. George was there. Who is to say that he didn't follow us out to that beaver pond and then take a shot?"

"I don't know, just seems too hard to believe. God knows George is not my favorite person, but still I just don't seeing him, a respected researcher and doctor, doing something like that."

"I know, but as Sherlock Holmes says, when you have eliminated the impossible, whatever remains, however improbable, must be the truth."

Egan gave a wan smile, "Okay, my dear Watson, but I don't think we've done too much eliminating. We need more information."

Gail looked hard at Eric for a long minute. "Okay, here's what we do. I think we need to check out the in vitro clinic."

"Yeah, you're right. We can start by checking out everything we can find out about the research. I'll see what I can find in the medical literature. Maybe Michael will be willing to cover me for a couple hours today so I can go to the library."

"Sounds good Eric, but I think we also have to go to the source. Maybe we should go to the clinic. During third year orientation, the dean told us that we should take advantage of all the cutting edge stuff going on here. Visit labs, check out what's happening. He even mentioned the in vitro clinic specifically. What do you say we drop by today and ask for a tour? I'm a third-year med student trying to decide what area I want to go in, and you're a finalist for the O'Neil fellowship. It would be perfectly natural for us to want to ask for an inside tour."

"Okay, let's do it. We'll try to get away right after rounds, but why don't we go there separately and meet in front of clinic. In the meantime, let's get a little shut eye. Miraculously, my leg feels better."

"Hey, nothing miraculous about it. It's my healing hands."

Chapter Forty-Three
January 7, 2008

Prince Fasi was becoming rapidly schooled in the art of crisis management. Those closest to him were surprised to find how impressively he was handling himself during these first few weeks of his son's birth. From the moment he had lifted his face from his hands after crying in front of the doctor, the expression of resolve never left him and he approached his son's illness with single-mindedness. Starting on the day of his son's birth, he quickly mastered the details of his son's illness. In fact, he asked so many questions, that it made the neonatologist fearful that the prince was trying to uncover some wrongdoing on his part.

After learning the primary diagnosis, which was hypoplastic left heart syndrome, and having a handle on its basic anatomical and physiological implications, he plunged into the minutiae of his son's care, and soon the nurses were no longer surprised to find him noting a 1 cc per hour change in the IV rate or asking about whether he shouldn't have another dose of lasix, a powerful diuretic that helped get rid of extra fluid from the circulation so that the infant's heart could pump more efficiently. The fact that he had been an indifferent student at the university made his rapid acquisition of basic cardiac physiological principles all the more amazing.

Yet his involvement was not like the typical parent of the meddling, intrusive sort that presented the medical staff with a management problem more complicated than that of the patient himself. He was adroit. He quickly learned the hospital hierarchy and mastered the deprecatory yet charming manner that caused the hospital staff to look forward to their encounters with him. On two occasions he had caught minor errors he managed to bring to the staff's attention in a way that seemed collegial rather than accusatory.

It was now two weeks since the birth, and Fasi and Farah were sitting quietly together gazing at the incubator that contained their son. He no longer was connected to a respirator, but had two miniature cannulae in his nostrils delivering humidified oxygen and his breathing seemed mildly labored. His skin had a slight bluish cast.

"Fasi," began Farah. "He looks so normal. I still can't believe this." Fasi looked at her briefly, patted her hand and returned his gaze to his son. After a moment Farah spoke again. "Do you think this is a punishment for what we did? Was it so wrong to want a boy so much?"

"No, Farah, no," answered Fasi in a firm voice while taking her hand again. "We did nothing wrong and you will see—everything will turn out okay. I have consulted with some of the best doctors abroad, one of whom will come next week. He will be cured, I am certain."

Fasi and Farah stared hard at each other, with tears welling up in her eyes. Finally, they both returned their gaze to their son thinking and remembering all they had done to have him.

Chapter Forty-Four
September 2, 2008 7:00 AM

They had been sleeping two hours when, Egan gradually became aware that his cell was chirping.

"Egan, here."

"Eric, it's John Oden."

"Dr. Oden. Nice to hear from you."

"Eric, please, I've told you. Call me John."

"Okay, John. What's up?"

"I was wondering whether you could brief me on what if anything you found out about the meningitis cases. Remember, you promised to stay in touch."

Egan let out a long sigh of relief. "Sure, absolutely. I could use some support right about now. Actually, I'm free right now."

"Great, do you want to come over to my office?"

Egan got up and after writing a note for Gail who was still deep asleep, he headed toward Oden's office.

Ten minutes later, Egan was sitting across from Oden in his rather modest office. His desk was piled messily with charts, journals, and miscellaneous papers. On the walls were several large pictures, almost poster sized of John Oden pursuing various extreme sports: rock climbing, off trail skiing. The largest showed him hang gliding off of Yosemite's El Capitan.

"That's amazing!" exclaimed Egan as he stared at Oden's picture in midair, a wild grin on his face.

Oden smiled. "Oh, it's nothing. But I tell you there is no feeling like it, to be suspended high above the earth gliding and slowly rising on a thermal wind current. Well, anyway, let's return to earth, shall we? Tell what you've found out."

Oden was no longer smiling and he was looking intently at Egan.

"Well, there have been some new developments. I found some other cases and all but one are linked to Dr. George's in vitro clinic."

"Are you kidding me? What possible connection can that have?"

"Well, I have a theory and please, hear me out. It may strike you as bizarre."

"Don't worry about that."

"Protein F, I learned recently, is integral to the structure and function of the blood brain barrier. Protein F, which I know from a previous research project I was involved in, also plays a role in the barrier of the uterine membrane before embryo implantation. So I began to wonder if some sort of technique that is used in the in vitro clinic that apparently greatly enhances implantation could possibly inadvertently affect the nascent blood brain barriers of the implanted fetus."

Oden exhaled a long low whistle and sat deep in thought for some moments while Egan eyed him nervously wondering if Oden would explode the way Newhouse had.

Finally Oden began in calm measured tones. "This is, as you said, farfetched, but it has a certain kernel of plausibility. But, we have to be very careful here. Dr. George is very powerful and in vitro is not only his baby, so to speak, but a tremendous revenue generator for the medical center. We have to be realistic here. First off, we have to be extremely certain of all our facts before going forward. Can you show me everything you've gathered?"

"Absolutely."

"Good. In the meantime, we keep this totally under wraps."

"I understand. But I should tell you that I've already talked to Dr. Newhouse, and he may have already talked to Dr. George."

Oden raised his eyebrows. "Maybe I can talk to Newhouse. I'll help you anyway I can. I owe you."

Egan left Oden's office, feeling better and took energetic steps toward the pediatric floor.

"Hey, Eric, wait up."

Egan stopped and looked back and saw Michael. He slung his arm around Egan. "You, my man, are always in such a rush. Where the hell are you heading?"

"Up to peds, for rounds. Michael, you were next on my list. I need your help."

Egan stopped and put his hand on Michael's shoulder. They faced each other.

Egan outlined his concerns about the in vitro clinic.

Michael shook his head with quiet amazement. "Quite a kettle of fish. You can count on me to help in any way I can. One question: Why not leave all this to the discretion of Newhouse? You have properly pointed out a possible cause and effect to the proper person who has promised to look into it. You know as well as I do that the wheels of scientific advancement grind rather slowly, and if a possible connection of these sick babies with the in vitro clinic becomes widely publicized, it will virtually shut down the whole operation, entirely appropriate if you're right but if you're wrong..."

"Exactly the point: There is a tremendous amount at stake here, and Newhouse didn't exactly promise to look in to it. To my mind, if there is even a small chance of a connection with the in vitro clinic, by all means shut it down until you know for sure. Believe me I trust and respect Newhouse, but I feel compelled to carry on my own investigation."

"Okay, buddy, whatever you think."

Chapter Forty-Five
June 2008

"Excellent, Joyce, excellent. Your cervix is tightly closed and the baby is in good position."

Dr. George stepped back from the examining table. He pulled carefully on each digit of his right hand, and slowly, meticulously, slid off the surgical glove. He stretched the glove before releasing it and it flew several feet before dropping neatly into a waste basket.

"Nice shot," commented Joyce as she sat up swinging her legs around to the side of the table.

"Thank you. I never miss. I take care of one of the Knick's wives and do you know that Jack Jones, the point guard was between me and the waste basket. I was able to fake right and then shoot left and got it in."

Joyce laughed appreciatively as she stood up.

"Joyce, we'll leave you to get dressed and then you can join John and me in my office."

Joyce slowly put on her clothes with a half-smile on her face. As she buttoned her shirt over her large abdomen she patted herself and broke into a huge grin. "I can't wait!"

Soon she joined the two men who were engaged in such a spirited discussion of the Knicks' prospects in the coming season, they didn't notice her entering. "Boys, boys, can we just this once focus on this?" she said while pointing at her belly.

"But, darling, we're talking about the Knicks. This is probably going to be their best chance in ten years." John stood up and put his arm around her while stroking her abdomen. "Just kidding. Dr. George tells me that things are going quite well."

"Right you are," echoed George. "Please, sit down and let me give you the details. Joyce, you were made to have babies. At 36 weeks, your baby is doing fantastic. Heart beat strong and steady, good size. As I said before, your cervix is tightly closed so I am quite confident you will carry this baby to term. Joyce, you are positively glowing. I, as you can imagine, see hundreds of pregnant women—most are happy, but you take it to a whole new level."

Joyce grinned. "I have wanted this for such a long time. I just can't wait. It's all I think about. Everybody at work is laughing at me because I spend so much time smiling and daydreaming."

"As you know, your amnio was absolutely normal. You still don't want to know the sex of the child?"

"No," answered John, "boy, girl whatever—as long as he or she can hit the outside shot, then I'll be perfectly happy. And speaking of outside shot, what do you think of Jeremiah Rudolph—52 percent from three-point range?"

"Men!" exclaimed Joyce with a laugh.

Chapter Forty-Six
Janaury 15, 2008

Prince Fasi was at the side of his son, waiting impatiently for the specialist he had arranged to fly in from Europe. It was not that he did not have confidence in the local doctors. Indeed, he had been impressed by their skill and efficiency. But through what had already been extensive research, he had determined that his son's care required expertise that was probably available only in a few places in the world. Therefore, he'd sought out one of the top European pediatric cardiac surgeons and had persuaded him to fly down to render an opinion on his son's care.

The prince looked over his son's monitors for the tenth time in as many minutes, and leaned over to give Ali a gentle kiss. He got up and began to pace around the room. His ears perked up as he heard the sounds of several footsteps in the corridor and he fought his impulse to race into the hall. Instead he settled into his chair and reached for his book so that by the time Dr. Wilson, the cardiac surgeon strode into the room, he was the picture of relaxed royalty.

Dr. Wilson was accompanied by a troupe of the top cardiologists and surgeons of the hospital. The prince got to his feet and regarded the doctor as he walked over to greet him. He was tall, towering over all the local doctors, strongly built; with short blond wispy hair. The prince reached out his arm and they shook hands.

"Dr. Wilson, it is so good of you to come," said the prince in a tone that was warm and welcoming but with a studied casualness as if he was greeting a neighbor who had come over for tea.

"Prince Fasi, the honor is all mine."

"I trust your flight down was comfortable?"

"Oh yes, quite. Your jet couldn't have been better equipped. It was good of you to have all his records and x-rays on board for my review."

"And your conclusions?"

"Well, Prince, I certainly have some, but let me examine your son and then I will discuss it all in detail with you."

Dr. Wilson approached the bedside. The group of doctors with him began to move with him, but the prince spoke up.

"Gentlemen, if you would be so kind as to leave us for now and allow the doctor to conduct his exam in private. Do not worry, I have arranged for Dr. Wilson to conduct grand rounds later this afternoon and he will be at your service for case discussion and consultation."

Dr. Wilson took careful note of the monitors and observed that the heart rate was elevated, and the blood pressure was a bit on the low side. The baby had a slightly bluish cast signifying a lack of oxygen in the blood despite the generous amounts being supplied from the large tank nearby. The baby's abdomen was distended and a gentle palpation revealed an enlarged liver and spleen. He took his stethoscope and listened intently moving the head of the stethoscope from spot to spot over the chest for a full five minutes. All the while, his facial expression merely showed intense concentration like that of a museum aficionado studying an old master, but did not reveal anything about what he was finding.

The prince watched him work with a similar attention. The doctor's demeanor was calm and dispassionate, as he went about his business, unhurried, seemingly unaffected by the fact he was thousands of miles from home working under the gaze of royalty. The prince waited patiently until finally, Dr. Wilson looked up from his exam and the two men exchanged glances.

"Dr. Wilson, would you care for some coffee?"

"That would be most welcome."

"Well, sir, let us adjourn to the next room where refreshments are waiting."

They crossed the corridor to a large private room that was resplendently outfitted by a large gold coffee urn, fine china and an assortment of delectables on an ornately styled silver tray. The prince waited until the doctor had settled into a chair with his coffee and food and then sat across from him.

"Prince," the doctor began, "your son is not well. Let me start at the beginning, though much of this you may already be familiar with. First of all, there is no question about the diagnosis: this is hypoplastic left heart syndrome. The heart, of course, is the pump that circulates the blood throughout the body and maintains the blood pressure, just like a water pump in a house. In this condition, the whole left ventricle of the heart is poorly formed: the chamber is smaller, the walls thinner, and the muscle weaker."

"Excuse me, doctor, but why does this become manifest only after birth. Doesn't the heart start beating and pumping early in fetal development?"

"Excellent question. The fetal circulation is quite different in that the lungs are bypassed and the two ventricles share in the job of providing circulation to the body. Once the baby is born, with that first breath the lungs open up and a radical shift occurs in which the province of the right ventricle becomes solely that of pumping blood to the lungs and the left ventricle becomes solely responsible for the body." Dr. Wilson paused for a moment, wondering if he was going into too much detail, but the prince's facial expression indicated complete attention and interest and he continued. "Now the two pumps work in tandem. The right ventricle pumps blood to the lungs and all that blood is then delivered to the left ventricle which sends it on to its nourishing mission to the rest of the body. In your son's case, the left ventricle was woefully unprepared for this sudden shift of burden, which is why he became sick so shortly after birth. His doctors, I must say, were quick to make the diagnosis and have delivered exemplary care."

The prince merely nodded slightly acknowledging the complement to Saudi medicine, but said nothing.

"What we are faced with now is simply pump failure: the left ventricle does not have the strength to pump out whatever is delivered to it. Thus, we see all the signs of backup of the blood: crackles in the lungs, enlargement of the liver and spleen. The situation as it stands now is not compatible with long-term life."

The prince stared at him as if to will different words out of the doctor's mouth. He got up, strode around the room for a moment, wiping a tear away as he went. Finally he returned to his chair. "Doctor, I appreciate the complete honesty of your report— something I don't always get locally. But tell me, is there no hope? Surely there is something that can be done."

"Well, there is no definitive medical treatment. There is plenty to do to prolong life and palliate the situation. There is an operation that in the right hands would considerably improve heart function. The best course is perhaps the most difficult: a complete heart transplant."

"A heart transplant." The prince murmured almost to himself and looked up with an excited look on his face. "Well, then, a transplant it will be. How soon can this be arranged?"

The doctor appeared momentarily startled by this quick enthusiasm for radical surgery. "Now wait a second. This is not something to go into lightly. First, you should know that finding a suitable heart for transplant is a long, and if you'll excuse me, heartbreaking process. There are simply very few infant hearts available. Second, transplanting replaces the problem of an inadequate pump with a host of others. Massive quantities of medicines have to be given to quell the rejection process. It is by no means an easy or quick solution."

"But," interjected the prince, "it appears to me to be the only solution. Indulge me, doctor, with a best-case scenario. Is it possible with a heart transplant to live a normal life, not probable, but merely possible?"

"Yes, certainly, but—"

"Well then," interrupted the prince, "it's settled; a transplant it will be. Now tell me; where can we go to get a heart?"

Chapter Forty-Seven
September 2, 2008 1:00 PM

Egan's head dropped forward for the third time in ten minutes, and he jerked himself awake.

Michael reached over, pulling away the chart that Egan was working on. "Listen, Eric, give me your patient list and I'll cover you. Can I make a suggestion? You're exhausted. You go home and catch some Zs. You'll be able to think more clearly after some rest."

"Michael, I appreciate it, but I'm okay."

Michael laughed. "I was in the morgue yesterday at an autopsy, and I saw more animation in the faces down there than I see in you."

"I'm okay."

"Listen, macho man. I said I'd cover you. That's what friends are for."

Egan stared at him for a long minute and finally took his on call cell and in a motion of surrender handed it over to him.

Egan got home early in the afternoon and fell into a deep though restless and dream-filled sleep. He dreamed that he was in the hospital, his cell going off constantly and nurses beseeching him at every turn. He ran into the ICU, where he was grabbed and suddenly found himself stretched out on a bed. One nurse inserted an IV while another a Foley catheter into his bladder. Two doctors intubated him. He tried to shout "I'm not the patient here." but the tube in his trachea prevented him. He could hear voices murmuring above him and he recognized Newhouse, Oden, Michael, and Barrett all surrounding the bed. Then he noticed at the head of the bed Dr. George, autopsy knife in hand and he heard him ask, "Does anybody mind if I start the autopsy a little early?" Egan tried to scream as the knife came down to start a sternum to pubis cut.

He awoke with a start and it was completely dark. He brought his hand up to his mouth and with infinite relief realized that there was no tube and it had all been a dream. He felt momentarily confused and unsure of where he was. He heard a faint scratching sound and briefly he thought it was the familiar sound of mice gnawing. His heart, however, began to pound as he realized that the scratching had a metallic quality and he looked over at the handle of the door of his studio apartment which was partially illuminated by a shaft of light from a street lamp and it appeared to be moving slightly. The door began to open and Egan let out an involuntary shout. At that moment, two men burst into the room. With nylon stockings over their heads, they moved toward Egan.

Egan had fallen asleep fully dressed, including his sneakers, a fact he was grateful for as he embarked on a plan of action conceived during the seconds that had elapsed between the abrupt invasion of the two men and their steadfast approach to his bed. In one smooth motion he rolled off the bed and flung himself out the window, which fortunately was wide open, and onto the fire escape.

This sudden action surprised the two men who had been fooled by Egan's sleepy appearance. Their momentarily delay in adjusting to this transformation of half-awake body to athletic leaping gymnast was just enough to allow Egan to get down two floors and onto the ladder which lowered rapidly to a height where he could jump. He landed awkwardly on the hard pavement and fell forward painfully as he felt a jolt at the site of his wounded calf, but fear banished the pain from his consciousness and he emerged from his low crouch like a sprinter and tore out of the alley, spurred on by the sounds of the two men scrambling down the fire escape.

He came out of the alley at full sprint to find a completely deserted street and he decided to race toward Central Park, some five blocks to the west, a route he was familiar with. Despite the cold fear he felt, he had the presence of mind to slow down slightly and settle into a more relaxed lope. He calculated that he had enough of a lead to afford this and he had had enough of a glimpse of the men to form an impression that they were heavy set, certainly muscular, but built for short bursts of speed, not a long chase. He thought of a cheetah that could achieve bursts of speed up to 70 miles per hour, but quickly tired and thus any antelope that got a good jump could escape.

His world reduced to the few feet of pavement in front of him and his only sensations were the sound and feel of his hard breathing and the steady pulse of his pounding footsteps. He had taken one quick backwards look and seen the two men at full sprint, probably gaining slightly, but a full 75 yards back. Predator and prey, this biological relationship had never seemed more real to him and he briefly panicked and started to race faster, but then reason again prevailed and he returned to his previous more relaxed efficient gait.

He approached the park, took one long look up and down Fifth Avenue hoping to find someone, anyone, who could help him, but the street was as deserted as all of the streets before had been. He entered the park on a small asphalt path that was full of curves and adjoining woods that he thought might afford him a hiding place. He had taken one more quick backward look before entering and was gladdened to see that they were now a good hundred yards back and more significantly, their running stroke appeared more choppy and labored. This sight gave him the energy to redouble his speed.

He ran down the circuitous path and was quickly out of sight of his pursuers. He spotted a heavily wooded dark area and scooted in and lay down on the damp earth and leaves. He took a couple of deep breaths and tried to control his breathing, willing himself to be still and quiet. His pounding heart filled his head but was superseded by another pounding, that of his pursuer's feet on asphalt as they got closer. Egan held his breath as they passed him and the sounds of their footfalls began to fade.

He exhaled a sigh of relief, but remained where he was, partly cautious, partly exhausted and overwhelmed by the events of the preceding 20 minutes, which had propelled him so rudely from a warm comfortable bed to this cold, damp, insect ridden spot. He began to feel ants crawling up his legs and stopping at his wound which had began to throb and small flies feasted on the sweat on his brow. He was about to get up and brush off the insects when he heard footsteps again approaching, now at a more leisurely pace and voices of two men. He laid shock still as the two men paused to light cigarettes not more than 5 feet from where Egan lay.

"Damn, where the hell did he go?" said one of the men. "Fast motherfucker wasn't he?"

"This is not good. Doc is going to be plenty pissed off about this. He will not be happy, no question about that."

"Should we keep looking?"

"Naw, he could be anywhere. Come on, we might as well get going."

The two men continued on their way and soon Egan was alone again. Doc! He exclaimed to himself. Those men were sent by somebody from the medical center. Their voices sounded vaguely familiar, but he couldn't quite place it. A mosquito hummed and nestled into Egan's ear, and feasted in peace as Egan, preoccupied with his predicament, hunkered down mentally trying to figure out a plan of action.

Clearly, he thought, something is not kosher with the in vitro clinic. The varied dimensions of his dilemma, running the gamut from thugs to academicians, threatened to overwhelm Egan, but he steeled himself and thought, Shit, I'm a Malloy Center resident, trained to deal with any crisis. I can handle this.

Whether bravado or true conviction, its effect was the same: to mobilize Egan out of the dirt and onto his feet. A single swat took care of the mosquito on his ear and he could not help for a fleeting moment wonder if he had any more chance than that mosquito against the behemoth which was the Malloy Medical Center and its in vitro clinic. But that thought was as transient as the death agony of the mosquito on his ear. He brushed off the dirt and set off down the path going deeper into the park. His mind, like any good resident, had sorted out immediate priorities, from those that could wait to those that needed immediate attention. His cell phone was sitting uselessly in his apartment. I need shelter, he thought to himself, and I can't risk going home. In fact, I can't even go back to the East Side. Those goons may be lurking.

The hospital was out too for the same reason. His reverie continued as he walked deeper into the park in the opposite direction of the two men. He resolved to hike southward to 59th street and to then decide where to go from there. He realized he had no money on him. He thought of Gail.

Bit of a trek down to her place in the village, but he had been undaunted by longer hikes in less hospitable conditions. Just having a destination calmed his nerves and he fell into a steady rhythmic gait which got him quickly out of the park and began to consume downtown streets. He turned his predicament around in his mind compulsively, thinking first of steps to ensure his safety, then of ways to learn more about the in vitro center and the research that surrounded it.

Finally, he reached Gail's block and like a horse approaching his stable, he quickened his pace. After five minutes of ringing and knocking, the door opened and with profound relief found Gail looking at him with open-mouthed astonishment.

"Eric! What on earth? Come in."

She threw her arms around him, and Egan moved by this welcome held on tightly and sobbed briefly against her shoulder. Gail said not a word, but led him to the couch, kicking her foot backwards to close the door. His disheveled appearance with twigs, leaves, dirt, and even insects in his hair and clothing made it obvious to her that some sort of misadventure had occurred. They sat there for some minutes as Egan tried to compose himself, taking occasional deep breathes while Gail gently rubbed his neck. He tried to talk, but his voice kept cracking.

Egan told her about the chase. When he finished, she sat quietly, looking at him. She took his hand. He resisted briefly, but allowed himself to be lead toward the stairs and into a cavernous bathroom with a large circular Jacuzzi. She helped him out of his clothes and settled him in a deliciously warm tub, with jets of water massaging his aching muscles. She took a cup and poured warm water over his head and began to massage shampoo into his tangled dirty hair, pausing occasionally to remove a wriggling ant.

"Boy, you're lucky I'm not the squeamish type. What were you doing, lying in an ant hill?"

His eyes were half closed as he reveled in the sensations of warm currents against his body and Gail's fingertips on his scalp, but shivered slightly as he thought back over his escape. As a resident, he was not unused to charging headlong out of a dead sleep in response to an emergency, but he was still ill-prepared for the singular transport from bed to damp earth and now improbably to heavenly comfort.

"Close your eyes." She dunked his head to rinse off the shampoo, briefly causing him to choke, his response time slowed by the stultifying effect of his exhaustion. Soon he was toweled off, robed, and sitting in front of the upstairs fireplace, a restorative glass of brandy in his hand. He stared meditatively in the fire for several minutes and then looked up as Gail joined him on the couch.

Her bedroom had a large Persian carpet on the floor and the bed was a large oak framed double bed with ornate carvings on its headboard and covered with an antique quilt with matching pillows. He looked at her and inhaled her scent. It all comes down to this one moment, this apogee of evolution, these genes percolating down through the generations, coding for a myriad of proteins and enzymes that activate the exquisite machinery that allows us to ambulate, talk, see, smell and mate. All these chemicals organized into a grand symphony for this one purpose, echoed over and over again over eons: a black widow spider mating and afterwards eating her mate, a fish spewing spawn over a bed of eggs, a female orangutan taking her third partner of the day deep in the trembling brush.

Wordlessly, they undressed each other as they neared the bed leaving a detritic trail of jeans, briefs, and panties. They embraced and tumbled on to the bed. He could feel the descent from higher cortical centers of his brain to the more primitive areas dominated by the senses. Their movements at first mammalian in nature underwent an ontogenetic descent into more primitive, convulsive reactive motions, an evolution in reverse ending in a primordial ocean as waves of pleasure swept over them.

Chapter Forty-Eight
September 3, 2008 6:30 AM

Early the next morning Egan awoke just as first light appeared and for some time gazed at Gail sleeping. He felt aglow from the night before and was tempted to wake her, but he was reluctant to disturb such a pretty slumber. As he stared intently at her face, her eyes blinked open and she smiled. Egan reached out to stroke her shoulder and they began to gently explore each other's bodies.

Gail looked into Egan's eyes and, spent from the rigors of the night before, was content to make a slow languorous inspection of his cheeks, lips. Her hand stroked the side of his face, feeling the texture of his beard, the rise of his nose, the angle of his mandible.

"Zygomatic arch," he whispered to her as she touched the bony buttress below his right eye.

"Sternocleidomastoid, pectoralis, deltoid," he said softly as she continued her anatomical explorations to his neck, chest, and arm. She paused as her hand encountered a rough raised pigmented area on his left shoulder.

"Becker's nevis. A benign pigmented lesion," Egan told her with a smile.

She reached his abdomen and her fingers found a slightly raised scar. She could feel Egan's abdominal muscles tighten slightly and she looked up at him. Egan put his own hand over hers on top of the scar.

"Surgery when I was fifteen."

Gail continued to look at him, guessing from his suddenly pensive manner, that there was more.

He continued. "My mother developed end stage kidney disease early in my childhood."

"How old were you?" she asked while stroking her fingers lightly along the scar.

"I don't remember exactly when, but as long as I can remember, she would disappear into a back room twice a week where we had a dialysis machine. She made no big deal about it, but it was clear to us kids that we were not to disturb her during that time. She must have compartmentalized it because she didn't act the role of a chronically ill person, at least not in front of us. She underwent two transplants, but rejected both of them.

"When I was fourteen, I got involved in this honors biology project and I chose transplant immunology as my topic. Through the lab I was assigned to, I was able get myself tested for histocompatability antigens and guess what—I was a perfect match for my mother. Took quite a bit of persuading, but I was eventually able to talk my mom and her doctors to take me as a donor. I told her, 'but Mom, you gave birth to me—I just want to return the favor.'

"I donated my left kidney. My mother did well post op and for a few blissful weeks the dialysis machine just gathered dust in the back. Mom moved around the house with renewed energy, great color, every trip to the bathroom a celebration of her ability to produce urine."

Egan stopped talking, his lower lip quivered slightly and a single tear made its way from his right eye, and accelerated down his cheek and became lost in the tangled forest of his beard. Gail watched quietly, her turn to listen. "She developed a high fever the day after her forty-fifth birthday. At first we figured it was the flu, but soon it was clear even to my mother that more was going on and she was rushed to the hospital. It was an acute rejection crisis and within days the kidney failed and had to be removed. She seemed to give up after that and within a month or so she was gone. Somehow I can't quite get over the feeling that she was rejecting me or that my kidney failed her. Crazy huh?"

He looked at his watch. "Oh, shit; look at the time. I'd better get a move on." He sprang from the bed and scrambled for his scrubs that were scattered about the floor. Gail also sprang out of bed. "I'll go with you."

As they walked quickly toward the hospital, they discussed a plan for the day. Egan would go to rounds, and then they would meet up and go together to the in vitro clinic.

* * *

As he entered the hospital, he groaned inwardly as he saw Barrett who appeared to be dressing down one of the interns. Egan tried to avoid him, but it was too late. Barrett had already spotted him.

"Ah, Dr. Egan, gracing us with your presence. How nice!" Barrett said in a loud voice. Then, eyeing his rumpled, dirt-stained clothing added. "But you didn't have to dress up for the occasion."

"Good morning, Doug. I had a bit of an accident in the park this morning when I was running. I'm going to change into some scrubs."

"Wait, I have a little matter to discuss."

Egan sighed, but stopped and thought to himself, Barrett, you are the least of my problems.

"Egan, I know you consider yourself the top resident around here, and I admit you manage from time to time to stumble upon some rather interesting diagnoses, but that does not give you license to leave the medical center in the middle of the day. I was looking for you yesterday and could find neither hide nor hair of you."

"You weren't the only one," murmured Egan.

"What was that?"

"Oh, nothing.

"Let's face it, Egan; life here in the big medical center is not all peaches and cream. The point is you can't just take off in the middle of the day. We're talking responsibility to patients here."

"Barrett, for Christ's sake, I signed out to Meiselman."

"Mieselman?" snorted Barrett, with a short staccato laugh. "He has his hands full just servicing the nurses up on 8w, let alone handling his load and yours. You know the rules: Let me know if you have to leave the hospital."

Egan brought himself to an erect stance and giving a sharp salute said, "Ja Vol, Herr Kommandant, requesting permission to enter the bathroom to take a leak. I promise to think only of patients while my bladder empties." Egan spun around and walked quickly down the hall.

Barrett called after him: "Egan, wait, I haven't finished!"

Egan ignored him and continued on, his mind already deeply engaged in his plan for the day.

Chapter Forty-Nine
September 3, 2008 7:30 AM

Egan, as usual, joined rounds in progress. Johnson looked up and opened his mouth to remonstrate, but something about Egan's steely expression coupled with his obvious exhaustion caused him to pause and merely nod in greeting before turning back to the chart in his hand. Egan listened with half an ear and even when presenting his own patients, part of his mind was obsessing over the in vitro clinic. The rest of him was on automatic pilot. Thankfully rounds ended sooner than usual. He assigned tasks to the interns and medical students and abruptly left them, surprising them since he usually pitched in to help.

He headed toward the library resolving to learn as much as he could about the research underpinnings of the in vitro process hoping that it would give him some sort of clue.

He found a computer terminal half-hidden in the stacks and began to do a search. He started by entering Dr. George and soon was scanning articles written by him. He found himself impressed with the quality of the science and he read more carefully than he needed to the articles before him. He traced the research that had resulted in increasing refinement in the in vitro technique. After an hour or so he had a handle on the biochemical underpinnings. He read a series of papers that Dr. George had published while in Boston before he was lured down to New York. He looked at each article carefully, looking for a reference to protein F, but could find none. He yawned and stretched and put his head down on the desk.

Egan opened his eyes, feeling a cramp in his left jaw where it had been in contact with the hard desk surface. Saliva had pooled onto the Formica and had soaked the left part of his beard.

"So, you're awake."

He lifted his head. It was Gail. His mouth gaped open in a long yawn while he reached to pull her to him. She kissed the top of his head.

"You poor baby, you are so tired. But you got to wake up. We've got a lot to do. Here, let me show you something." Gail pulled out of her book bag a small, cylindrical device.

"What is that?" asked Egan with a puzzled expression.

"This is a small video camera, designed for secret surveillance."

He took it in his hand. "It is so small. It doesn't even look like a camera."

"Of course not, stupid. Remember it is for secret surveillance."

"I'll ignore the stupid part because I can't wait to hear just where you got this. Are you a CIA agent in your spare time?" his expression and tone showing that he was not only surprised but impressed by her resourcefulness.

"Believe it or not, this is hospital equipment. Remember that case of Munchausen's by proxy? I spent some time with Dr. Jason the child abuse expert discussing the case and she showed me the equipment. It's used to surreptitiously observe parents in the hospital room to see if they are doing anything to harm their child. She showed a videotape of a parent of a child who had had several episodes of stopping breathing and they were monitoring the baby in the hospital for possible sudden infant death syndrome. The video showed the mother looking around to make sure she was alone and then leaned forward with a pillow and placed it over the baby's mouth and nose long enough to set off the apnea alarm, which of course brought the hospital staff running. Really impressive. So I managed to borrow the equipment."

"Gail, you are amazing."

"Eric, you can complement me later. We have to get a move on. A guy named Carl who's a physician's assistant in the in vitro clinic said if we get there by 12, he'll show us around. Dr. George, by the way, is doing a scheduled c-section, so he won't be around."

* * *

They were greeted by Carl, a handsome man in his thirties, with a colorful silk tie, firmly knotted at the top and secured below with an ornate silver clip with a depiction of the Greek goddess of fertility, Aphrodite. He led them through the plush waiting area which was as always full of affluent and anxious looking couples. Both Gail and Eric couldn't help staring at one wall taken up entirely by a large fish tank. He guided them into the inner sanctum through a sturdy oak door. They walked down a long corridor that was ornately decorated with small statuettes which appeared to represent many cultures.

Carl stopped and turned to them. "This is our hall of fertility. And all these are goddesses of fertility from all over the world. As Dr. George says, we have the best technology in the world, but why not hedge our bets." He paused to smile and bowed slightly with his hands together in front of his chest to one of the statuettes.

"Take this one for example. That is Parvati, a Hindu goddess." He took a few steps and stopped before another. "And over here is Pachamama revered by the Incas."

Gail pointed to a wooden statue of a svelte woman with the head of a cat. "Who is that?"

"Oh that's one of my favorites. Her name is Bast, an ancient Egyptian goddess. I like to call her a "bast from the past.""

Eric and Gail both laughed politely at the joke. Eric looked at a porcelain depiction of a rather plump severe looking woman.

"That's Frigg, Odin's wife, in charge of fertility in Scandanavia."

They continued down the corridor. "In here are fairly standard exam rooms with what you'd see in any obstetricians office with ultrasound and the like. Let's proceed to the heart of the operation." They passed a door that had in large letters "Blake George MD"

"There's the boss's office."

They entered a large laboratory room. There were several white-coated technicians each leaning over microscopes.

"Here's where it all happens. Fertility evaluations like sperm counts in this area. Over there is the sterile room with positive pressure ventilation where the actual fertilization takes place."

"Wow!" exclaimed Egan. "This really looks like state-of-the-art equipment. Gail, check out this ultracentrifuge."

Egan, who had spent long hours in labs doing research began to examine the equipment with the air of a car enthusiast at an automobile show. Carl, delighted with his enthusiasm, launched into a long technical description.

"Excuse me, Carl," Gail interjected. "Can you tell me where the bathrooms are?"

Carl, bent over the ultracentrifuge, pointing out some of its features, gestured back toward the "fertility hall" they had just traversed. "Go to the right, the third door down on the left."

"Thanks, I'll be right back."

When Gail got back, the two men were still in front of the centrifuge engaged in an animated discussion of its features and comparing it to other models.

Gail laughed. "What is it about machines that fascinate guys so much?"

Carl paused and looked at his watch. "My goodness, where did the time go? Unfortunately, I don't have too much more time. Dr. George is due here in a half-hour and I have to prepare some slides for him. Tell you what, let's take a peak at the cryovault where embryos are stored and then call it a day. You can always come back another time."

"Sounds good to us" Said Egan. "We really appreciate all the time you spent with us."

They walked quickly toward another room dominated by a large walk-in freezer. "We won't actually go in, because there is a whole procedure to ensure that there are no temperature changes, but over here is a window where you can see most of it."

They spent some minutes peering into the freezer with neatly numbered containers covering the four walls from floor to ceiling.

"Each one of those has an embryo. There's a whole new generation in there, biding their time," said Carl with a smile.

* * *

After leaving the clinic, Egan turned to Gail. "So?"

Gail put her finger to her lips and they walked silently. The medical library was just one flight down and they took the stairs and Gail led Egan deep into the stacks to the small nook where they had first kissed.

"OK, out with it. Were you able to set it up?"

"Yes. I put one in George's office and another one in the corridor just outside the lab."

"Wow." Egan emitted a long low whistle. "Risky business. Christ, if someone finds them and identifies them as hospital equipment, the trail leads right back to us."

"Believe me, I know," said Gail, leaning forward in a whisper. "But George's propensity for ostentatious cultural artifacts gave me lots of choices for concealment. Anyway, it's a chance we have to take."

Egan shivered slightly and felt a dull throb in his leg at the site of his wound.

"That's quite an operation they have there. Did you notice that the so called fertility hall was fairly wide and then abruptly curves and narrows as it approaches the fertilization lab?"

"Yeah, struck me as somewhat unusual, but I assumed that the wide part was just to give more room for the fertility goddesses and the curvature was just to get around Dr. George's humongous office."

"You maybe right, Gail, but remember your anatomy. What does it remind you of?"

Gail thought and then exclaimed. "Fallopian tube!"

Chapter Fifty
September 3, 2008 2:30 PM

Egan took the call as he was walking down the corridor toward the pediatric floor. He had left Gail in the library to continue the literature research he had started that morning. "Hi, Dr. Egan, this is Dolores in OB at University. According to the schedule, you're on for the DR today."

Egan groaned inwardly. He had forgotten and with his sore leg acting up, he was looking forward to an afternoon not punctuated with sprints to the delivery room, particularly two blocks away at University Hospital. University Hospital was a part of the medical center, but a world apart. With a worldwide reputation for giving cutting-edge care in a rather luxurious setting, it attracted the infirm from upper crust households throughout the globe.

The residents, while spending most of their time at the main teaching hospital of Malloy, rotated for a month or two at University, enjoying the plush on-call rooms and spectacular food, but hating the schizophrenic difference from Malloy and being at the beck and call of the private attendings, the wealthy demanding patients and the highly paid nurses. Unlike at Malloy, where the residents ruled the roost, the residents did not even do a simple venipuncture without checking with the private attending physician.

"If you say so, Dolores."

"Dr. Egan, your enthusiasm is contagious. Anyway, right now the labor board is pretty quiet."

"So you're just calling me to tell me to just relax? That's very kind of you."

Dolores laughed. "Not quite, there is one little thing."

"There, that's more like the Dolores I've grown to love."

She laughed again. "Oh, Dr. Egan, if I was only twenty years younger. But anyway, Dr. George has a woman in labor, one of his in vitros, first pregnancy, no problems, but a bit of a VIP. He just thought she and her husband would feel a wee bit more comfortable with peds in the room."

"I see. How soon do you need me?"

"Her labor has been progressing nicely overnight and the baby's head is starting to crown, so if you could get here in half an hour that would work fine."

"Okay, I'll be there. I should look at the bright side. I'll get to see you."

Dolores was laughing as he signed off.

Half an hour later, as Egan neared the delivery room, he could hear the typical sounds of a delivery: a woman's low moans punctuated by sharp outcries, a man's voice tinged with panic. "Honey, breathe; you can do it," the cajoling intonation of the obstetrician "Joyce, you're doing fine. Okay, here's your contraction; push, push!" Egan went to the sink and began to scrub while continuing to listen for any signs that there were problems developing. After scrubbing, he dried, put on a surgical cap, mask, and gloves and he entered the delivery room.

Dr. George looked up. "Here's the pediatrician. Just routine. John and Joyce, meet Dr. Egan, one of the pediatric residents who will be checking your baby."

"A pleasure to meet you," said the father seated next to his wife's head. Between pants, the woman managed a brief smile and nod.

Egan greeted them both and stepped over to the resuscitation table. He turned on the overhead radiant warmer and light and spread out a hospital receiving blanket. He began to meticulously look at all the equipment to make sure that nothing was missing and all was in working order. He could hear the woman's moans decrease in intensity signally the end of a contraction. He was carefully testing the ambu bag for any leaks, when he sensed a presence next to him. He looked up and was startled. Dr. George was standing next to him. He leaned forward until his mask was almost touching Egan's.

"No dramatics; do you hear me?" hissed Dr. George in a low whisper. Before Egan could answer, the woman cried out and George scurried back to his stool. "Okay, Joyce, this is it. I can see the head, push."

Egan's forehead had broken out into a sweat, and he began to feel the familiar dread of an oncoming panic attack. His medicine was deep in his scrub pocket which was covered by the large delivery room gown he was wearing. The father's voice penetrated the roar that was beginning to rise inside his head. "Breathe, Joyce, nice cleansing breaths, breathe away the pain." The woman had a smile on her face that reminded Egan of a medieval painting with Madonna in adoration of the newborn Jesus. Egan found himself breathing in sync with the mother and the sense of panic began to recede.

"He's coming. Okay, Joyce, one more push."

A baby covered with mucous and blood slithered out in a whoosh of amniotic fluid wet and glistening like a newly caught salmon into George's waiting arms. Egan smiled to himself, thinking no baby like this would ever appear in a medieval painting or in a Gerber commercial.

After cutting the umbilical cord, George held up the baby for the parents to see. The baby let out a loud, lusty cry, which was music to Egan's ears. George brought over the baby to the resuscitation table and whispered to Egan. "Just a quick check, and then give the baby to the mother." Egan merely nodded, his irritation concealed by his surgical mask, as he began to suction out the amniotic fluid from the baby's mouth. He wiped off the rest of the baby and took his stethoscope and listened to the lungs and heart. He wrapped the baby in the blanket and carried him over to the parents who emitted familiar chortles of pleasure.

"Oh, darling, look at him. Let me hold him." Egan placed him into the woman's arms and stood gazing at the mother's beatific expression and he thought to himself that he had never seen anything so beautiful in his life.

Chapter Fifty-One
September 4, 2008 5:00 AM

It was still dark early the next morning when Egan awoke next to Gail who was still asleep. He thought for a moment to turn over and sleep for the hour left before his alarm was due to go off, but his mind, a restless cauldron of thoughts and worries, not to mention the throbbing pain in his leg, made sleep out of the question. He got silently out of bed, dressed quietly, and tiptoed downstairs without waking Gail.

He walked to the hospital. In the ICU, he headed toward the isolation room, but stopped short when he saw that both Mr. and Mrs. Gold were in the room with Newhouse and appeared to be engaged in a deep, serious conversation. Mrs. Gold, head in hands, was sobbing while Mr. Gold looked grimfaced at Newhouse as he talked. Egan could not catch the low tones of Newhouse's conversation, but could surmise that there had been some sort of devastating setback. He backed up and found the resident in charge of the ICU.

It was Dr. Richter.

"What's happening with the Gold baby?"

"Egan, what are you doing here? Aren't you off call?

"Yeah, but I admitted the Gold baby from the ER, and I couldn't sleep so I decided to swing by and see how he was. It looks like last rites in there. What the hell happened?"

"We're not really sure. To all appearances, the baby was turning the corner. During the night the baby abruptly began to show signs of increased intracerebral pressure. We, of course, hyperventilated the baby and even gave mannitol, but strangely that seemed to make it worse. We think he herniated, because his pupils are fixed and dilated and there are now no signs of brain activity on the EEG. So

Newhouse is talking to them and actually is hoping to get their consent for organ donation."

"Organ donation?" asked Egan in a surprised voice. "Aren't we being a little hasty here?"

"Well, you know as well as I do that once it gets to this stage, it is really quite hopeless, and if you leave these babies comatose on a vent too long, the organs start to deteriorate. Besides, there is a baby over at University Hospital that is a perfect match."

"A match? How the fuck do they know that already?"

"Hey, watch your language," answered Richter backing up a step. "You know how aggressive Newhouse is. He automatically sends blood for histocompatability typing on every ICU admission. That way, if God forbid something happens, we can act quickly. I know," continued Richter, eyeing the growing look of horror on Egan's face, "but think about it. It is really quite progressive, and transplants that have transformed adult medicine now are increasingly saving kids' lives."

"Do you," broke in Egan shaking his head, "also automatically send their measurements to the undertaker just in case? It probably would greatly speed up the logistics and paperwork in the unlikely event of a tragedy."

"I don't think that's funny. It's completely different."

"I don't know. I think if I was an ICU patient battling a serious illness, I would not find it relaxing to have potential transplant recipients coming by and rooting for my demise so they can get my kidney or liver. It is a bit like living in a house under threat of foreclosure and having potential buyers poking through your house just waiting for your financial collapse. By the way, does informed consent enter this picture at all?"

"Well, the consent form is actually an all-purpose one that has been carefully crafted and does mention this. It also emphasizes that this is a teaching hospital and major cutting edge research facility and so I think people are willing to give us wider latitude."

"I'll bet it is carefully crafted. Nothing like doctors and lawyers working together for the betterment of mankind."

"You are awfully cynical. Anyway, here comes Newhouse, he can explain the ethics of this more cogently than I."

"You know, that's okay. I've got a ton of paperwork over on peds, which I've been avoiding for weeks. I'll catch you later." And with that he hurriedly rushed out of the ICU.

* * *

"Where's he going in such a hurry?" asked Newhouse.

"Oh, he claims he's got paperwork, but probably anxious to get back to that cute medical student he has been carrying on with."

"I see. The hormones do rage in these residents," said Newhouse with a smile. "But I must say his expression was not that of someone running to meet his lover."

"Why Dr. Newhouse, I never have known you to show the slightest interest in the resident's romantic lives."

"Well, I'm quite interested, of course more so in some than in others," continued Newhouse giving her a flirtatious smile.

Richter colored slightly, but the welcoming smile of her face indicated that she clearly enjoyed this sort of attention.

"But seriously, Joan, what was he upset or angry about?"

"First of all, I don't think he had been aware of the deterioration in the Gold baby, but what really seemed to set him off was the speed with which the transplant was being arranged."

"I see. Did you tell him per chance about the automatic typing policy?"

"Well, I did. Is that a problem?"

"No, not really. I prefer that only the more mature residents like yourself know about it, who can, uh, appreciate the overarching purposes of the program." He reached his hand out and gripped her arm as talked. "Dr. Egan is brilliant, but between you and me, at times he fails to see the forest for the trees. But no problem, I'll have a discussion with him later. Now, my dear, we have work to do. The consent is all signed. Call the transplant coordinator."

Chapter Fifty-Two
September 5, 2008 6:00 AM

Egan's paperwork, in restful repose in his in-box, was in no danger of being disturbed. Instead of going to peds, he headed toward the postpartum ward at University, occasionally pausing to rub his leg. Once there, he scanned the chart rack and found the one he was looking for and began to study it. After ten minutes of careful review, he put it down, lifted his head and stared into space for a moment. He looked again at the front of the chart, muttering to himself, "Room 602." He got up and headed down the corridor. He stopped at room 602, pausing a moment before proffering a tentative knock. There was no sound from within the room, so he knocked again and opened the door slightly.

"It's Dr. Egan, the pediatric resident."

A sleepy male voice answered. "Sure, come on in."

He entered the room. On the hospital bed dominating the room, was a dark-haired woman that was a much more relaxed version of the woman he had seen the day before in the delivery room. She was asleep on her back with a swaddled infant cradled in her arms. Near the bed, the father was stretched out on a cot, his head up looking inquiringly at Egan. Egan took a glance at the brand new mother on the bed and was struck by the look, even in repose, of utter contentment on her face, a half smile, her cheeks with a beatific sheen, and was so transfixed by the scene that it was a long moment before he turned back to the man on the cot who was now smiling as well.

"They're beautiful, aren't they?"

"Well, yes," answered Egan, coloring slightly. "I'm sorry to disturb you so early in the morning, but I was in the delivery room when your baby was born and I just wanted to do a follow-up check on him."

"By all means. I'm sorry that I didn't recognize you. So you were that masked man who came in to save the day."

Egan suspected that there was a hint of sarcasm, but the smile that accompanied it, was so warm it somehow didn't bother him.

"Yes, that was me, the lone ranger." He answered with a sheepish smile. He looked at the mother and baby again. "Gosh, they look so peaceful. Perhaps I should come back a bit later."

"Don't worry about it. Hey, Joyce, the doctor is here to examine our son." Her eyes opened and her smile became radiant.

"By the way," continued the man while leaping agilely off the cot and extending his hand toward Egan, "I'm John Maitland. This is my wife Joyce and my son Jason."

"Pleased to meet you all." He stepped closer to the bed. "Can I take Jason for a moment? I can examine him right here in the bassinette." Joyce sat up and handed the baby to Egan who placed the baby gently into the bassinette. He slowly unwrapped the thin swaddling blanket in an attempt to not wake the baby. He removed the hospital issue infant shirt and for a moment simply looked at the baby. Joyce arose from the bed and joined her husband on the other side of the bassinette.

"Do you mind if we watch?" asked John.

Egan looked up at them standing, arms around each other with broad smiles. "Of course not. In fact, it's good that you watch so I can explain some things about your baby as I go along."

"Oh, good," answered Joyce while pulling her husband closer and giving him a quick kiss on the cheek.

Egan looked back down at the baby. "Okay, first part of the exam is to just watch the baby for a moment. He appears quite comfortable; his color is a healthy pink except for a bit of a blue cast to his hands and feet which is normal. He is breathing effortlessly, but notice the slight irregularity."

They leaned forward closer. "Watch his chest going up, down, there, did you see it speed up for several breaths? And now it's slowing down."

"Oh, yes, I see it." said Joyce. "Is that okay?"

"Absolutely. That's called periodic breathing, which all infants do. Next thing to observe is the muscle tone. See how his arms are flexed at the elbows and the legs at the knees and hips, like a frog? That's normal and tells me that his muscle tone is sufficient to sustain that posture." Egan looked at the couple, their rapt attention evident on their faces and continued.

"Now let me take advantage of his sleeping to get a good listen to his heart and lungs." He took his stethoscope that he had draped around his neck, placed the ear pieces and leaned forward and placed the diaphragm onto the baby's chest. After a moment of several re-positions, he looked up. "The heart sounds fine and the lungs are clear." He palpated the baby's abdomen and ran his hand along the suture lines of the baby's skull, pausing over a soft area on the top of the head. "This is the anterior fontanelle. A baby's skull is made up of plates of bone that are not fused yet. That gives it some flexibility to allow it to squeeze through the birth canal. The anterior fontanelle is where four different bones meet. Hope I'm not boring you with all this."

"No, not at all," said John. "This is fascinating. A question about the fontanelle. Should we be careful about touching it?"

Egan smiled. "Babies are not nearly as vulnerable as you may imagine. The fontanelle covering is like thick leather. Here, check something else out. Look really closely at the fontanelle and tell me if you notice anything."

They both peered closely. "Why it's moving!" exclaimed Joyce.

"Absolutely" said Egan. "The baby's heart is pumping blood into the brain and the pulsations are transmitted to the cerebral spinal fluid that surrounds the brain which is just under the fontanelle. So that tells me that your baby's brain is well nourished with blood flow."

"Doctor," said Joyce with a smile. "Isn't he beautiful? We waited so long for him and I just can't believe we have him now."

"He is beautiful," Egan answered. "And that's a professional opinion," he added with a laugh and the Maitlands laughed as well, almost giddily.

Egan watched the couple for a moment, transfixed by the sheer delirious pleasure that the couple exhibited with their new baby. "So you waited a long time. I saw in the chart that you used in vitro. I'm very happy for you." He paused for a moment. "I said before that babies are less vulnerable than we think, but you should know that they are a bit more prone to infection than older children or adults. So if Jason develops any fever, you should seek medical attention right away. In fact, you can feel free to call me. I'll give you my cell number." He reached into his pocket and handed him a card.

"Well, that's awfully kind of you, but we do have a private pediatrician."

"I understand. It's hard to explain, but I have a feeling of responsibility toward babies when I attend them in the delivery room. You can call me as well and anyway if you call at 3 AM, I'm more likely to be awake and alert than your private."

Maitland looked at Egan for a moment. "Do you have some reason to be more concerned than usual?"

"No, not at all. But do feel free to call. Again, congratulations." Egan turned toward the door and as he reached for the handle he grimaced and instead of the door knob, he grabbed his calf.

"Hey, are you okay?" asked John.

"Yeah, I'm fine. I injured my leg a couple of days ago, sort of a freak accident and occasionally my calf muscle just cramps up. It's a long story." He straightened up and tried to smile through his pain.

"Here, let me get the door for you," said John.

"Thanks, and don't hesitate to call me," said Egan as he left the room and started down the corridor. John Maitland stood at the door watching him limp down the hall until he turned the corner and was out of sight.

Chapter Fifty-Three
September 2008

"Fasi, darling, please sit down and try to relax. Your constant pacing is making me nervous."

The prince ignored his wife's admonition and continued to walk energetically up and down the room. He took a look at his watch and muttered, "Ten after ten, and he promised to call me by ten at the latest."

Farah continued to watch her husband. She was still trying to get used to the man her husband had become. His intense preoccupation with their son's illness was on the one hand very gratifying and she admired this strong, competent leader who had heretofore not been evident. On the other hand, she missed his easy charm and humor. All their conversations now were about his son and his medical care, not that she was indifferent, but just once she wanted to laugh and talk about something else.

She got up from the settee, and intercepted her husband.

"Darling, you have to try to relax. Our son is not going to get better overnight. I don't want you to burn out. By the time our son is cured, you'll be a wreck. Where will that leave us?"

She could sense that her words were having an effect. His shoulders sagged and he turned around in her embrace and held her tightly.

"So you believe he will be cured?"

"Yes, darling, he will be. I know it."

The phone rang and the prince wriggled free from the embrace and pounced on it.

"Yes, this is the prince."

The prince listened intently for some minutes and then broke into a wide smile. "That's wonderful. We will be on the next flight."

The prince hung up the phone, turned to Farah and clasped her in a tight embrace, his eyes closed and smiling. Farah's eyes were wide open staring at the far wall. "Allah, forgive us," she said under her breath.

Chapter Fifty-Four
September 10, 2008   11:00 PM

Joyce stood over the bassinette watching Jason, who was sleeping peacefully. John came up behind her, slipping his arms around her waist and pulled her toward him.

"Isn't he beautiful? I just can't get enough of him."

"Yes, he is," answered John while nuzzling her neck. "And so are you." He gave her stomach a gentle squeeze. "And getting smaller by the minute."

"Why thank you, but I have to give Jason the credit for that. Nursing is a great weight loss tool. It's better than liposuction."

"Actually, it literally is liposuction—it involves lips and suction and the direct removal of fat."

"Along with some protein, carbohydrates, and all the other nutrients a growing baby needs," Joyce added while turning around to face John and putting her arms around his neck. "This is so surreal. I just can't believe that we are in our apartment with a baby. Every time he cries, I go, whoa, is that really our baby? I can't think about anything else.

"You know, Fred called me from work and he was in the middle of telling me about this tort case I was working on before the baby was born and I realized I hadn't heard a word he had said and that I didn't really care. I'm not sure I can go back after three months. All I want to do is stare at Jason and take care of him."

A slight sound from the bassinette caused them both to look again at the baby. "Oh, look, isn't that cute the way he roots around with his mouth? Looks like he wants to eat. Christ, it's only been two hours."

"Honey, I don't think my milk is in. Do you think you can do it this time?"

"That joke, while mildly amusing the first time, pales considerably by the fiftieth," said Joyce as she began to unbutton her shirt and unclasp her nursing bra. She bent forward and picked up Jason and carried him to a nearby rocking chair. Jason continued his increasingly energetic rooting and Joyce, once settled into the rocker, positioned the baby's mouth next to the nipple of her breast. The infant frantically bobbed his head until his mouth found just the right position and began to suck vigorously while Joyce began to rock gently.

"Honey, I'm going to the kitchen. Do you need anything?"

"Sure, a cup of herbal tea would be nice. Thanks." John left the bedroom.

Some twenty minutes later he returned to find both mother and son asleep. With a smile, he put down the cup of tea and carefully removed Jason from Joyce's arms and walked over to the bassinette where he placed the infant, and returned to Joyce.

"Come on, darling. Time for bed."

Joyce awoke with a panicked jerk looking frantically around. "Where is he?"

"Joyce, Joyce, it's okay, I put him to bed."

"Oh, God, I thought I'd dropped him or something."

"Come on, let me put you to bed. Everything is fine."

Joyce allowed herself to be pulled to her feet and padded over to the bassinette before collapsing on her bed. "Christ," she murmured, "I never really knew the meaning of the word 'worry' until I had a child."

"There, there," said John while stroking her cheek. "Everything will be fine." Her eyes slowly closed. John pulled the sheet and blanket over her shoulders and soon was fast asleep himself.

Some four hours later, Joyce stirred partially awake, vaguely aware of a feeling of pressure and her hands went to her chest. She awoke more fully and realized that the sensation was that her breasts were full and tense, with leaking milk having already soaked through her bra and onto the sheets. She sat up and listened, turned on the bedside lamp and moved quickly out of the bed and over to the bassinette.

"What's going on?" asked John sleepily from the bed.

"Sorry. I woke up because my breasts were engorged, and I got worried because usually Jason starts crying and wanting to nurse long before that happens. But, he seems to be breathing and okay." She bent and picked up the infant. "Come on, buddy, you've got to nurse whether you want to or not. Mommy is suffering." She placed him at her breast.

"John, I think something's wrong."

"Oh, honey, I'm sure everything is okay," answered John groggily.

"John, wake up. He doesn't seem right. He won't take the breast."

"For goodness' sake, Joyce," exclaimed John, sitting up. "Calm down."

"Calm down yourself. I think he feels warm."

John without a word got up from the bed, padded into the bathroom and returned with an infant thermometer. "Here, Joyce, let's take his temperature and then we can all go back to sleep."

They placed the baby on his stomach, and John inserted the thermometer tip and then waited for a beep and removed it and peered at the small digital screen. John paled.

"What is it?"

"It's 101.2."

Chapter Fifty-Five
September 11, 2008 2:00 AM

Egan was in a deep state of sleep when he gradually became aware that his cell phone was chirping.

"Hello, Dr. Egan here."

"Dr. Egan, this is John Maitland. I'm so sorry to wake you, but I'm having trouble contacting my pediatrician and you did say we could call anytime."

"Absolutely and I meant it. What's going on?"

"Our baby has developed a fever. I'm sure it's nothing serious, but Joyce is quite worried."

Egan could feel his heart beginning to pound in his chest.

"How much fever?

"Little over 101."

"How did you take the temp?"

"With a brand new digital rectal thermometer."

"So it's probably accurate. How does the baby look otherwise?"

"Okay, I think."

"Feeding normally?"

"Well, actually, he's overdo for a nursing and doesn't seem that interested."

"Mr. Maitland, how far are you from the hospital?"

"Ten blocks or so."

"I want you to bring the baby to the hospital pediatric emergency room as soon as possible. I'll meet you there."

Egan rolled out of bed and quickly got dressed. Minutes later he was en route to the hospital. He sprinted into the front entrance of the ER. Thankfully, it was quiet.

"Hey, what's going on?"

It was Tina. "I'm glad you're working tonight. Listen, a ten-day old baby with fever is coming over momentarily."

"Should I wake the ER resident?"

"That's okay, no need to disturb him. I'll do the workup."

"Okay, I'll get out the spinal tray and the culture bottles."

"Great, I'll help you."

Within minutes everything was laid out, and Egan began to pace with occasional pauses to look at his watch. Then he heard the sounds of running footsteps in the corridor.

Ten minutes later, Egan was lifting his eyes from the microscope, his face set in a grim frown. "Tina!"

Chapter Fifty-Six
September 11, 2008 3:00 AM

Egan burst into the treatment room. Both John and Joyce looked up, startled, from chairs next to a gurney. Their infant was in Joyce's lap.

"Your baby has early meningitis."

"Oh, my god," said John while reaching for his wife while her face convulsed in quiet sobs.

"I'm sorry to be so blunt, but we have to act quickly. I'd like to get an IV in and start antibiotics right away."

Tina stepped forward to take the baby. Joyce gave him a kiss and handed him to her, then collapsed back into her chair, her sobs increasing in intensity. Tina placed the baby on the gurney and immediately Egan looked for a vein. He could feel his heart pounding and he willed himself to pause for a moment, remembering that old saw, that the first pulse the doctor should take in an emergency is his own. Tina straightened out the infants arm and Egan put a small tourniquet above the elbow then began to gently palpate the crook of the elbow.

"I think I feel one," he whispered and without another word reached his hand out. Tina placed an alcohol swab into his hand which he used to clean the skin over the vein. He extended his hand again for the IV catheter and needle that Tina had at the ready. He took a deep breath, exhaled slowly, and he could feel his pulse slowing down. He remembered reading that sharpshooters timed their trigger squeezes to occur in between heartbeats lest the faint vibration alter the bullets course. He plunged the needle and immediately felt the pop of the needle entering the vein, then holding his hand absolutely still, used his thumb to advance the catheter. He removed the needle and jabbed it into the mattress to keep the sharp point out of harm's way and nurse and doctor with ballet-like coordination taped the minute catheter into place with several thin strips wrapping around the hub designed to hold the precious venous access firmly in place.

"Dr. Egan, do you want me to prepare the ampicillin and gentamycin?"

"We'll go with ampicillin, but I'm going to push cefotaxime instead of gentamycin to cover pneumococcus. I already have it drawn up—400 milligrams. Go ahead and draw up 200 of ampicillin."

Egan took from his side lab coat pocket a fluid filled syringe and attached it to hub and began to slowly push the fluid into the baby's intravenous line.

"Is he going to be all right?" Joyce's soft voice coming from behind him jolted Egan. He could barely will himself to turn to face her. In his mind's eye, he could see her beatific smile and when he turned, he looked at a face with grief and worry etched into every furrow. He looked at her speechless for a moment and at John, ashen faced who had his arms around Joyce.

"Your son has bacterial meningitis which is potentially a very serious disease, but we have caught it incredibly early in its course. Just to give you some perspective, I admitted a baby a couple of weeks ago with meningitis who had in the spinal fluid moderate bacteria and 850 white cells, which is considered very early. Your baby has only 75 white cells and scant bacteria, so I'm very hopeful that the antibiotics will be very effective."

"Doctor, I have the ampicillin ready."

"Okay, thanks, Tina. Mr. and Mrs. Maitland, we'll sit down and talk but first I've got to do a few more things. Jason will be admitted to the ICU and will get the best possible care."

Joyce collapsed into her husband's arms. John held her tightly and looking at Egan said, "Doc, do all you can. Jason is everything to us."

Egan reached his arm out and clasped his shoulder.

Twenty minutes later having given the additional meds, written IV orders and performing a careful reexamination of the infant, Egan picked up the phone and dialed the pediatric ICU.

"Hey, Jane, this is Eric Egan. I'm down in the ER with a baby with early meningitis. Yeah, I know, another one. Listen, who's the on-call resident for the ICU. Michael? Great, can you get him to the phone? Thanks."

While he waited for Michael, he leaned back in his chair and stared at the ceiling. Then hearing Michael's voice he sat up putting his elbows on the desk. "Michael, it's Eric. I hate to add to your workload, but I have a baby with early meningitis." Egan quickly outlined the clinical details and then paused for a moment listening.

"Yeah, I know, I'm not on call, but the father called me." Another pause. "Well, I gave it to him. Anyway, Michael, that's not important now. I want to get this kid up to the unit as soon as possible. I'm so glad you're up there. Watch this kid like a hawk. I can't deal with another brain dead baby." Pause. "Yeah, I know, but with everything that's going on—in fact I may just watch the baby myself." Pause "Okay, maybe you're right. I'll go home and sleep for a while, but promise me you won't leave the ICU. Okay, thanks, buddy."

In ten minutes, Michael strode into the ER, looked over the chart and orders, did his own exam and sat down with Egan and the Maitlands.

John and Joyce, now composed and holding hands, listened intently.

"You're in good hands with Dr. Meiselman. I'm going home to sleep but will check in with Jason in the morning."

"Thanks, doc," said John standing up and reaching to clasp Egans hand with his two hands. "We are so grateful you came in on your off time."

"Happy to do it," answered Egan. He left the room and with one backward glance saw the Maitlands leaning forward, listening

intently to Michael. Their faces were solemn and cleared-eyed, perhaps hopeful and Egan could only imagine the bottomless sorrow
that a parent confronts when contemplating the possible loss of a
child. He could not get Joyce's face out of his mind as it had been that
early morning shortly after the birth.

Chapter Fifty-Seven
September 11, 2008 5:00 PM

"What? I don't believe it!" shouted Egan into the phone. "You can't treat meningitis any earlier. It's not possible. What the hell happened?"

"Eric, I don't know exactly. Apparently his kidneys suddenly failed which then caused an abrupt increase in intracranial pressure. They just finished doing an EEG which is flat line," answered Gail who was sitting at the nurse's station approximately ten feet from the bed of Jason Maitland who lay shock still with a ventilator hissing and surrounded by doctors and nurses.

"I'd better get over there. Did you talk to Michael?"

"Yes, he is baffled and pretty upset. Eric, the transplant coordinator is here and I believe he has already talked to them. Joyce left sobbing ten minutes ago with John right behind her."

"Shit, this is déjà vu all over again. I suppose they already have a recipient."

"Well, yeah, the kidneys are shot, but the heart is in good shape and apparently there is a kid from Saudi Arabia over at the VIP wing who needs one."

"I don't believe it. They couldn't have gotten back the histocompatibility tests yet."

"You're right, but the blood groups are identical. And that may be close enough."

"Gail, I'm getting dressed as we talk. Sit tight and tell Michael not to let them do anything until I get there. I'm going to the VIP wing first."

"Eric, be careful."

Egan took quick steps as he headed toward University Hospital. He arrived there and found his way up to the main pediatric ward.

"Dr. Egan," exclaimed a tall redheaded nurse, "what are you doing here? I thought you had finished your rotation here for the year. How nice to see you."

"Mary, it's nice to see you too. I missed the abuse that you all dish out, so I put in a special request to come back."

"Abuse, ha! We treated you royally and you know it."

"Mary, I'm actually here to find out about a patient, I don't know the name, but I believe it's a child of about ten months old from Saudi Arabia with congenital heart disease. He's due for a transplant and we think we have found a match."

"Oh, are you on the transplant rotation? I thought that only third years or fellows were eligible for that."

"Mary," said Egan smiling, "for an exceptional resident like me, exceptions are made. I talked my way onto it."

"You are a glutton for punishment. The kid's name is Ali Fasi, and we are talking major VIP. He and a rather large entourage are down in the Carlton suite."

Egan sat down with the chart and carefully went through it. He learned that Ali Fasi had been born with a hypoplastic left heart and had required lifesaving surgery in the first few days of life. He had endured three other trips to the operating room in his young life in an increasingly desperate attempt to correct what life had so cruelly apportioned to him. After the third procedure his heart went into failure, and now Egan could see he was on a long list of medications designed either to increase the pumping strength of the heart or to help the kidneys excrete the extra fluid and thus lessen the heart's burden. Since then, it apparently had been a grim wait for either death or a transplant. Egan knew that the odds were not good; donor hearts for babies were almost nonexistent. Egan looked at the date of the admission and noted that he had been admitted just two days before.

Egan closed the chart and looked thoughtfully at the ceiling. He was startled to feel fingers digging into his shoulders and he jumped.

"Boy, are you tense," said Mary, who had come up behind him to give him a soothing massage, a service she bestowed upon a few honored residents.

"Sorry, Mary, I've had a run of on calls you wouldn't believe." Egan settled back in his seat to enjoy the massage. He could feel the gentle pressure of her breasts against his shoulder blades and he luxuriated in the sensation.

"Mary, this is heavenly, but Newhouse will kill me if I don't finish here." Egan got up and went down the hall toward the Carlton suite. The suite consisted of three rooms: an outer one, which was the hospital room proper, albeit luxuriously outfitted; an inner room that functioned as a living quarters for family members; and a small kitchen. The door was partially open, so he poked his head in and found himself facing a group of some ten people of various ages and genders. The patient was sitting up in the hospital crib. There were several people seated together companionably talking in low tones. A man with a swarthy complexion stood upon seeing Egan and approached him with a polite smile.

"Excuse me for intruding," began Egan, "I'm Dr. Egan, one of the residents on the transplant team."

"A pleasure, Dr. Egan," answered the man in accented, but precise English. "I am Prince Fasi and this is my wife, Farah." He gestured to one of the woman on the Queen Ann couch. "And excuse me if I don't introduce you to everybody, but they are my family."

Egan bowed slightly to the group who all regarded him with mild interest.

"Sir, er, prince. I am just doing routine weekend rounds and just checking on how your son is doing."

"Ah, yes, rounds. I've already learned how important rounds are in an American hospital. But excuse me for asking, my experience has been that the doctors round in groups, large groups like a Bedouin family moving from oasis to oasis."

"Yes, you are quite right, but this is Saturday and usually it is done alone since it is the weekend."

"Oh, yes, I understand. The rest of the team has already gone to the Hamptons?"

"Exactly, but somebody has to hold down the fort and that's me."

"Hold down the fort. I'm sorry, this is an idiom I am not familiar with."

"Sorry, prince, I just mean I am on duty," said Egan as he tried to hide his impatience with this conversation. "Anyway, how is your son doing?"

"He is doing well. He is comfortable. He will be so much better after the transplant. He has suffered so much in his young life. When we heard about the heart, we were very excited and our jet took off immediately and here we are."

"What day did you hear? I'm just curious."

"Oh, I believe it was Thursday."

Egan's face was impassive, but inside his brain was spinning. Thursday was the day he admitted Jason with meningitis.

"Well, prince, we are mighty excited also. Let me examine your son."

He approached the crib, where the ten-month old eyed him warily, but thankfully allowed Egan to listen to him without crying. He noted the large surgical scar in the front of his chest, the slightly rapid breathing and bluish tint to his lips and extremities that identified him as a cardiac patient as surely as if he had a written sign on him. Upon touching the stethoscope to the front of the chest, he heard a loud whooshing murmur, sounding like a mighty river trying to push through a narrow canyon. He listened intently trying to separate out and classify each of the different sounds, which was made more difficult by the intensity of the murmur.

He closed his eyes and leaned forward, his forehead furrowed in concentration and held his breath. There, he could just barely make out the first and second heart sounds, S1 and S2 and finally he was aware of a third extra heart sound, S3, usually a sign of a failing heart. He began to breathe again and his auditory attention began to wane as he became aware of input from one of his other senses. It was an odor, distinct, but hard to characterize. Without thinking he leaned even closer so his flared nostrils were just above the boy's chest and sniffed. Yes, there was a faint but definite odor of fish. Suddenly remembering that the boy's father was watching, he jerked up with an embarrassed smile. The prince merely smiled benignly back at him.

"Yes, I know. He smells slightly of fish. We have noticed it since he was just a few weeks old. But it's quite faint, isn't it? You are actually the first doctor to notice it. I'm thinking that when he gets his new heart, perhaps it will go away. Whatever, as long as he is healthy I don't care what he smells like."

"You're right it is quite faint and of no significance. Anyway from a cardiac standpoint I think he is quite stable today. Do you have any questions?"

"I don't think so. Oh, will Dr. Newhouse come by later?"

"I'm not sure. But you can be assured that whether he comes or not, he is following all the details of your son's care with his usual meticulous attention."

"I know. Doctor, before you go I have a little gift for you." He reached into a drawer where Egan could see several small gift-wrapped boxes and handed him one.

"Prince, please, you don't have to."

"No, I insist. You cannot refuse. To do so is very insulting in the Saudi culture," he said with a smile.

After a few more minutes of polite sparring, Egan left defeated carrying the small gift. He opened it as he walked. It was a Rolex watch.

Chapter Fifty-Eight
September 12, 2008 6:00 PM

Egan left University Hospital and began to walk, his head down, deep in thought, toward Malloy Medical.

"You bastard."

The voice intruded harshly upon his intense internal preoccupation and he jerked his head up from the sidewalk he had been staring at as he walked and found himself eye to eye with John Maitland. Maitland stared at Egan with hostile intensity, fists clenched. Before Egan could recover enough from his confusion to utter a single word, Maitland's right fist had swung in a wide arc and landed squarely on Egan's chin sending him spinning backwards.

Somehow he remained on his feet and had just enough time to exclaim, "What the hell?" when a charging John Maitland was upon him. Down he went with Maitland on top, his head hitting the sidewalk with a resounding thud.

Maitland began to pummel him with his fists while Egan held his arms up trying to protect his face. Suddenly it was over, like a summer squall that had spent itself. Maitland's hands dropped to his side and he rolled off of Egan while emitting loud sobs. Egan sat up rubbing his chin, totally nonplussed and merely sat watching Maitland heave with his face buried in his hands. Finally, Egan reached a tentative hand to Maitland's shoulder.

"Mr. Maitland, what is going on?"

Maitland sobbed another minute and then looked at Egan and winced when he saw the bleeding on his face.

"Shit, I'm sorry. Despite everything, you don't deserve what I did."

"Despite everything? What the hell are you talking about? Listen, I know that your baby took a serious turn for the worse and you have every reason to be grief-stricken, but Jesus." Egan began to rub his chin which was beginning to ache.

"You really don't know? Didn't Dr. Newhouse talk to you?"

"I have no idea what you're talking about."

"Well, I think you know that they began to have trouble controlling the pressure in his brain and things got worse and worse until they told us he was brain dead."

Maitland paused for a moment looking away from Egan, taking deep breaths as he attempted to regain his composure. Finally, he turned back to Egan and continued. "When Dr. Newhouse told us that, we were of course shocked. Apparently, they are already talking about him as an organ donor."

"Yes, I heard all that."

"Well anyway, Joyce and I asked questions about how this could have happened and finally Dr. Newhouse told us of the mistake you made."

"What? The mistake I made? For Christ's sake. I made the diagnosis, started treatment right away. Newhouse actually gave me effusive praise for my handling of the case, I mean your son. Even you and your wife were thanking me, don't you remember?"

"You really don't know anything about this," Maitland said shaking his head. "Well, Dr. Newhouse actually pulled out the chart and handed me a lab slip. It showed an extremely toxic level of gentamycin and he said the only explanation is that you mixed up the doses of the antibiotics and that you gave ten times the normal dose of gentamycin which severely damaged his kidneys and caused a sudden retention of fluid, which led to the brain to reach pressures that on top of the meningitis went past the point of no return." Maitland's words tumbled out of him at an increasingly rapid rate and an increasingly angry edge returned to his tone.

Egan could only look at him, dumbfounded, unable to speak as he searched his memory banks frantically, trying to picture his actions in the ER. "Gentamycin?"

Chapter Fifty-Nine
September 13, 2008 9:00 AM

Egan entered the room located on the eighth floor. A small plaque was mounted above the door: "The Doris Levy Pediatric Conference Room - in memory of Doris Levy MD, chair of pediatrics, 1952 -1960."

The Levy room, modest in size, but located near the pediatric wards, served as a handy refuge for residents with a free half-hour to read, or as a site for impromptu conferences. It was book-lined with an eclectic mixture of modern texts and older books apparently from Dr. Levy's private collection. Every bit of wall space not taken up with book shelves had period portraits of various pediatric chairmen stretching back to the 1800s. Labeled by recent residents the "ghost room," it nevertheless was a popular refuge and Egan often found himself folded into one of the overstuffed chairs reading a journal, occasionally looking up to gaze at one of the mustached men on the walls. Also at one end of the room was a small conference table that was used often to conduct oral exams and thus one side of the table had several chairs for exam proctors while the other side contained just one chair, the hot seat as it was known.

It was to this seat that Egan was directed to by Newhouse with a silent gesture. He sat down, the room quiet except for rustling of papers and the faint hum of the cooling system. A bead of sweat formed on his forehead as he surveyed the panel before him. Dr. George was sitting upright, perfectly groomed and was engaged in a minute examination of his fingernails. Doug Barrett, leaning forward on his elbows, tapping the sides of his cheeks while his foot beat out a different rhythm, looked away when Egan looked at him. Newhouse was in the middle, a sheaf of papers in his hands, his gaze

fixed just over Egan to the back of the room. Egan shuffled restlessly in his chair, unable to find a comfortable position. He looked
above the group in front of him at the array of bow-tied, monocled,
bearded former chairmen portraits that seemed to be all staring at
him with stern disapproval. The continuing silence seemed interminable to Egan. Finally, Newhouse broke the silence with a clearing
of his throat. "Dr. Egan, I think you have an idea of why you have
been summoned here.'

"Well, yeah, I do, though it would have been nice not to have
learned about it after getting punched by an angry father."

"We are sorry about that. It was, uh, inadvertent and unfortunate."

"Wait a minute, Mr. Maitland told me you pulled the chart out
to point out exactly what I did wrong."

"Dr. Egan," broke in Dr. George whose gaze had left his nails to
bore into Egan. "That is a minor point. I suggest you just calm down
and we will not be diverted from our purpose here, to review your
care of a baby, who I delivered by the way and who now lies brain
dead down the hall." George half rose out of his seat as he spoke.

"Everybody calm down," said Newhouse putting a restraining
arm on George's shoulder. "Let's review the facts, shall we?"

Newhouse stopped to gaze at the chart in front of him and
continued. "Baby Maitland presented to the Emergency Room on
Thursday with signs and symptoms of a serious infection. Dr. Egan,
for reasons that are not clear, came in when he was not on call from
home to evaluate the baby, which by the way, is against hospital
rules. The attending should have been notified."

"Jesus," began Egan becoming red-faced, but Newhouse held his
hand out to silence him.

"Dr. Egan, you will have plenty of time to defend yourself, but I
must ask you for now to simply listen. Anyway, you made the diagnosis of meningitis. You started an IV and immediately pushed an
antibiotic that you drew up yourself, which also is against hospital
policy. The nurse should have drawn it up."

"For Christ's sakes," Egan broke in no longer able to restrain himself, "but Jack—"

"I'm Dr. Newhouse to you. Language, Dr. Egan. To continue, the antibiotic you drew up was gentamycin, four hundred milligrams which is ten times the therapeutic dose."

"No, no it wasn't gentamycin, it was cefotaxime, 400 milligrams."

"I'm sorry, Dr. Egan, but we have every reason to believe it was gentamycin. Anyway, isn't gentamycin standard at this age for a baby with sepsis or meningitis?"

"Yeah, yeah," answered Egan, "but I could see the bacteria for myself on the microscope slide, it was definitely pneumo. So I chose cefotaxime, I'm sure of it."

"Aren't you just a bit too sure of yourself?" interposed Dr. George. "Should a second-year resident be making a decision to deviate from an accepted antibiotic protocol based on a ten-second scan of a slide?"

"Dr. George, we'll get into that, but let's stick to outlining just the facts." Newhouse said. "Dr. Egan, isn't it possible that you simply in the heat of the moment grabbed the wrong bottle?"

"No, I am quite certain that I pushed 400 milligrams of cefotaxime. You can ask Tina. She was right next to me."

"We did ask Tina, and she could tell us that you said it was cefotaxime. Like we said, she didn't draw it up herself, you did."

"I'm sure it was cefotaxime."

"Well, then, hotshot, explain this," said Dr. George as he slid a sheet of paper toward Egan. The paper wafted off the table did a double flip and landed at Egan's feet. He bent over, picked it up and peered anxiously at it.

It took him a moment to comprehend what he was looking at; the printed words were just a meaningless jumble as he listened to the pounding of his heart. Finally the words leapt out at him "gentamycin level 10.2—toxic range above 3.4". He blinked his eyes disbelievingly, and hot tears blurred the words before they came into focus again.

"This is unbelievable," sputtered Egan finally finding his voice. "I'm sure I drew up and gave cefotaxime and in fact I believe it's in my note."

"Well, yes it is," said Newhouse, "but look, nobody is saying you did it intentionally. I'm sure you thought you were giving the right medication, but there unfortunately is indisputably the lab value you have before you."

Egan stared at the laboratory sheet again trying to will with his eyes a different number. How on earth could he have done such a thing? He wracked his brains trying to reconstruct that morning, to conjure up a visual memory of the antibiotic vial that he used to inject from, but could not come up with a focused image. He was sure, yet now doubt began to creep into his thinking and he began to mentally castigate himself as flashes of the baby on the respirator, the Maitlands tortured expressions began to crowd out all other mental images.

"Dr. Egan," continued Newhouse, "our committee conferred prior to you coming in and I think I can safely speak for all of us in saying that nothing that you have told us changes the regretful but inevitable decision we have come to." Newhouse paused to look briefly at the other panel members who all nodded in assent with Dr. George's head bobbing being particularly energetic.

"It is with considerable pain that I inform you Dr. Egan, that as of" Newhouse paused to look at his watch, "9:35 AM, you are suspended from the medical staff pending a full investigation. During this investigation, you are prohibited, I repeat, prohibited from stepping foot on hospital grounds or contacting any of the hospital staff."

Chapter Sixty

September 13, 2008 3:00 PM

Gail found him sitting under a tree in Central Park at one edge of a large meadow where in happier times he would go for a run or a Frisbee catch. Egan looked up with a wan smile.

"You know I have been looking for you and calling you for the last three hours."

"I know, I picked up the phone a dozen times, but couldn't bring myself to call you back. Suspended. I feel so utterly worthless and ashamed. All I have wanted since I was fourteen years old was to be the best doctor I could be and now that has all gone up in smoke. All I can think about is the Maitlands and their baby. Like Newhouse has said, the devil is in the details. I do everything right and make one lousy, stupid mistake. I don't think I can ever again look a parent in the eye and ask them to entrust their child's care to me."

"Eric, don't talk that way; you are a wonderful doctor."

"Yeah, yeah, and everybody makes mistakes, right?"

"You're damn right. But I'm not so sure you even made a mistake."

"Ah, Gail, it is so nice of you to try to make me feel better, but I have agonized over this and I can't think of any other explanation for that high gentamycin level. Christ, to seize someone from the brink of death and then to carelessly—like a fireman tripping on the way out of a fire and dropping the victim he just rescued back in to the inferno."

"No, listen to me. You're not the only one agonizing. Damn it, you could have called me. I thought we had a really good thing going. Do you really think I love you one iota less even if you did make a mistake? Are you so full of yourself that you think you can nobly suffer alone and not think for a moment of what I'm going through on your behalf?"

Egan looked at her for the first time and their eyes held each other for a long moment.

Finally, Egan reached his arms out and Gail slid into his embrace.

"Christ," whispered Egan, "I'm really fucking up on all fronts."

"Listen." Gail's voice broke the calm interlude of their embrace. "There is something that I just can't fathom. Why did they order a gentamycin level? I mean you wrote in your note that you had given cefotaxime and that is the antibiotic that was continued in the ICU. I mean, a fairly sick baby in the ICU can go into kidney failure for any number of reasons. Presumably, they would test for it only if they knew the baby had received it."

"Gail, how do you know all this?"

"Well, rather than sit around waiting for you to call, I took a fine tooth comb to the chart."

"They let you look at it? I figured that it would have been sequestered or something."

"No, the chart is in the ICU. Amazing how a medical student can fly under the radar. Nobody said boo when I went in there. Anyway, there is no mention of gentamycin in any of the ICU notes."

Egan's face took on an animation that had been absent for several hours. "Gail, I think you're right. It is odd. And I'll tell you something else that's odd and I have been too busy feeling sorry for myself to even give it any thought. There is an infant over in University Hospital that is apparently a match for the Maitland baby's heart."

"Yeah, I heard that. What is so odd about that?"

"I went over to University just before the shit hit the fan. This baby's father is, from what I can tell, a wealthy Saudi who was summoned here before the Maitland baby became brain dead. Can you imagine that? Have them fly over all the way from the Middle East just for the possibility of a heart?"

"That is really strange. Eric, something is going on and I can't help but think that you are being scapegoated. Look, we've got to do something."

"Like what. I'm fresh out of ideas. I'm on suspension so I can't do any more poking around."

"Hey, how about the surveillance video? It has been a few days since we last checked it. Maybe there is something on it."

"Well, it's been a big nothing so far, but what the hell. Let's see if there is anything new on it."

They went back to her apartment and went up the stairs and into a small study. She turned on the computer on top of an ornate oak desk.

"Okay, Eric, here goes nothing." She activated the video software and soon on the screen was a view of the inner sanctum of the in vitro clinic. "This video cam," she explained, "as you remember becomes activated by movement and then continues to record for fifteen minutes after movement has ceased. The date and time of each segment are up top here."

Egan looked at the top of the screen. "So this view is from two days ago."

"Right."

Dr. George's handsome features filled the screen. He was alone and settled down to do what looked like routine paperwork. They watched in silence for some moments. Egan was in awe of the quality of the images on the screen and of Gail's mastery of the technology.

"Wow, this is getting ugly."

Dr. George had paused in his work and now was engaged in a prolonged, assiduous excavation of his right nostril. He worked calmly and with the ease of a man who is completely certain that he is unobserved. His hard work was finally rewarded and he gazed at his right finger with a look of quiet satisfaction on his face.

"Well, Gail, we have definitely nailed the man. Wait until the dean finds out that besides delivering babies he delivers boogers."

Meanwhile, Dr. George began to work on the other side.

"Time to fast forward," Gail said.

They spent the next hour spot checking various points of the video log and then viewing a part of it. They were able also to hone in on portions that contained sound and listened to portions of what seemed to be routine conversations about the in vitro work.

"Okay, now we are up to Sunday evening. According to the log there is a forty-five minute stretch of movement after nothing most of the day."

Egan exclaimed. "That's Dr. Newhouse." They watched as Newhouse entered the room dressed in scrubs and a surgical cap.

"He must have come in to do some sort of procedure in the ICU, but what is he doing in the in vitro clinic?"

Newhouse appeared to be looking around quickly and then turned toward the door. His voice, deep and resonant startled Egan in its unexpectedness.

"Come on in, my dear," they heard Newhouse say. "I think you will find what I have to show you quite interesting."

Gail and Egan waited expectantly and finally another figure loomed in of the screen.

"Why it's Richter," said Egan. "I guess she must be on call."

They continued to watch as Newhouse and Richter talked. Newhouse was explaining the immunology of transplant rejection and it soon became apparent that they had been working together in the ICU on a four-year-old four days after a liver transplant who had just weathered an intense rejection crisis.

"Is that fairly clear?" Newhouse said a large smile clearly visible on the screen.

"Oh, yes," answered Richter, somewhat breathlessly. "You really are an incredible teacher."

Newhouse reached out and patted her hand. "And you, my dear, performed flawlessly in there."

"Oh God, here it comes," said Gail.

"Here comes what?" asked Egan with a puzzled expression.

"You are obviously not a woman."

"I'm flattered that you consider it obvious, but quite honestly can't see what's coming."

"He's hitting on her."

"Newhouse? I can't believe it. He is a real straight arrow, married, two young kids."

Egan's voice trailed off as he observed the figure of Dr. Newhouse lean forward, while the hand that had previously been placed on hers for some solicitous patting now had a firm grip and was pulling Dr. Richter closer to him. Their lips met in a long, increasingly passionate kiss.

Gail nudged Egan in triumph. Egan sat open-mouthed in astonishment, not out of naiveté, but there was something in the smooth, practiced manner with which Newhouse had maneuvered the young resident into his arms that sharply contradicted his own image of the man: consummate doctor, teacher, and researcher, his resolute demeanor bespoke a man consumed with patient care rather than that of a seducer planning his next conquest.

Egan and Gail watched transfixed by the scene in front of them. Newhouse broke away for a moment, and began to slowly pull off Richter's scrub top. She lifted her arms and he pulled it over her head and off, pausing to gaze appreciatively at her black bra. He reached behind her back with the air of a man carefully unwrapping a precious gift. Richter closed her eyes and shivered slightly as Newhouse's exploring hand gently caressed her breast before sliding back fingering the bra strap. His other hand at the back of her neck pulled her forward for a brief kiss. He had during this brief kiss expertly undone her bra with his right hand and now his left hand slid down from her neck and he began to ever so slowly pull the ends forward.

"Jesus, this guy is a pro," muttered Egan, no longer able to contain himself.

As Newhouse pulled the straps forward, Richter's breasts became increasingly visible and he slowed his movements even further, like a wine connoisseur pausing in anticipatory excitement before popping the cork. In one final movement he removed the bra and the soft grunt of pleasure he emitted was clearly audible.

"Michael was right," murmured Egan, gazing at the extraordinary resolution that represented the apogee of thousands of years of mankind's technological advancement.

"What did you say?" asked Gail.

"Oh, nothing important.

Chapter Sixty-One
September 13, 2008 5:00 PM

"So what we have learned so far is that Blake George is a fanatic about nasal cleanliness and Newhouse is not exactly the paragon of virtue we thought he was. Those two facts while quite fascinating in their own right don't advance the ball one iota," said Egan as he walked next to Gail, with his head down and his hands in his pockets. They walked silently along a narrow asphalt path in a wooded area of Central Park. The path eventually led downward to open meadow adjoining a small duck pond.

They sat down on the grass and watched as a duck noisily chased a rival across the surface of the pond and then quiet reigned.

"We should be getting back," Gail finally said after twenty minutes of silence.

"Gail, I'm going to stay here a bit longer. It's so peaceful here. I need to think things out."

"Are you sure?" she asked doubtfully. "Are you going to be okay? You look discouraged. Listen we only looked at about half of the video cam. We should review the rest of it. Who knows what we will find?"

"Sure, sure. I'll be fine, I just need to relax. Meet you at your place in a couple of hours."

She walked away, hesitantly, pausing once and continuing after Egan waved her on.

After she left, he sat leaning against a tree and fell asleep, the chronically exhausted resident. When he awoke, the trees on the west end of the meadow were casting long shadows. He stretched and as he craned his neck upward to loosen the crick there, he could feel the cool breeze against the tiny beads of sweat that had formed in the folds of his neck while sleeping so awkwardly against the side of the tree. He wandered into the meadow full of buttercups, lupine and Queen Anne's lace. Bees flitted from flower to flower. There was a buzzing that after some time he realized was from locusts. He leaned over to examine a small beetle that had climbed laboriously to the top of a dandelion. Nearby ants were dragging a huge dead dragonfly. He was briefly started to see a praying mantis camouflaged expertly in the grass, standing utterly still while waiting for some hapless insect to wander within range. A microcosm of nature, thought Egan.

He stood up and walked to the edge of the meadow and peered into the dark recesses of the woods. What an idyll, thought Egan, so different from the frantic, urgent rhythms of urban residency. He lay down on a soft bed of moss at the end of the meadow, chewed on a twig of sassafras and stared up at the blue sky punctuated by occasional billowy clouds. His mind obsessively turned over and over the memories of the past few days.

The baby with meningitis now apparently irreversibly brain damaged, the baby with kernicteris, the baby who died in the ER, being chased all tumbled together in an inchoate jumble. He got up and wandered down to the bank of the pond. A dead carp lay belly up at the ponds edge. A faint whiff of rotting fish caused him to wrinkle his nose and then he was transported in his mind to the moment when bending over the Maitland baby during the spinal tap and the first drops began to drip from needle's hub. He remembered the odor wafting from it.

"Oh, my God," he said aloud and turned abruptly to run.

Chapter Sixty-Two
September 13, 2008 6:30 PM

Egan rushed out of the library, rounded a corner, and nearly collided with Michael coming from the opposite direction.

"Eric, as usual, you're in a big hurry. What's going on?"

"Michael, am I happy to see you. We have to talk."

"I'm all ears. Talk away."

"Not here."

They walked to the elevator bank with Michael taking several quizzical sideline glances at Egan. They rode to the 12th floor and entered Michael's on call room.

"Michael," began Egan with an urgent whisper, "they are clones."

"Who are clones? What are you talking about?"

"The Maitland baby and the Saudi baby are clones."

"What? How is that possible?"

"Look, Michael, I know this all sounds incredible, but let me explain. The Maitland baby and the Saudi baby both have an extremely rare metabolic syndrome know as trimethylaminuria, or fish odor syndrome. They lack an enzyme that oxidizes trimethylamine into an odorless derivative. I had noticed the odor on the Saudi boy, but it only recently hit me that the same odor was on the spinal fluid of the Maitland baby."

"But, Eric, does that prove it? I mean it all seems extraordinary."

"I know, but I was just in the library reading up on this. Trimethylamiuria is not only quite rare, it is virtually nonexistent in people of Northern European or Eastern European ancestry as the Maitlands told me they are when I took a family history. It can't be just coincidence. Joyce Maitland's uterus was implanted with the clone of that Saudi baby for the express purpose of providing a donor heart."

"This is all too much to take in," said Michael shaking his head, "though your reasoning is very persuasive. Oh, shit, my cell is vibrating again. Let me just see what that's about."

He opened his phone and punched in rapidly and then peered at the small screen for a moment and then snapped it shut.

"Nothing that can't wait. Anyway, tell me from the beginning how you figured this out."

"Well," answered Egan rubbing his chin as he considered his words, "my curiosity was first aroused when I diagnosed the Gold baby with pneumococcal meningitis. Pneumococcus, as you know, is a somewhat uncommon pathogen at that age and this was a baby with apparently no risk factors. Quite honestly, my interest was merely on clinical grounds. At the time, I wasn't invoking conspiracy theories to explain the unusual findings. What I did was simply something I have done in the past when confronted with an unusual case which was to investigate a bit and see if there were any other similar cases."

"So I did a record search and found that indeed there were other cases over the last two years, certainly a much higher number than you would ordinarily see even in a busy center such as ours. I began to wonder if there was some sort of common epidemiological thread and I at some point noticed that they were all from Dr. George's in vitro clinic. I knew that he had recently pioneered a new technique and of course my first thought was perhaps there was something in the technique which quite unexpectedly had some sort of adverse effect on the baby's immune system."

"But, Eric, excuse me for butting in," said Michael, "did you think at the time that George was doing this purposefully? I could understand, I suppose, that if there was something wrong with the side effect profile of the in vitro technique, that perhaps, considering how lucrative in vitro is, there may exist a strong temptation to deny, perhaps even unconsciously, that there was a problem."

"Absolutely. Certainly my original thought was that it was totally inadvert. In fact, I began to postulate that the same factor that allows the sperm to more easily penetrate the ovum and thus achieve fertilization or implantation may also effect the nascent formation of the baby's blood brain barrier. Three facts led me in that direction. First, the only unusual infection was meningitis. If a problem of the immune system was involved, I would suspect that other types of infections would also occur. Secondly, I learned that protein F is intimately involved in the structure of the blood brain barrier as well as in the barrier to fertilization. Thirdly, there was a case of kernicterus at unusually low levels of bilirubin, which implies a perforate blood brain barrier. The baby was also from Dr. George's in vitro clinic."

"That seems quite plausible," said Michael. "So what was it that made you think it was being done on purpose?"

"I'm getting to that. Last week, the Saudi child was admitted to University Hospital with a diagnosis of hypoplastic left heart syndrome—in need of a heart transplant. I found out that the Maitland baby who I diagnosed with—guess what—pneumococcal meningitis at a very early stage and who should have recovered, instead went on to suffer severe brain damage and was put on life support and, get this, was to be the donor—apparently a perfect match. This child, from the Middle East, was told to fly over here, before the Maitland baby even had arrived at the ER! I believe those pricks gave the baby a large shot of gentamycin and blamed it on my clinical error."

"Brilliant," said Michael.

"Yes, brilliant," echoed a voice just outside the room that Egan immediately recognized with a start as that of the familiar Boston twang of Dr. John Oden. Within seconds, he was in the room. On either side of him were Bob and Ray and in a flash Egan realized it had been they who had chased him into Central Park.

Egan gave a quick look at Michael, and his cold eyes and icy expression offered not a hint of ambiguity. He read in his face cold ambition and resolve. He glanced around frantically, looking for any avenue of escape.

"I wouldn't try anything. My two friends here are awfully good at what they do. Now turn around and put your arms behind you. I mean now."

Egan reluctantly turned his back on Oden, his mind frantically trying to comprehend this sudden turn in events. His thoughts were interrupted by a sharp pull on his wrists and he realized that his hands were being tightly bound behind him. Once incapacitated, he was led over to the on call bed. Egan gave a sharp involuntary shiver as he looked up at Oden.

"So, Eric, here we are. Your brilliance, olfactory and otherwise, has gotten you into deep trouble. I am truly sorry it has come to this but you have left me little choice. It's a pity. You are as talented a resident as I have ever had the privilege to meet, but I have the sense that despite your iconoclasm and originality, you are deep down a traditionalist, unable to comprehend a calculus that would sacrifice young infants in order to save more fully formed conscious children."

Oden looked hard at Egan and then turned away. "Oh spare me that sanctimonious look. Medicine has always involved a tradeoff, the greatest good for the greatest number. We are on the cutting edge and on the balance we are saving lives."

"Oden," Egan broke in, "I saved your son."

"Yes, you did, and for that I am eternally grateful. I couldn't have handled losing another son."

Egan looked at him with surprise for an instant, but then remembered what Oden had told him in the coffee shop just a few weeks before. "Yes, you heard me right. I had a son, a beautiful baby boy, but stillborn due to a botched delivery by the famous Dr. George. He was just as arrogant then as he is now. I held my dead son in my arms, and I vowed that day to get justice. The pompous fool. I was a fellow in his lab at the time along with Newhouse in Boston. Early on in animal trials, I discovered a serious problem with the first crude elaboration of protein F: that it had an unfortunate effect on the blood brain barrier of the developing fetus.

"With refinement, I was able to eliminate that unfortunate side effect and I went on to develop the method which has resulted in Dr. George's phenomenal success in his in vitro clinic. I quickly saw the possibility for revenge. I would allow him to enjoy the initial success. Since only I knew the refinement required, I planned to later substitute the initial version of protein F and watch his empire collapse into a boiling cauldron of lawsuits and recriminations. But it was Michael, then a young medical student working with me in the lab, who came up with the brilliant notion that a flawed blood brain barrier would create a sort of a programmed obsolescence. A baby is born and at some point becomes brain dead either by toxins or bacteria while the other vital organs remain in pristine shape. So I decided to delay my revenge on George."

Egan in a steely calm voice that belied the situation broke in. "I have no illusions about what you are going to do to me. But rather than give me your ridiculous rationale, I'd rather hear the details of what you did. I think I understand parts of it. Clonal embryos were implanted in order to become future organ donors. You used the early protein F derivative to create in vitro babies that would get sick within weeks to months. Most would return to the hospital of their birth, I guess to provide you with patients to perform heroics on and as a steady source of organs for Newhouse who was in on it too. Is that it?"

"My dear, Dr. Egan, my assessment of your cognitive abilities if anything has been short of the mark. You have done a masterful job of figuring this out." Oden broke into a broad grin. "But please, you flatter Dr. Newhouse. He really does believe that the reason his transplants work so well is due to his meticulous care."

Oden paused over to look at Bob and Ray. "He has no idea that his two loyal nurses actually work for me supplying me with information and allowing me to manipulate him like a marionette master. Here is how it works: A young baby is born with, say, severe congenital liver disease or as in the case of the Saudi baby with hypoplastic left heart—conditions that do not result in a neonatal death, but considerably shortened life span."

"Can you think of anything more cruel? To provide palliative treatment to those patients so they can survive to say the age of thirteen—a life filled with multiple hospitalizations, operations, heartache for the parents. Instead this parent finds out about my, ah, service. I, using the baby's DNA, create a clonal fertilized egg and arrange to have it implanted into a mother at the in vitro clinic."

Egan stared hard at Oden. "But it's George's clinic."

"I told you, he's a fool. It's a simple matter of switching embryos the night before implantation. He doesn't know a thing about it."

"How do the babies get pneumococcus?"

"Michael would simply slip into the nursery, nothing unusual for a resident, and inject a small number of pneumococci into the baby before discharge. From animal experiments we learned that we could fairly predictably produce meningitis within two to three weeks. The baby returns in extremis and the appropriate organ is harvested. True, the organs are a bit small, but they quickly enlarge and they can't get rejected!"

"For God's sake," interjected Egan, "how on earth can you, as a physician, justify this monstrous scheme?"

Oden calmly regarded him. "You really don't get it. Can't you see that by sacrificing young babies, we are saving other lives? Infanticide has been practiced for eons by various societies for the greater good. A group of Eskimos in days of old would sacrifice a newborn if the available food would not justify increasing the population. I imagine you are in favor of abortion—how different is this? It is really a question of where you draw the line. What is the real difference between a twenty-week fetus and a several week old baby? Anyway, these babies are clones of the organ recipients and technically are not related to the parents at all."

"I imagine the mothers of these babies would beg to differ."

"Dr. Egan, as enjoyable as it is to discuss medical ethics with you, my time, I'm afraid, is running short. I do most regret that this will be our final meeting."

Oden turned to leave after pausing for a quick whispered communication with Michael, who silently nodded his head.

"Sorry, my friend, life's a bitch and then you die."

Egan merely turned his head away.

"It's a pity. We could have worked together. I did so enjoy our philosophical ramblings during so many late nights in the hospital. But I sensed in those talks an old-fashioned adherence to traditional societal mores and a rather pristine aversion to making big money. You must know that I am the ultimate opportunist. Can you picture me treating patients in a suburban practice enduring the nags and demands of the worried well for a mere pittance or toiling in the academic byways hoping that the dean will grant me a three percent per annum raise? No, that's not me. I have bigger plans and unfortunately you are not in them. I loved you like a brother, but unlike you I am unencumbered by sentiment and also unlike you I know when it is time to move on."

"So it was you that injected the gentamycin into the Maitland baby?"

"Yes, it was I. Rather brilliant, no?" answered Michael with a grin.

"You bastard." And Egan was on his feet, charging Michael with his hands still bound tightly behind his back, his head pointed forward. Michael momentarily startled, rapidly regained his poise, neatly sidestepped him and dealt him a blow to the side of his head. Egan fell to the ground, a piercing pain shooting through his head taking him to the verge of consciousness. He lay for a moment where he fell stunned by the impact, but his anger fueled a convulsive, ill-advised roll to his feet.

Michael turned and gave him one swift kick sending Egan cascading back to the floor, his jaw impacting the hard floor. He lay there with hot blood from his mouth mixing with his sweat.

Soon a gurney emerged from the on call room pushed by two muscular men dressed in scrubs. On it laid a prostrate figure, firmly encased in a strait jacket, eyes glazed, and mouth slightly agape and drooling. This was a sight that excited no particular attention as it made its slow but steady course to the psychiatric wing.

When they got there, the attendant told the ward clerk, "It's Dr. Egan. Poor chap made a disastrous medical error and was suspended. He had a complete psychotic meltdown. He is heavily sedated and should not be allowed to wake up. He could be violent."

Chapter Sixty-Three
September 13, 2008 7:00 PM

Gail paced nervously in her study and looked at her watch for the fifth time in as many minutes. She leaned forward and pushed the play button on her message machine and listened for the second time to the message that had greeted her on her arrival to her town house.

"Gail, I think I have it. I'm leaving the library. Wait for me and I'll explain all."

She continued her pacing now dialing Egan's cell number for the third time.

"Shit," she said aloud as once again she heard his voice telling her to leave a message. "Where the hell is he?" Her eyes fell upon the computer screen on the desk.

She opened the web cam recording and began to view from where they had left off. She fast forwarded through twenty-four hours of routine activities until she got to the night that the Maitland baby had gotten sick. A light turned on and a figure in blue scrubs strode into the room. Gail looked at the time that the scene had been recorded: 3:15 AM. The figure turned toward the web cam and sat down. It was Michael. He picked up the phone on the desk and punched in some numbers.

"John, Michael here. Sorry, I know it's late. The Maitland baby was admitted with meningitis." Michael paused, listening and then continued. "I know it was earlier than we expected, but the parents called fucking Egan. No, I don't know why." He listened again. "Unfortunately, the baby is doing quite well. Egan pushed meds down in the ER." He listened again. "Gentamycin? John, that's a great idea."

Gail turned off the computer, made one phone call and raced out the apartment.

Chapter Sixty-Four
September 13, 2008 8:30 PM

Gail placed a small piece of chocolate into her mouth, chewed it thoughtfully, and took a couple of deep calming breathes before knocking.

"Come in."

She entered and saw Michael lounging on the on call room bed.

"Well, Gail, how nice to see you. Now why this sudden urge to see me?"

"Michael, I'm worried about Eric."

"I'm worried about him too," he said, shaking his head grimly.

"I think he is getting paranoid. Ever since he was suspended, he's talking conspiracy and coming up with all these strange theories that explain how that baby got the gentamycin."

"Well, his ego really took it on the chin. Can't really blame the poor fellow."

"Well, I'm having trouble relating to it. He's calling me at all hours. I'd hate to break up with him at such a time, but I'm not sure how much more I can take."

"Well, well, the truth hurts, but when it's time to move on, it's time to move on."

"Maybe you're right," she said looking down at the floor and then looked up again into Michael's eyes. She put her face into her hands and began to sob.

Michael took her in his arms. "There, there, it will be okay."

Gail clung to him, burying her face into his shoulder. She lifted her head and looked at him with her lips parted slightly. Michael, so expert at reading signals and generally decisive about acting on those readings now hesitated, and peered suspiciously into her eyes but found himself hypnotized. His head leaned forward at a pace barely perceptible but inexorably closer. Their lips met, first gently and then with more force.

"That was sweet," murmured Michael pulling back to look at her with a smile. He moved in for another kiss. Abruptly he pulled back again now without a smile, but with a puzzled anxious expression. He ran his tongue over his lower lip and reached up with his hand. Gail stepped back from him and watched him with a fixed stare. Suddenly he looked at Gail with panicked eyes but now with a look of comprehension. He was too skilled a physician not to recognize the early signs of anaphylaxis.

"You bitch! What did you do to me?" His voice, becoming increasingly hoarse failed him at the end of this sentence and he broke into a paroxysm of coughing. He collapsed to the floor, his hand and arm hitting first, his med alert bracelet, which proclaimed his severe allergy to peanuts, clanging against the hard wood floor. Gail simultaneously reached each hand into a different pocket and held aloft in her right hand a half-eaten Reeses peanut butter cup, and in the other, a syringe.

"Listen carefully, you bastard, because you have very little time. I have a syringe loaded with epinephrine, enough to reverse the anaphylaxis."

Michael, his lips now grotesquely swollen, looked at the syringe with pleading hungry eyes and sat up abruptly, reaching for it. Gail took a step backwards keeping it out of his grasp and he fell back again consumed by another paroxysm of coughing.

"Save your energy. Tell me where Eric is."

Several minutes later, after Gail had injected the epinephrine, the swelling had begun to go down and Michael's breathing began to ease as Doug Barrett, who had been waiting outside the on-call room, placed the last knot in the rope that had Michael secured to the bunk bed.

"That should hold you, you prick. You really sang like a canary," He said before sprinting out the door and catching up with Gail.

"Let's hightail it to the psych ward and get Eric out of there before something happens to him. After that we'll go directly to the dean. Gail, you have the video?"

"Yeah, it's right here on a thumb drive. But let's hurry. If anything happens to Eric, I will never forgive them."

* * *

Doug Barrett pressed the buzzer again at the entrance of the locked psychiatric unit, this time letting it ring a full thirty seconds. Finally, an attendant opened the door.

"All right, all ready. You don't have to lean on the buzzer."

"Sorry, we've got to see Dr. Eric Egan right away."

"Just who are you anyway? He's in a locked room. He's not allowed to have visitors. Apparently he attacked one of the residents and he's a bit banged up."

"I'm Doctor Douglas Barrett, chief resident in pediatrics. It's vitally important that I see him right away."

"And who are you, young lady?"

"I'm Gail Roscoe, a third-year medical student." she said smiling at him. "We'd be most grateful. Dr. Egan is a pediatric resident."

"Well, it's against regs, but okay, I'll let you in for a brief visit. He is totally out of it. He's in a morphine-induced coma."

They followed the attendant down the hallway. Barrett whispered to Gail, "Good work. Your smile would open doors anywhere."

He led them to a door, waved a badge at the security box and the door opened. Egan was on a bed, flat on his back, his arms and legs in restraints and appeared to be unconscious. A large hematoma distorted the upper right side of his forehead and his eyelids were swollen and red.

"Oh God," exclaimed Gail and ran to him.

Barrett turned to the attendant. "We'd like to sit with him a while in case he wakes up."

Gail began to sob. Barrett gestured toward her. "Can we be alone for a short time?"

"I suppose that's okay, Dr. Barrett. But I really should call the psychiatrist."

"That would be fine. Go ahead, make your call. We'll be fine."

The attendant left to go down to the nurse's station.

Gail jumped to her feet. "We don't have much time." She pulled out a large syringe from her lab coat pocket, disconnected the IV at its hub, and replaced it with the syringe.

"Okay, narcan, do your thing." The opiate antagonist flowed into Egan's bloodstream and like an invading army of ninjas tackled each molecule of morphine and rendered it inert.

Within thirty seconds, Egan's eyes flew open with a startled, panicked expression.

"It's okay, we're here," said Gail while stroking his head.

"Gail and Barrett?" He looked at them, appearing completely nonplussed.

"It's okay, Eric, he's with us. Now listen, we have to get out of here right away. We'll help you up. Do you think you can walk?"

"Yeah, I think so." The memory of Michael and Oden and his anger fueled him and he sprang to his feet. The three of them ran headlong down the corridor.

* * *

Howard P. Yodell MD, PhD, dean of the medical school and one of the nation's top medical leaders, phone in hand was listening grim-faced. In front of him were Doug Barrett, Gail Roscoe and Eric Egan sitting in chairs facing his desk and watching him intently. Dr. Yodell's world had been rocked some 20 minutes earlier when the motley trio had breached the outer secretarial barriers to the dean's inner sanctum. The dean had barely expressed his shock at such an abrupt invasion of his office, when the laptop computer with the incriminating video which Barret had placed on the desk in front of him began to capture his attention. Dr. Yodell hadn't become one of the nation's preeminent physician leaders by being slow on the uptake and he had quickly grasped the situation. Doug, Gail, and Eric in alternating short staccato bursts had told the dean all they had uncovered. The dean had picked up the phone. "Get me security, stat!"

Now the dean slammed down the phone. "The hospital is on complete lockdown. Luckily, we have an efficient system since we occasionally have to invoke it to prevent kidnappings from our nursery. Every exit is locked and will be manned by a security personnel. Oden is in the building, since he was caught on a surveillance camera near the front entrance just 20 minutes ago. Meiselman may have gotten away."

"But," exclaimed Gail, "he should be tied up in the peds on call room."

"Unfortunately, he managed to untie himself. Security found the cords and duct tape scattered on the floor. We've alerted the police so it should only be a matter of time. Oden is the big fish here and I'm sure we can get him."

"We can help," said Barrett, springing to his feet.

"Hold on there, Doug; he could be dangerous. He may have figured out that we're on to him."

"But Dean, who knows the nooks and crannies better than a resident. Look, assign me to one of the security men and I can help."

"I'll go with you," said Gail.

"Me too," said Eric, speaking for the first time.

"Dr. Egan, you have done enough and you're in no position to do anything but rest over here on my couch."

The phone rang and the dean picked it up on the first ring. He listened for a long moment. "Thanks, let me know of any new developments."

He turned to Gail and Doug. "Oden's office shows signs of a rapid gathering of items so he probably knows that we're looking for him. The head of security has assured me that he could not have left the building unless he has learned to fly."

Doug was bouncing on his feet. "Let's go."

"Okay, Doug and Gail, I told security of your offer to help. They're sending one of their guys. I want to go the main security desk." He turned to Eric who was now comfortably ensconced on the couch. "Will you be okay here?"

"I'll be fine."

The three left the office.

Egan looked around the office. One whole wall was covered with framed diplomas and various honors, one signed by the president of the United States. He closed his eyes and rubbed the bruised area on his forehead.

He began to drift off to sleep. *To fly.* The dean's words suddenly echoed in his mind and he abruptly sat up, fighting an attack of vertigo. He remembered the large poster-sized picture in Oden's office. He got to his feet and steadied himself for a moment and dashed out of the office, startling the dean's secretary as he flew by her.

He raced to the elevator bank, pressed the button several times, then gave up and ran to the stairs. He took the last flight of stairs two at a time and paused at the top to catch his breath before slowly opening the door to the roof of the hospital.

At the far end of the roof, near the landing pad for the helicopter, stood John Oden. He had just strapped himself to a large hang glider. Egan saw that it was too late to stop him, so he watched as Oden, a man he had so admired just days before, leapt off the precipice.

Egan ran forward to the edge and watched the bright red glider catch a rising gust of wind. The glider did a wide arc and then floated out over the East River where Egan had spent hours rowing his scull.

Egan could not help but admire the preternatural skill that Oden exhibited while smoothly guiding his glider down the river towards the New York harbor. He took out his cell phone, and rapidly made some calls as he watched as Oden sought out rising air pockets. Within minutes, he spotted a police boat giving chase and then another.

"He can't stay up there forever." Like Icarus before him, Oden had flown too close to the sun. It was only a matter of time.

Chapter Sixty-Five
September 16, 2008 4:00 PM

Egan and Gail walked out of the medical center. It was late afternoon. A cool early fall breeze hit them and Gail pulled her sweater a little tighter.

"First cool day. Better start getting the old ski equipment out. By the way, Gail, do you ski?"

"As a matter of fact I do. I was, uh, a competitive skier in high school."

"Really. Were you any good?"

"Well actually I was Middle Atlantic slalom champion my senior year."

"Gail, is there anything you don't excel at?"

Egan stopped and looked at her and thought how little he knew of her. The early days of their relationship had been consumed by the travails of the past few weeks. Now that things were settling down he looked forward to learning all he could about this remarkable woman.

The rest of the day was consumed with talking with various authorities and medical center officials. Despite vigorous attempts to contain the story, it spread through the hospital like a California canyon wildfire. There was a lot of awed congratulations and back-slapping, especially from the medical students and residents, but less so from the fellows and junior attendings. Virtually none was from senior attendings who were too engrossed in the dimensions of the scandal and who wondered if their institution would survive it. Through it all, despite the considerable relief, he felt saddened and numbed by his experience. He thought about Michael, his "best friend" and wondered where he was now.

He continued to look at Gail and she held his gaze. The breeze, licking at the back of his neck, caused Gail's hair to dance around her face. He pictured them on the slopes together, Gail far ahead schussing down with perfect form.

"Will you allow me to keep up with you when we ski? I like to stop and look at the trees and the view."

She looked back at him. "Yes, I will." She exclaimed and grabbed him in a furious embrace.

Chapter Sixty-Six
September 18, 2008 7:00 AM

"Doug, can I come in?"

Egan stood poised outside the chief resident's door. He appeared rested and refreshed having been given three days off to sleep. He paused for some minutes before the door reflecting upon issues of trust and how easily both individuals and institutions can abuse it.

"Hey, Eric, come on in. You look like a walking advertisement for the three-day leave act for all medical residents. Have a seat."

"I just wanted to, uh, apologize…"

Barrett held up his hand. "Eric, no need for that. Look, why don't we start over? You are a hell of a doctor and I guess it has been hard for me to admit it."

"Doug, so are you. So, friends?" He held his hand out and they clasped and held it for a long minute.

"Friends."

Egan left Barrett's office feeling that he had a new friend. He walked the familiar corridors and soon found himself on his ward. He saw the team already on rounds, the nurses charting, aides scurrying in and out of rooms and he smiled in pleasure at the pure routine of it all.

"Dr. Egan, are you waiting for a special invitation? Rounds have been underway for five minutes."

"Yes, sir!" Egan ran to join the group and listened intently to the case presentation.

Epilogue
Several Months Later

In Vitro Couple Granted Custody

(New York, NY) Today in Superior Court in lower Manhattan, Judge Roy Shapiro ruled in favor of John and Joyce Maitland in a custody dispute with Prince Fasi of Saudi Arabia. This was the first of many cases to be adjudicated that came out of the huge scandal that enveloped the Malloy Medical Center in vitro fertilization clinic in which women were fraudulently implanted with cloned embryos for the expressed purpose of becoming organ donors. The baby that Joyce Maitland brought to term became ill with meningitis and as a consequence became brain dead. His heart was harvested and successfully transplanted to his identical clone, the son of Prince Fasi.

It was this son that the Maitlands sued for custody of, arguing that the circumstances which caused such "egregious suffering and harm to the Maitlands" mitigated against the Prince retaining custody of his biological son. Judge Shapiro apparently swayed by this argument, invoked King Solomon when he stated that the Prince was willing to "almost literally cut one baby in half" which "effectively terminates his parental rights in a civilized society."

After the ruling, the Prince had to be restrained as he shouted in anger, vowing "international repercussions." John Maitland and his wife Joyce, wearing maternity clothes, left the court hand in hand in the company of Dr. Eric Egan and Gail Roscoe, the pediatric resident and medical student who unearthed the scandal. They had no comment for the mass of reporters assembled outside the court.

In a related development, the FBI announced they had evidence that Dr. Michael Meiselman was, as recently as one week ago, in Botswana, though his current whereabouts remain unknown.

CPSIA information can be obtained at www.ICGtesting.com
Printed in the USA
BVOW06s1427231115

428084BV00008B/83/P